W9-DGC-510

Long Live *the* QUEEN

Also by Saundra

Her Sweetest Revenge

Her Sweetest Revenge 2

Her Sweetest Revenge 3

If It Ain't About the Money

Hustle Hard

A Hustler's Queen

A Hustler's Queen: Reloaded

Anthologies
Schemes and Dirty Tricks (with Kiki Swinson)

Published by Kensington Publishing Corp.

Long Live the QUEEN

SAUNDRA

www.kensingtonbooks.com

DAFINA BOOKS are published by

Kensington Publishing Corp.
119 West 40th Street
New York, NY 10018

Copyright © 2022 by Saundra

To the extent that the image or images on the cover of this book depict a person or persons, such person or persons are merely models, and are not intended to portray any character or characters featured in the book.

This book is a work of fiction. Names, characters, businesses, organizations, places, events, and incidents either are the product of the author's imagination or are used fictitiously. Any resemblance to actual persons, living or dead, events, or locales is entirely coincidental.

All rights reserved. No part of this book may be reproduced in any form or by any means without the prior written consent of the Publisher, excepting brief quotes used in reviews.

All Kensington titles, imprints, and distributed lines are available at special quantity discounts for bulk purchases for sales promotion, premiums, fund-raising, and educational or institutional use.

Special book excerpts or customized printings can also be created to fit specific needs. For details, write or phone the office of the Kensington Sales Manager: Kensington Publishing Corp., 119 West 40th Street, New York, NY 10018. Attn. Sales Department. Phone: 1-800-221-2647.

The Dafina logo is a trademark of Kensington Publishing Corp.

ISBN: 978-1-4967-3879-0
First Trade Paperback Printing: December 2022

ISBN: 978-1-4967-3880-6 (e-book)
First Electronic Edition: December 2022

10 9 8 7 6 5 4 3 2 1

Printed in the United States of America

I would like to dedicate this book to my loving mother, Inez Patricia Patterson Diggs. No words can express how much I miss my mother. One of the most caring, giving persons God ever created. Mom, I dedicate this book to you. You are loved and missed, but you will always be in our hearts. Gone but never forgotten.

Acknowledgments

First, I would like to give honor to God and thank Him for His Grace and Mercy, He gets all the glory because without Him nothing would be possible. And I truly believe that. To my daughters DJ and CJ and my husband, Onester, I love you three to the moon and back. DJ, stay in them books that degree coming soon. To my dad and stepmother, I love you both, and I really enjoyed your first visit to Indiana. Little sis did that long drive and did not blink. LOL! To all my brothers and sisters: Roy, Cardell, Angela, Saidah, and O'Raefo, I love you guys and keep supporting me. To my stepdaughter, Oneisha, you already know I love you, girly.

Shout out to all my family and friends. I also want to shout out my nieces, Zaleika, Corlunda, and Corlexus, I am so proud of you three ladies. I watch you now with your own kids and see how hard you work for a better future, and I smile, I love y'all. To my niece Mya, you graduated this year Class of 2021; proud of you, niece, and I love you. To my nephew Travis first let me say how proud I am of you graduating Class of 2021. And now I'm even prouder to say you serve our country, I love you and wish you nothing but success. To my nephew Cardell, AKA Lil Carl, just know we love you and support you no matter what.

I would like to thank my editor Norma Hernandez thanks for being there when I have questions and easing my mind while I complete my projects. And thanks to my Kensington/Dafina family for your continued promotion and support of my work. Shout out to my readers who continue to support me book after book. Thank you for the love you show. Without you all this could not be possible, and I thank you so much. Latunya Jones, here you go. I know you on the edge of your seat and I know Kim Harper is right behind you. LOL Enjoy

What can I say—this writing journey is one filled with ideas and more passion than I can describe. It brings me absolute joy. Being able to share it with others is the icing on my cake. *Long Live the Queen* is here to take over. A page-turner to the end and even then, you will beg for more. So sit back, relax, and get ready to turn the pages, from your favorite author.

Saundra
One Key Stroke at a Tyme!

Chapter 1

POP, POP, POP, POP, POP, POP, POP, POP, POP, POP, POP

So many bullets rang out I lost count. But I suddenly felt arms I recognized as Marlo's wrapped around my waist. My body folded into his as he pulled me backwards. The bullets stopped and all movement seem to instantly cease as the smell of gunfire filled my nostrils and clouded the air.

"Bab, you okay?" Marlo's words blew down the crease of my neck and into my ear. Still feeling some type of way about him withholding that Pablo was his father, I took a swift step away from his embrace. My eyes landed on Salvador's bloody, bullet hole-filled body, hunched over and lifeless, with all the color drained from his face. His henchmen lay in a pool of their own blood, dead. Other unknown men stood around glaring at the bodies with their guns still drawn as if they expected the bodies to move. I glanced over at Marlo, whose eyes were also now glued to the bloody scene at hand.

"Mane, what the actual FUCK!" he yelled, his eyes now on the tall Hispanic man, who looked to be about fifty, with curly hair and a small cherry like birth mark on his right cheek. And just as if he had just realized who he was Marlo mouthed, "El Guapo." The name slid out of his mouth in a gruff but surprised tone.

Just as I had never met Salvador before until that day, I had never met El Guapo. I was aware of them both and their quest to be the one and only at the top. A position they both hungered, and I should say battled, for. And now it seemed settled in blood, and death. Just moments before Marlo and I were standing face to face with Salvador as he laid out his plans for us to rule as King and Queen of LA and Miami's drug distribution. And here now, bold as shit, El Guapo stood before us voicing the same demand as we stood in a pit of blood, and uncertainty.

"Precious, I know you have seen me blowing up your phone." The sound of Promise's voice tossed me back into reality. But a hint of anger still tingled up my spine from those previous events. For a second, I had forgotten where I was. Staring out of my bedroom window for about the past hour I had been replaying those moments in Peru over and over in my head. I could only vaguely remember getting off the plane in LA and driving home from the airport.

The ride back from Peru was almost a blur as well. I had all but refused to discuss anything with Marlo besides the game plan for the new position that had been forced on us. To be honest there was nothing we could do. We had a duty that was bigger than us, we were employers, people's livelihoods depended on us. We were how they ate. But our employers were no longer available to provide for us so that we could provide for our own. The life on which our bread and butter depended was now El Guapo. And he had christened us the new life that would oversee all supply and demand in our areas. It was simple, may our businesses rest in peace. And to be honest, possibly us. So here we were back in the states and our plane ride discussion revolved around that. Our approach had to be strategic. First things first, we had to meet with Crew leaders to let them know we were the new Pablo and Penelope, the new point of contact for collection and distribution. This would bring shock and jealousy, among other things. But one thing was for certain: none of that would change what was to be.

Before departing, Marlo and I decided the first meeting would be held in LA, so he would arrive promptly in twenty-four hours. He only had time to stop in Miami and pack another bag. Next up, I would head to Miami to be in the meeting that would be held there. It had to be clear to the Crews that we were bosses in both LA and Miami. In the meantime, I would have Mob schedule the meetings in LA.

"Precious." Promise said my name again when I didn't respond to her, but this time there was concern in her tone. I blinked back my thoughts and quickly ran over in mind what she had said so I could provide an answer.

"I'm sorry. It's my phone, I think the ringer is still off." I was nonchalant about my phone hiccup. I had thrown it on the bed when I had strolled in my room, its existence not important to me at the time. I had only used it once since I touched back down in the states to call Mob. But I did remember turning the ringer off before we met with Salvador. I never wanted my phone ringing when I was in a meeting.

"I knew something was up. I rang the doorbell and was about to use my key until Rosa opened the door to let me in. What's up with you today? Why are you standing here in a trance staring out the window? I know it is a beautiful day outside. But . . ." Promise took steps that brought her closer into my space. The concerned grimace on her face confirmed she knew something was up with me. I knew I had to come out with it because she was stubborn and would never let it go.

I sighed as my right arm came up and my hand went to the back of my neck. I could feel the tension built up, like a tight knot trapped. I rubbed lightly in the area, and pressed down a little to ease some of it. "Shit has been crazy." I finally released with my eyes closed as the slight massage I gave myself took some pressure off. I slowly re-opened my eyes. And made a quick mental note to schedule an appointment at the spa, to have them massage that stubborn tension right out. "Pablo and Penelope are dead. They were killed."

"What?" Promise eyes grew wide and confusion burst from them. "I mean do you know what happened?"

I shook my head with disappointment. I couldn't believe I just had to say it, it still sounded strange coming from my mouth. Pablo and Penelope were some of the most connected people I knew. To say they had been killed was a bit much, simply unreal. "Plies." His name tasted sour in my mouth. "Turns out he was a snake."

Shock was Promise's reaction, it was clear she was at a loss for words.

"Yep, that bitch ass nigga wasn't shit, not an ounce of loyalty. He was offered money to kill Clip just to get him out of the way. And he would have carried out the act, but somebody beat him to it."

"Hell naw." Promise head shook right to left. "But Clip was his boy."

"Like I said, he was a snake. Only money and position mattered to him. Marlo and I were summoned out to Peru to meet with the big boss, Salvador. That is where I have been these past few days. And guess who's already there when we arrived? Mr. Plies himself. Bold as flies claiming a pile of shit. Salvador said he needed someone to watch his distribution and spy on me for some time now. You know, when I first burst on the scene. Clip refused to do it. So, Plies jumped at the chance to be somebody and took the job. Long story short he didn't get to Clip fast enough, but he murdered Pablo and Penelope for Salvador. Now Salvador, who wanted Pablo and Penelope out of the picture, had a plan for Marlo and me to take over in their position."

"What do you mean take over in their position?"

"Salvador had plans to make Marlo and me the major distributors for LA and Miami."

"Why you say, 'had?'" Promise had been around me long enough to know my meaning in other words. She paid attention to detail when I talked.

"Salvador sucks dirt now and forever," I confirmed with certainty.

"Sucking dirt?" She repeated the words as if to replay them back in her head for confirmation. Her eyes fell back to me. "What the hell happened to him? Or better question. Who happened to him?" Promise's eyes squinted at me.

"El Guapo killed him." I confirmed to ease her suspicion. I knew she thought right away I had finished him off. And while I would have liked to be the one to pull that trigger, the fact was El Guapo beat me to it.

"Okay this too much for me." Promise threw her hands in the air to wave everything I had said off. "Where the hell is Plies's rat ass at? I'll pop a cap in him myself." Her statement made me burst out with laughter. She laughed too. My sister was my keeper at the drop of a dime.

My tone went back to the seriousness the matter caused for. "No worries. Snakes don't crawl long in this game. Plies is sucking dirt for now and forever also." My statement was clear.

"Good. Wait, who did him the honor?"

"His sponsor, Salvador."

Promise sucked her teeth. "See? What goes around comes around. Weak ass nigga."

"A true fact. The proof is in the bullet," I added.

"Oh, and this all works all for the good of you, now you don't have to work for Salvador who clearly was a snake too."

"Well, actually Marlo and I are now employed by El Guapo, who now holds Salvador's power and has the same demands of us as Salvador," I announced to her dismay. The immediate frown on her face confirmed that. I had laid out everything but purposely I had left out the part about Pablo being Marlo's dad. I was not prepared to discuss that secret that had been kept from me. I didn't even want to think about it but couldn't shake it.

"Damn, this is all a mess."

"Some would say so." I finally stepped away from the window. I walked over to the bed and picked up my cell phone. I had called Mob on the way from the airport and told him we needed to meet up. I had to get going. "Listen, I have to meet up with Mob. As usual I have business to handle, you know that never ends. But we'll talk later." I looked over at my twin then made a quick exit from the room before she could question me.

Chapter 2

In the garage I jumped in my new white Ferrari 488 with Red Interior, while the garage door eased up, I slid on my Tom Ford sunglasses. I backed up just as Promise reached her black Porsche. She glanced over at the Ferrari and smiled. She was crazy about this car. I planned to get her one just like it for our birthday. I slowly drove down my driveway and made the interstate my destination. I knew rush hour was about to approach and I didn't want to be a victim of it. I veered onto the freeway and let my Ferrari rip. I was in the mood for some speed, then a nice drink.

Downtown traffic was already deep. People were getting off work and in a hurry. I pulled up to a red light, and the vehicle next to me honked their horn. I glanced over at the blue minivan sitting stuck waiting on the light to change, and the white young blonde woman who was driving let her window down and yelled. "I love your car so much." Then she gave me a thumbs up just as the light turned red. I was not in the mood, but I forced a smile before stabbing out.

I pulled up to the Bird & Bees bar, a hot spot in downtown LA. The crowd was always thick, but I been cool with the owner since DaVon had introduced us, they had been close. So, all I ever had to do was call ahead and one of their best tables was reserved for me. Soon as I took a seat Mob strolled in.

"What's up Precious? Mannn that Ferrari out there lookin' sweet and hot. When you gon' let me bend some corners?" Mob always wore a serious look, so everyone always assumed he was mean. But he really was a sweetheart. Around me, he softened and would smile or even ask me to drive my whip. We were cool like that.

"You already know you can borrow that car whenever you ready," I said. The waitress approached the table with our drinks. I had ordered two cognac shots for us both. I knew we would need them. At least I did. I had not had a drink since before Peru. And with the situation at hand, I really needed one. If only to mourn Pablo and Penelope, which I had not done yet. There had been no time. Business had to be handled first.

"A'ight. I'ma slide to pick it up one day." He grinned, then looked down. "Damn, wait, two shots. This must be deep." Mob sat down and ate me up with his stare. "Come on now, Precious, drop the bomb. You can't sit there and make me sweat."

"Drink up," was my words to him. I picked up one of the shot glasses in front of me and put it to my lips and sucked down the brown liquid with intense energy.

Mob's eyes never left my face, but he picked up one of the shot glasses in front of him and gulped it down. He set his empty glass on the table.

The brown liquid warmed me. I was ready to talk. "We have some major changes that are taking place as we speak. Marlo and I are now in charge of major distribution, and all collection for LA and Miami."

Mob's head moved a bit to the left. "Major Distribution of the product?" He seemed shocked and confused.

"Yes, the word has come down and we are now the link. Just like that." Mob's eyes grew wide then I could see the question on his face. Why was I meeting with him only? Where was Plies? After all, he was my right-hand man. And ever since he had assumed his position he was at every meeting as he should have been.

"That's not the only change. Plies was out of pocket like a motherfucker. He now sleeps forever." I knew I didn't have to explain beyond that.

Mob's shoulders seemed to sink as if I had dropped a bag of bricks on them. He appeared to suck in a breath. "Hell naw." He finally released. "That nigga betrayed the code? Went against the grain?"

"Dirt in the ground, snake flat on his belly. He murdered Pablo and Penelope." I picked up my last shot and downed it. I signaled the waitress over. "Please bring me two more." I realized I needed to slow down on the drinks, but I really needed it. I could literally see Penelope and Pablo's faces. In a way, they were the last connection I had to DaVon. I could remember the first time he introduced us on my first trip to Miami. Things were so different then. I was different then. I was an innocent girl, a regular citizen with regular dreams. Now . . .

"I'll take two more as well. Damn, I can't believe that nigga had the nuts to kill them." Mob looked disgusted, then downed his last shot. He released a small grunt as it wet his throat. "I shoulda known that nigga was a fake. How da fuck I let that slip me?" Mob balled up his right hand. His pinky ring was shining so hard the lights from the ceiling bounced off it. "Pussy ass niggas can't spell loyalty these days. Wish I coulda put that nigga to sleep myself woulda been my pleasure. Fuck boy." I had known the information about Plies would bother him, nothing bothered a hustler more than knowing someone they trusted with their lives was a snake. When you on the streets making moves, getting money, claiming territories, you are for sure racking up enemies just as fast as you can do all three. Someone is always gunning for your spot. So, you need the ones you hustle with to watch your back. Because all situations are life or death. And to find out they were the enemy all along. It leaves a stain that's hard to get rid of. Sometimes forever.

"So in lieu of all that, I'm going to need you to set these meetings up with the Crew leaders. You know what must be done. And you are familiar with them all, correct?"

"Ah, hell yeah. I know them all. Clip made sure of that. He told me I was to always know the leader of the pack."

"Good. I need you to reach out to them and set it up, like for tomorrow. I know this is super last minute but this shit gotta be done quick. Ain't no way around it. All they need to know is they must make this meeting; their product depends on it. But you are not to disclose no more than that."

"Got it. What about the spot and the time?"

We paused the conversation as the waitress returned to set the shot glasses on the table. She exited and I continued, "Well, that is going to work the same way it does when we meet with our own crew. I will let you know about an hour before the meeting. You will tell them then. Marlo will touch down tomorrow. I'll have my final decision then."

"A'ight. I'll start reaching out asap. Don't worry, I got you."

I nodded because I knew Mob could do it. We finished off our drinks then parted ways. I had to go by the dry cleaners to check on one of the pressors Katrina had been complaining about. I wanted to grab the warranty paperwork to take home to review. She had called the company to come out to look at it. But according to her it was acting up again, and they had been out twice already. I wanted to see exactly what the warranty said before I made my next move, possibly with the insurance company.

"I see you in that pretty white piece of heaven today." Katrina was beaming as soon as I stepped inside.

The drinks had me feeling a bit more mellow, so I was able to give Katrina a sincere smile. Not like the one I had forced for the lady at the red light earlier. "What's up, K?" I noticed a tall, light-skinned, muscle-toned, medium-built guy, with a flat top haircut, standing close to the counter. He glared at me then back at Katrina. Something told me he was not a customer, and they were acquainted on a personal level.

"Same ol', wrapping up a few things before Regina gets here. But I want you to meet Lalah daddy, Kenneth. Ken, this is my boss lady Precious." I had guessed right.

"What's up." He spoke in a deep throaty tone that I thought was disgusting.

"Hi." I continued behind the counter and stood close to Katrina and looked him face on. His eyes seemed to get a bit shifty.

"Precious, you never met him before, but Mr. Larry did." She referred to my dad. "He met him more than once. Ken, you remember Mr. Larry back when you used to come up in here?"

"Yeah, sho' do. Your dad was nice. Always welcomed me when I came through." I wondered if that was a hint for me to welcome him. That was the shady way it came off. I decided to ignore that.

"That he was." I nodded. I wasn't sure about this Kenneth. I did remember hearing his name a few times, although I had never managed to be here at the dry cleaners when he came by. I also remembered that my dad didn't like him. From what my memory gathered he was not good to Katrina, and as my dad put it "not good for her." And if my memory served me correctly, he had gone to prison. I really didn't have time for pleasantries since I was on another mission. I excused myself to seek out that warranty. I was sure if he had just got home from lock up, they had some catching up to do.

Chapter 3

To say my head was banging when I opened my eyes the next morning was an understatement. Those quick shots I had taken at the Bird & Bees with Mob had kicked in. Not only was my head banging like it was being beat by a drum, but my stomach was twisting and turning so hard I had no choice but barf its contents up into my toilet. But I couldn't let that slow me down. Today was the first meeting and there was nothing getting in the way of that. So, after emptying my guts and popping two extra strength Excedrin I headed for the kitchen on foot, but the way my head was banging I seriously contemplated crawling there.

I nearly bumped into Rosa coming out of the kitchen. She was so short, sometimes I felt like I was towering over her. "I'm sorry, Rosa." I apologized, trying to hold my balance. My head seemed to swim from my throbbing headache. I rubbed my forehead and tried to breathe slowly.

"It's okay. Awww, I hate to see you suffer. Pfft." She sucked her teeth. "That pot of coffee you asked for is ready to go. Come on, sit down and I'll make you a cup."

"No, I got it, Rosa. I'll be fine, I just swallowed two Excedrin. I should be good in about five minutes."

"How about breakfast? I can scramble you up some eggs and bacon. A full stomach might suck up the pain and some of that alcohol."

"No, I'm good on the food too; this coffee is more than enough." The thought of food made my head pound even more. I was not in the mood to do no munching. I wanted silence and a cool breeze.

"Alright, yell or text me if you need me." She scrambled off with her AirPods in her ears. Rosa loved her music. It was common for me to find her doing a little dance while performing her duties. I loved her spirit around the house.

Grabbing a coffee mug from the cabinet I reached for the coffee pot and allowed the black liquid to fill the cup. I only mixed in three Splenda packs to rid it of that bitter taste. I normally had a cappuccino or plain coffee with about ten Splenda and plenty of creamer. But today I was on a mission to break this headache, so less sweet was okay. I wanted some fresh air while I downed my coffee, so I decided to sit out by the pool.

"*Just touched down. Got a few moves to make.*" I read the text that came through from Marlo. I sipped my coffee and took in a deep breath. The fresh air seemed to caress my skin, and seep into my pores—it was what I really needed. I wished I could sit there all day and do nothing but stare at the beauty. But even I knew that was a dream. I finished off my coffee, slid on my all-white Jimmy Choo heels to match my tight blue jeans, red fitted blouse, and my Gucci gold line chain purse, told Rosa bye, and jumped in my black Porsche.

By the time I pulled up to Promise's salon my headache was a memory and the caffeine had given me some life.

"Good morning, Precious," Lisa said as soon as I stepped

inside. She was sitting behind the desk batting those long lashes that she kept so flawless.

"Good morning." I smiled at her.

"Precious, I swear you be coming up in here lookin' like a supermodel. You and Promise need to hit somebody runway and let these chicks know what's really good."

"Nah, I like hot wings way too much," I joked. People have always told me how exquisite my facial features and body were. I had been called beautiful on more occasions than I cared to count. But my dad had raised me to focus on being a good person. So I never thought about my looks even when others raved about them. And to be honest I was glad I was not shallow or conceited. Those characteristics would do me no good in the life I led.

"Hey, Precious." Toya popped in the front. "You don't have an appointment with Promise, do you?"

"Nope, not today. What's up?" I knew if she asked me that something was going on.

"She called not too long ago saying she would not be coming in today. She had two appointments this afternoon, but she couldn't remember who. Lisa, can you check that for me and also call Prel and see if she can come in to do one of them. And I'll squeeze the other one in."

"Sure, I'll take care of that right away." Lisa started typing on the MacBook in front of her.

"Toya, did Promise say why she wasn't coming in?" I asked out of curiosity.

"Nope, she never really said. She just asked about her appointments." Toya hunched her shoulders.

"A'ight I'll give her a call. I'm out."

I jumped back in my Porsche and dialed Promise right away. I would have headed over, but the meeting was about to start soon, and I just didn't have the time.

I clicked my seatbelt and waited for her to answer.

"Hey sis." Promise answered the phone on the second ring. Her groggy voice told me she was still in bed.

"Girl, why you playing hooky this morning?" I wasn't used to Promise missing work. She was one of those people who came to work even when she did not feel well.

She laughed on the other end. "You must be at the salon."

"Yep. Thought I'd stop through this morning and show you my pretty face." I teased. Hearing her voice, I knew she was okay, so I wasn't worried anymore.

"Dang, well, I hate I missed your pretty face." She giggled. "I was going to call you once I got up. But I had this migraine this morning that was kicking my butt. So I said forget it."

"Ah, I had a headache this morning too but mine came by way of the too many shots yesterday."

"I wish mine had come from shots." She yawned. "I think I'm just tired. But I'm good though."

"A'ight you need anything at the moment?"

"Nah, just some rest. I took some pain meds. I'll be back kicking ass in a few hours."

"Cool, well, that meeting I told you about will start soon so I'ma head that way, but I'll come by your place later and check on you."

"Wait, what about your boy, Marlo, did he make it?" That was a question I did not want to answer because I did not wish to discuss Marlo. I also knew Promise would ask question after question if I didn't quickly shut it down. So I did.

"Yes, he is here. Listen, I gotta go. Get some sleep." My words were rushed on purpose. I ended the call before she could respond. I really wasn't prepared to see Marlo, but I had no choice. We had work to do, nothing else mattered.

* * *

I arrived on time for the meeting. Mob met me outside, joined by Don P. They were talking as I approached. My instructions had been clear. Case and Rob held down the inside along with a few lower-class henchmen who had hopes of coming up, all standing guard. I knew the Crew leaders would bring along a few of their henchman for safety. I mean everyone always wanted to feel like they had back-up which stood for status. And it was cool. They could bring along henchmen, but this meeting was closed to anyone but the bosses. So henchmen would remain outside the room.

"Everyone inside?" I asked soon as I was in earshot of Mob and Don P.

"Just as ordered." Mob stated.

"They a bit antsy though." Don P warned.

"Really, hmmph." I was amused by that bit of information. I swear men had no patience. This made me want to delay things just to fuck with them. But I was a professional. I wouldn't make them shit bricks for no reason. "Let's go inside." Just as we started to enter the building Marlo pulled up. He and Phil jumped out of a Mercedes truck. We stood back and waited for them to approach.

"Yo, this LA traffic ain't nice to a Miami nigga." Marlo grinned. He stepped in close to me, and his presence felt so welcoming. But I took a step back; being too close to him was making me weak. As usual, he looked good enough to chew up and swallow. He had on some clay-colored Givenchy trousers, with a fitted white tee, and a navy-blue Burberry blazer. Talk about suave and plain sexy. And he smelled so delicious, I had to count backwards to keep from swooning. I was captivated by his sheer presence. I needed this meeting to be over so I could be gone away from him.

"Well, we have to have something that sets us apart

from the rest of the world. Otherwise we'd be basic." I said it as a joke but wore no smile. Phil, Mob, and Don P all dapped each other up. I started inside, but Mob jumped in front of me. His presence meant something to our visitors.

Inside the room I set my eyes on all the major Crew bosses that had dealt with Pablo and Penelope the same as I had for distribution. Yeah, LA was full of wannabe hustlers who had different distributors from all over. But this room was full of what some might call my brothers, although we had no relationship besides institutional knowledge of who each other were. And until today that had been more than enough.

Sitting around the table glaring at us were Quavo, Stylz G, Rolla, Yellow Jack, and Boss. All of them had known me as DaVon's girl in the beginning. I was sure each one of them had some type of ambition to take DaVon's territory over when he was murdered. But we know how that story goes.

The antsy look that Don P had spoken of was definitely apparent. They were ready to get on with it and bounce. I too was ready to be rid of this room, so I jumped right to it once I was seated. Marlo sat in a chair right next to me.

"Fellows, I know this meeting is totally unexpected. Or you might say out of the ordinary, take your pick. I'm not sure what you heard or if you heard anything at all, but I'm not here to confirm anything." I would not be the one to confirm Penelope and Pablo were dead. Truth be told, I was sure they probably knew more than I did. That's how it usually was. "Now I know all of you are familiar with me as I am with you. Not sure if you all are familiar with Marlo?" Silence, no one said anything. I expected that.

Marlo's eyes fell on me then rolled on all of them. His voice followed. "I'm Marlo, as Precious said. Miami born and hustle. But it's a new day. Precious." He tossed it back to me. I was hoping he would go on. Just speaking about the change brought me back to Pablo and Penelope reality.

"As you all just heard, it's a new day. What does that mean?" I asked the question I knew they were brewing to ask. "Marlo and I are your new distributor and collector." The glares they gave me, I felt like they were looking straight through me or were just dumb and didn't get it. And I personally didn't have time for that. I decided to be clearer. "We are the new Pablo and Penelope. All our product will be coming down from El Guapo. If Salvador's on your mind? Get him off." Their stunned faces told me they got it. "So, for what you need you will have to go through Marlo and me. Whatever changes need to be made to keep shit in order we send down the order. We in charge." That had to be said. The words no crew boss ever wanted to hear.

Yellow Jack, whose name described him and his banana-colored skin tone and face full of freckles right to a tee sucked his teeth. He gave a chuckle that was full of combativeness. I kept my composure and waited to see what mistake this fool was about to make. His eyes fell to Marlo. I watched in slow motion as his red lips moved. "Listen, I ain't taking orders from nobody who don't look tougher than my thirteen-year-old daughter."

The already quiet room seemed to get quieter. I was sure I heard a cricket chirp. Marlo looked around the room, his eyes nearly falling on everyone in attendance. A smile slowly spread across his face as if he was just catching on to Yellow Jack's insult. "Oh, that was meant for me?" He chuckled. But that chuckle carried something that sent a chill up my spine.

Yellow Jack lips attempted to stretch into a smile but before it was complete I watched as Marlo's right hand came up gripping a gun and a bullet released from the chamber landed right between Yellow Jack's eyes. His eyeballs bucked, his body jerked, his brains splattered from the back of his head, his head fell forward as the blood drained out the side of his mouth. Nobody moved or even looked at him long. The message was crystal clear.

"Anybody else?" I asked, just for clarification. Turns out nobody else had a thing to say aside from asking when they could get their next shipment. After filling them in on what we knew for now, I had another issue to address. We were fully aware of everyone's territory and what was going on. That was now a part of our job.

"Rolla. You have a few murders in your territory and it's going to bring unwanted heat, so the beef or whatever going on needs to come to a close. Get that under control like yesterday."

"We workin' on that. No doubt," he assured me. That was it for me, and Marlo had nothing else, so we ended the meeting. Mob set things in motion to handle Yellow Jack. His henchmen were dismissed. For their own safety, they complied. Trying to stand up for him would only have ended with them being chopped to pieces beside him. I would let them know in twenty-four hours who would be heading up their territory now. That was that.

Outside I tried to quickly head for my vehicle, but Marlo caught up to me. "Precious, slow down." Reluctantly I slowed my pace. I had planned on being out of sight before he could recognize I had dipped. Mission failed.

I turned around to face him. "What's up?" I tried to be nonchalant. I wanted to hold up my hand and tell him to keep his distance. This way I wouldn't be sucked up again by his delicious, enchanting scent.

"I see you in a hurry. But can we at least grab a drink a lil later . . . you know . . . so we can talk. We really need to discuss some things." This was why I didn't want him to catch me alone. I had avoided this conversation on the long plane ride back from Peru and I was still intending to avoid it for as long as possible. My thinking cap was on, but I said nothing. "Listen, I get on a Learjet later tonight back to Miami. So . . ."

Then the perfect excuse jumped in my head "Aye, I already know you have to get back. But I can't later, time is tight. I have to go check on Promise, she's not feeling well." I looked off quickly before looking back at him. "Yeah, gotta go see about her." I followed up. He knew I was trying to avoid him, but I didn't care. As long as I got out of it.

"Okay . . . okay . . . well listen. Send Promise my best. I won't hold you." I nearly turned around and took off running to my vehicle. Because if I looked at him any longer I would without a doubt give in.

I decided to stop and pick up some Hibachi before heading to Promise's crib. She answered the door wrapped in a pink and black Chanel throw blanket. She had told me on the phone that she was fine, but she looked the opposite in person. "Are you sure you're okay? You look like hell."

"Oh, gee thanks." She played like her feelings were hurt.

"Hey, I'm just saying." I hunched my shoulders and grinned.

"So brutal." She smiled. "No, really I'm fine. I feel much better. And thank you for bringing me this food. I am so hungry." We went into the den. I set the food down on the ottoman before sitting on the couch.

"It's the least I can do to get my sissy pooh well. Besides, I'm hungry too." I grinned.

"I got some Merlot in the refrigerator on chill, go grab it and some glasses." I went into the kitchen as fast as my feet would take me. My stomach was growling like an angry lion. Promise had pulled the food out the bags by the time I came back from the kitchen. I popped the bottle and filled both our flutes.

"So, how did the meeting go?"

"Good. I'm glad it's over."

"That's what's up. How is Mr. Marlo?" I wanted to scream *stop bringing him up*.

But instead, I replied "Good." Then quickly sipped my wine long and hard, hopefully, she wouldn't press me to elaborate. "Ahh, this is good and cold. I can't wait to finish off the bottle." I could only hope Marlo was finally off Promise's mind. Although knowing my sister, I truly doubted it.

Promise sipped her wine and then picked up her plate. "Marlo still in the city?" I had to fight to keep from rolling my eyes. The girl never gave up or in.

"Yeah, for a minute, he leaves out tonight. Gotta get back to Miami and the business. He wanted to go for drinks, but I told him I couldn't go."

"Why? I know not so that you can bring me food. Please say you didn't." She looked as though she might frown.

"Well, that and I just wasn't feeling up to it. Besides, I still have to go out to Miami. I'll see him then." I put a sauteed shrimp into my mouth and chewed. All this talking wasn't helping food get into my stomach and I didn't want my shrimp to get bone cold. Promise just continued to stare at me. I could feel her investigative eyes on me.

"What happened when you ventured out to Miami? Besides the obvious that you explained?" It was so hard to hide anything from Promise, but I still would try. I was just not ready to discuss Marlo no way no how.

"Nothing really, shit just got crazy." There was one thing I had to admit to her though. "But to be honest with you I'm really not ready to go back to Miami just yet."

"How long are you supposed to be out there for?"

"Two days to handle business. But I'm not ready to be alone with Marlo right now." I could not believe I was admitting that much. But I had to. I was desperate.

Promise screwed her face up with confusion. "Why? You need to stop tripping off Marlo. "Pfft." She sucked her teeth. "Tell you what. I need a getaway. I'll go with you, this way I can be like some kind of a distraction for you." I nearly jumped in her arms—that was exactly what I was hoping she would say. And she only had to say it once.

"I'll book your flight tonight. We leave tomorrow." The relief I felt was immense. Promise would be my saving grace from Marlo. "Wait, but what about the salon? You leaving last minute and all?" I had forgotten all about her business, I was so worried about myself.

"Toya got it, no problem. It's all good." The smile on her face reassured me. And l was desperate for her to go so I wasn't asking too many questions. *Miami here we come* was my only thought.

Chapter 4

The plane's landing gear hit the runway and slightly jerked my body, and I sank deeper into my first class seat and glared out the window. Promise sat next to me smiling so hard one would have thought she had won a prize and it was inside the airport waiting on her arrival. My mind drifted back to when she had volunteered to come with me to Miami. She had run and packed her Louis Vuitton bags five minutes after she agreed to go. And then she had rushed me off to go home and follow suit. It appeared she wanted to go just as bad as I needed her to go. Soon as we were off the plane we sought out Hertz Rental Car, where we picked up the Mercedes truck I had rented. The Hertz agent took my ID, verified the information, and added the car insurance, then she gave us the key and we hit the traffic.

"Precious, I just googled it and there is a Krispy Kreme not far from here. Let's go by there before you take me to the hotel." We had just got on the interstate that would take us to the Ritz-Carlton.

"I swear you, those doughnuts, and these non-driving-ass Miami people." I hit my signal light and jumped over to the right lane where traffic was moving faster and more consistently. In the lane I had been in, the car in front of me seemed to keep hitting their brakes for no apparent reason that my eyes could see. And one driver wanted to ride side by side with me like we were conversating. I had things to do and had no time for these traffic games.

"Just get me to Krispy Kreme safe and sound." Promise grinned. "And yo' ass know you want a doughnut too." She added that bit of truth.

I laughed. "Sure do. Matter of fact I'll take three. So don't be trying to cuff the box, or I'll take it and sit on the entire box until it's soft enough for you to drink." I teased her. The girl could eat an entire dozen while I almost had to fight for one.

She laughed out loud. "Ugh! So fucking nasty!" She twisted up her face with disgust. "Okay, okay, I promise this time I'll share. You have my word. Now watch that damn grey Challenger trying to race you and shit . . . stupid ass hype."

"Ugh. These people. Showoffs, broke-ass losers." I sighed. I was aggravated, and I switched lanes for the sixth time.

After we checked into our two-bedroom Presidential Suite at the Ritz I told Promise I'd be back. I had a meeting with Mob. He had arrived on a flight late last night. Once again, I got out in the difficult traffic. Reaching my destination, I parked and made my way inside the Rum Bar where I had told him we would meet. I was led to a corner in the back where we would have privacy. The Rum Bar was big on cigars; they carried every flavor or style you could think of in a cigar. Mob held one up to his nose and sniffed the aroma of it as if it was a sweet potato pie.

"I hope you saved one for me." I pulled out my chair and sat down.

"No doubt. I'm not sure about the smell of some of these cigars but Precious, I think I'm in love with this place. Shit, I might never leave but if I do I swear I'll be back. These cigars and that rum. Man, I already had two drinks and I ain't been here thirty minutes."

"I know, I know, I've heard good things." The waiter came over and I placed an order for a drink. I picked up one of the cigars and sniffed. To me, it simply stank, but Mob was mesmerized by its goodness. I guess this was one of those things they called a man thang.

I looked at Mob. He had really grown into a man in the past few years he had been on my team. I remembered when I met him, he was working for DaVon, kinda like a protégé to Clip. Clip really brought him a long way, but he had to keep him close because back then he had a killer mentality. And did not take any nonsense. Clip taught him how to contain his anger and use other tactics to be a bet-ter hustler and leader. After Clip was murdered, I contin-ued to groom Mob, and I had been watching his growth. He was ready.

"Listen, I know you wondering why I brought you out here. And I want to thank you for coming. You have really stepped up, been there when I needed you, and you did whatever I needed you to do. No questions asked. You have proven your leadership and you have been more than consistent. I couldn't ask for a better right hand." Mob's eyes grew big at the words *"right hand."* I knew it was a big deal to him. "The position is yours if you will have it. You have more than earned it."

Mob blinked a few times. I could tell he was emotional, but he sucked it in and kept his tough composure. "I gotta say, I'm honored. DaVon always treated me well. When I started in this game I was lost. Full of anger, and I gotta say a danger to society. But with Clip and now you, I see a bigger, better picture that don't include only death. That's huge for me. I'll continue to do my best for you." Now I was emotional. His speech was deep. I knew I would be safe with him by my side.

"Of course, with your promotion, we need to do some moving around. Case will be moving into your spot, and Rob into Case's spot. I know I told you in the past I see potential in Don P, he is a major hustler, his grind relentless. So I want him to have Rob's spot, but I want you to continue to work closely with him."

Mob shook his head in agreement. "He has mad respect in the streets to be so young." He added.

"That's what's up. We got our work cut out for us with this new transition. But as always, we gone eat the grind. We not gone let the grind eat us."

"No doubt. That shit gotta be twenty-four, twenty-four. That's where these rookies get it twisted."

"But that's where we come in. Lead the grind and build."

"Fo'sho," he cosigned.

"Now in a minute we got that meeting with the Crew bosses here in Miami. Gone be the same update for them as LA. But tomorrow I need you to meet up with Phil, y'all got some businesses to handle out here. He'll fill you in."

"A'ight, bet."

I looked at my cell phone to check the time. "Welp, I guess I will see you at the meeting. You got the address in your GPS in case we get separated in traffic?"

"Yeah, I checked it out before I got here. These Miami people can't drive. And they crazy as shit behind the wheel."

"Tell me about it." I chuckled. I picked up my Cognac and polished it off. The waiter came over and delivered Mob a box of cigars I had special ordered for him. After paying the eight-hundred-dollar bill, I dropped a two-hundred-dollar tip for the waiter, and we headed out.

Traffic was just as unsettling on the way to the meeting as it had been since I left the airport. I had been traveling out here for some years now and the drivers seemed to be getting worse. And just as I predicted Mob and I got separated. I arrived a few minutes before he did but by the time I was climbing out of my vehicle he was pulling in beside me.

Phil came out to greet us just as we neared the building. "What's up y'all?"

Mob and I both said, "*What's up.*" The men dapped each other up. Then I added, "Is everything set up? I'm ready to get this over with." If it wasn't in my tone, it was in my facial expression. Nonchalant.

"These niggas is ready to go to. Marlo ain't here yet. He should be arriving soon though." Phil filled us in.

"Well, I'ma go ahead and get inside. It's hateful hot out here." I was not in the mood to sweat, so lounging in the sun had to be done with.

"Shii' I feel ya'. You know how Miami do." Phil opened the door and led the way inside. I noticed Marlo's henchmen all around outside the meeting room. And a few unknown faces of course from the other crews. Inside the room it was the same, some of the faces known, others unknown. Phil leaned into my space and start naming off the crew leaders.

"Left all the way around to the right end of the circle these niggas is, Rush, his crew stay hot for dumb shit like beefing over bitches, Killer's next to him but word on the street he ain't never killed shit." I would have laughed but now was not the time. The corner of Mob's lips tightened; it was clear he too thought that was funny. "Then you have Phat, he keeps a low profile in the streets but deals a lot of weight. Carlos, he definitely a major player and outsell all these niggas except our crew, he can't fuck wit' us. Then you just got your regulars Goone and Low."

All eyes were on us but that was to be expected so we started to take a seat. Then Rush asked Killer who he happened to be sitting next to loud enough that we all heard. "Yo who dis fine ass bitch, she can't be from the three o five." He rubbed his chin as if he was scoping a hood rat on a street corner.

No sooner than the words left his mouth I could feel Mob body heat as he started to make his move. Standing to the left of him I grabbed his right arm to stop him.

Without a word I took a few steps towards Rush. As I got closer, he smiled at me and continued to mouth his own destruction. "Yeah, bring that ass . . ." his lips were fixed to say more but before he can release another word I pulled my nine-millimeter from my back and smacked him across the face with the butt of the gun. The force was so strong it pushed him back and he fell out of his chair.

His eyes instantly jetted towards all the eyes of the men who watched him, his face turned from shock to anger as his stare turned to me. "Bitch, I'll kill . . ." He attempted to scream his threat, but I pumped two bullets into the center of his chest. I dead that drama right away.

"Damn that nigga dead," Low mouthed.

"Mane, let's get his ass up outta here real quick fo' he decompose or some shit." Goone stood up.

"Leave him." Marlo's voice boomed from behind us. I turned around and made my way back towards the front where Mob, Phil, and Marlo now stood. "And for those of you who don't know this is Precious. LA finest . . ." He looked over at Rush laying on the floor stiff. "And well you can see the rest. Watch your mouth and you will breathe. I know the word is out, so by now you have heard the game done changed. So as a confirmation, the new distribution for your product and collection is Precious and me. Straight like that." Marlo laid it out.

I said a few things and we opened the floor for questions. It was time to get to work. It was take it or leave it. I did hate that lives had to be lost over stupid shit. Yellow Jack and Rush's attempt to have balls had done nothing but made them casualties. Which was a waste. They were two hustlers who could have continued to come up and take care of their families which I was sure they did have. But all was well in love and the game.

"So, are you gone tell me what's really going on?" Promise asked. We were out to dinner at a famous steak place. I had showered and changed as soon as I had returned from the meeting, and we had headed out.

"What do you mean what's going on?" I cut a piece of my steak and tried to avoid being honest. To evade the question a bit longer I stuffed the steak into my mouth and chewed. It really was so juicy and good.

"Please don't play at being crazy. What's going on with you and Marlo?" She bit a piece of asparagus.

I took my time swallowing then pretended to think about her question. "Oh, Marlo, we good." I played nonchalant, picked up my champagne glass, and sipped.

Promise tightened the corner of her lips and gave me a sarcastic facial expression. "Look, we twins. You and I both know that we know each other all too well. I have let this charade go on too long. Now I known something has been bothering you ever since I found you standing in that damn window staring out at nothing. And since then, I have given you too many chances to share with me but you still beating around the bush. But tonight, my dear sister, is reveal night. Now spit it out or else." This time she picked up her glass and sipped the champagne from it.

I knew the jig was up. The waiter approached our table just in time. "Please bring two shots of Jack Daniels," I asked. I needed something stronger. The waiter smiled before he exited the table.

"This must be worse than I ever imagined if shots have to be ordered." Promise's right eyebrow lifted in a concerned manner.

"Nah, it's just time for something stronger and I know my twin don't want to be left out. So, I ordered drinks for two." We both laughed. But I stopped laughing and said, "Remember Marlo and I went to Peru, and we found out Pablo and Penelope were dead." I paused.

"Yeah. You shared all of that with me." Promise shook her head and waited.

"Well, that wasn't all the news . . . I found out that Pablo was Marlo's dad. And get this, he never said one word to me about it."

"Really? Pablo fine ass was his daddy?" Promise said as the waiter sat our drinks on the table then walked away.

"Yes, and I can't believe he lied to me about it. I thought he was a straight-up type of dude."

Promise picked up her shot of Jack Daniels. She seemed to think about it then set the glass down. "But Precious, was it really a lie? Like a deliberate one?" I couldn't believe she had asked me that. "Maybe he just never said anything. Maybe he had his reasons."

I had never considered that. We were sleeping together but that didn't mean I thought he owed me his life story. But Pablo was a major part of both of our lives. He was our boss; we spent a lot of time with him and Penelope in mixed company.

I shrugged my shoulders. Now I was uncertain. But I was sure of one thing. "I just feel like he could have said something. In our line of business that bit of information is major." I could not downplay that.

"I get it . . . it's a sensitive situation. I'm just trying to analyze it from a different way. But I don't think avoiding him is the answer."

"What makes you think I'm avoiding him?" My question had all the trappings of me feeling guilty of what I was accused.

"Oh, let me think. You do not want to face him alone. All but falling on your knees and crying to get me to come out here."

My jaws dropped open. I could do nothing else but smile. All the while I thought I was keeping her at bay with my silence about the situation. "You knew?"

"I know everything about you, I wish you would stop making me remind you of that."

"I guess you do. You and your investigative nature." I teased.

"I do have that talent as well." She laughed. "But for real though. You need to let him explain. Let him tell you why he never shared. I'm sure he has a good reason."

"Let him explain?" I gave her a look. That was the reason I was avoiding him because I simply was not in the mood to talk about it. And here she was with that suggestion. There was nothing else to say. I picked up my shot glass and downed my Jack Daniels. It burned my chest but eased my thoughts. What a good feeling.

Chapter 5

"You geared up for this meeting?" Marlo turned to me with a mocking smile. We were about to sit down on a love seat sofa. Once again, I was hesitant to sit so close to him but since we were about to do a Facetime call with El Guapo I had no choice. El Guapo of course wanted to see both of our faces, there was no questioning that. So instead of dwelling on that small inconvenience, I made getting it over with my main concern.

"Yeah, there is no other place I'd rather be." I gave him the sarcastic tone and answer he had hoped for. I looked around the room at the nice Italian furniture that had been placed in it. Exquisite art pieces had been flown in straight from art galleries, according to Marlo. Each room had a different look to it. This one was definitely plush. I had been here a few times with him on business. And honestly the house still intrigued me at times. It sat in the middle of the hood. The outside had chipped powder blue paint and broken concrete steps that led to the front door, which had no screen door. No one would who had never been inside would imagine how nice some of the rooms were decorated. And its purpose was even more interesting. It was used for murders, meetings, celebrations, you name it.

Marlo had his lips set to respond just as his phone lit up. It was time. I breathed a silent sigh of relief we could get this over with.

El Guapo's face flashed on the screen. The screen immediately started jumping back and forth. This annoyed me, the first sign of the meeting going on longer than need be. Marlo held the phone mid-air and shook it a bit as if that would make the phone stop flashing. El Guapo tried to speak but it blinked again casting his figure and voice out. Then suddenly it was clear. "Hey, this thing not gonna work?"

"Shi'dd I guess not," Marlo replied. I said nothing. I just made sure my face was visible. Time was wasting away.

"So, no smoke signals coming from the states. Everything on schedule. I like," El Guapo finally said. I took this as a statement not a question.

"Everything is handled as ordered," Marlo confirmed.

El Guapo nodded with approval. "I hear some people had to meet their destiny early?" El Guapo had eyes and ears everywhere but that was not a surprise. I wondered who the carrier might be.

We knew it was a possibility that the casualties would be brought up. But Marlo and I had already decided if he didn't bring it up, we wouldn't talk about it. Because truthfully how we handled issues that arose was our business unless it disrupted El Guapo's money. We also knew El Guapo only wanted to discuss what he felt mattered to him. Allowing him to lead the conversation was best.

"Sometimes as you know bad apples exist. But we know better than to allow them to spoil the bunch." That was my two cents on that.

"Damn right," Marlo said. He always made it clear he had zero tolerance for bullshit. And that was not an easy lesson learned for some, until the bullet was busting their head wide open.

El Guapo nodded his head in agreement. "New product coming your way. I will be in Miami . . ." He kinda slowed his words as Miami slid out. His accent was deep but understandable. "Two weeks, be ready for my presence. Precious." He said my name as if a jewel was behind it. "Your collection will have to be in Miami, and you with it." Collection meant my money. So, the crews would have to get me cash on demand. Product had to be sold out, and ready to pay up. No questions asked.

"It will be there." I assured him.

We went over a few other things that were pretty much standard. Then finally but not soon enough it was over. The first thing I did was rise out of the sofa. I could feel his eyes on me as I slithered out of his reachable grasp.

"You in a rush again?" His words were at the back of me. I turned to face him.

"Somewhat. Promise flew out with me, so." I quickly played that card as I had originally planned before ever arriving in Miami. I knew what he wanted, and I thought about what Promise had said. But in the moment, I was still feeling some type of way. Even though I really wanted to shake it.

"Listen, we need to talk . . ." He paused. "No, what I mean is I need to explain. If you give me a minute, I can at least try." The puppy dog look on his face was making my resistance hard.

"It's all good. You really don't have to explain."

"Yes, I do. And first, let me just say I'm sorry for the way you had to find out about Pablo being my dad. I don't have any real excuse for not telling you besides I didn't know things would happen between us the way they did. Once they did I just . . . well . . ." He continued to pause and rubbed his hands together. "The situation itself is just complicated, always has been. And to be honest with you I really haven't spent a lot of time in my life speaking on it."

Suddenly I felt selfish. "Listen . . ." I held up my hand to stop him. In the moment I felt bad for making him explain the situation to me. I felt his pain down deep when he said it was complicated. That is exactly how I felt about my father withholding my mother's and Promise's existence. It was a stifling and deserted feeling that was almost unexplainable. And I would hate for anyone to suggest I explain it. "I get it, okay. Now please let's not talk about that anymore." My eyes begged him to hear me.

He smiled and I tried with all my might to match his. "A'ight. So, what you and Promise got planned for tonight? I know y'all ain't held up in no hotel while in Miami."

"Maybe dinner and a few shots." I kept it real. I toyed with the thought for a second Promise might be tired from all the shopping she had done. I had ordered her a driver and Miami was her oyster. But who was I kidding, that girl would be ready to hit the streets no matter what. There was just no way I would be able to keep Promise held up in a room.

"How about I get you both all the shots you can ask for? Come out and party at this hot spot with Phil and a few of the guys. It'll be fun."

One thing I knew for sure, Promise would curse me out if she found out that I had turned down a party and drinks of any kind. And it just so happened that I too was game for some fun and a night out in Miami could do it. Plus, I knew firsthand that Marlo knew how to have a good time, so it was a no-brainer.

"So, what do you think?" Marlo leaned into my space. He had to speak up loudly to be heard over the loud music, and other scattered loud voices that were close by, but I heard him well.

"It's cool, actually," I observed the spot and was feeling it.

"It's one of the hottest strip joints in the city." The name of the place was Pole Paradise, and Marlo's words had to be true because the crowd was thick. And as we made our way through the club to reach VIP, I observed mad money being thrown at the dancers. Top notch dancers to be sure, there was no debate they were bad. I had not seen one yet that didn't look like she could walk off the stage and onto a video shoot.

"You come here often?" I asked Marlo and continued to watch the dancers showcase their pole tricks. This one chick they introduced as Taste was banging on the pole, her skills were obvious. She appeared to fly to the top of the pole, she glided up so quick and fast. In one circular motion, she did a double flip on the pole, spun around, and started twerking on the pole from midair.

"Dammmm . . ." Phil yelled.

Promise's eyes bulged as she looked at Phil. "I got to meet her, that's one hard-working bitch." We all burst out laughing.

"That's why they call it Pole Paradise." Marlo said. Then looked at me. "I come periodically. Who wouldn't for entertainment like this?" Watching Taste do that trick I had all but forgotten I had asked him a question.

I smiled though. And he was right, entertainment like this was hard to come by. I was glad I had come; I was really enjoying myself.

"Marlo, thank you so much for inviting us." Promise beamed then winked at me.

"No doubt. Couldn't have you in Miami and not be a part of the hottest party in town."

After a few more drinks and twerking to a few more songs Promise said she had to go to the bathroom. She had finally gotten to meet Taste and two other dancers who had just left VIP putting on a personal show which landed them a quick ten thousand dollars from Marlo, Phil, and the crew. So, she yanked me off with her.

"Come on let's sit here for a minute." Promise suggested as we approached the bar. We had just come out of the bathroom and grabbed a seat. "I tell you I am having too much fun. I'm so glad I decided to come to Miami with you." She smiled long and hard.

"I'm glad you came. I probably would be in my room right now, having a drink and counting down the time my flight would leave." I had to be honest.

"Why would you stay at your hotel though? You still could have hung out with Marlo. He fun as hell."

I nodded my head. "He is," I admitted.

"Shit, Marlo my nigga. You better make sure we always kick it when we in his city or when he out in LA. No pressure . . . but how did the talk go you had with him? You never said anything. But we are here soooo . . ."

Clearly, our talk went okay. Because if not I would not be up in Pole Paradise getting my drink on. But I had not shared that with her because we didn't have time once I told her he had invited us out it was time to head out.

"It was cool. He explained about Pablo and why he didn't say anything . . . kinda the reason we expected." I hunched my shoulders.

"See, I told you. I'm glad you two sat down to talk about it."

"Yes, we are straight. And I understand why he didn't say anything. Nothing was intended in the wrong way."

"Here you go, one bottle of Krug, and it's our most popular flavor the Brut Rose." The tall cute, white, bartender was cut up with muscles, and wore a grin. He slid the pail full of ice with the Champagne bottle sitting on top, followed by two glasses across the counter in front of us. Both Promise's eyes and mine were fixed on him our heads turned towards each other at the same time. Our eyes both read clueless.

"We didn't order yet." I told him. He had given us someone else's order. But the club was packed, I was sure it was an easy mistake.

The bartender again showed us his grin. "Umm, it was ordered for you. Just look off to the right at the end of the bar." He instructed us.

A brown skin, medium build guy with a flat fade, met eyes with us.

Promise turned to the bartender. "Aye, we good." She glanced over in my direction. "A fifteen-hundred-dollar bottle of Krug. These Miami niggas just like the ones in LA. Do too damn much."

"Ain't that it." I agreed. I instantly thought of Quan's shifty ass. That had been his approach when he slithered into our circle. A bottle of very expensive Champagne had been his token of bullshit, that was meant to pull the wool over our eyes. I always wished I shot him on sight. Snake. It would have saved my sister and myself a lot of pain and be-trayal. But he was a lesson learned. "Let's get back to VIP." I stood so I could shake Quan out of my mind. Promise fol-lowed and we made the trek back to the VIP section.

The party continued back in the VIP. The drinks were plentiful, more dancers entertained, and the DJ kept us on our feet. Rick Ross's "Nine Piece" was blasting out of the speakers. "I'm smoking dope, I'm on my cell phone, I'm selling dope, straight off the iPhone." We all sang the lyrics along with Rick Ross. Promise and I twerked. Marlo bobbed his head, holding a cigar in between his fingers.

"Aye, Aye." Promise yelled. Her face was lit up with the good time she was having.

The Rick Ross song ended so we took a breather and sat down with Marlo and Phil.

"I really like this strip club; it seems more like a regular club. If it wasn't for the strippers, I would think we were strictly at a club," I said. Every strip club I had ever attended the atmosphere was Players Club, smelled like money, drinks, and thirsty niggas. This strip joint . . . the vibe was different. The girls had real skills and weren't just shaking their ass up and down and attempting fake half splits.

"Maybe you can turn your club back in LA into a strip joint. You know, bad bitches, a hot ass stage, and a few poles." Promise winked at me as she teased. "Shi'dd we could have these five nights a week."

Marlo laughed out. "Hey, I'm sure my man Money can give you some pointers on how to make it a success. All you got to do is say the word."

"Who is Money?" That was a name I had never heard someone be called. So I had to ask.

"He owns this place." Marlo answered my question and signaled the waitress over. He asked for shots for all of us. Just like that we partied on. We all were standing around gazing out the VIP window watching the stage with the current dancer. Suddenly, the brown skinned guy from the bar stepped inside our VIP area. Promise was bouncing to the music but she had caught a glance of him, she chilled and glanced at me.

"Everything good." He approached Marlo, he had to talk loud over the music.

Marlo was engrossed in lighting another cigar looked up, and grinned. "Yo Money, my man."

Promise turned to me and mouthed his name. "Money." We both knew he was the owner Marlo had told us about. My first thoughts were maybe that it is why he had sent us the Bottle of Krug down at the bar. Had he known we were Marlo's guest?

Marlo shook the guy's hand and continued. "Aye, you guys never let a brother down. They treat us like kings up in here every time we here. Guess you passed down the word?"

"Good, good. And what about your guests?" Money smiled and it was clear his eyes were glued to Promise.

"Shi'ddd they all good. Like I said, your staff roll out the best." Marlo closed the little space between us with Money on his hip and introduced us. From that point on Money permanently glued himself into our space and started up a conversation, but mainly with Promise. But I was cool with that. All the drinks I had set in, and I was feeling mellow and did not feel like chatting much. But eventually Marlo, Phil and I started chatting so I kinda separated from Money and Promise. The party continued, Money never left VIP, and he made it no secret Promise was his goal.

Chapter 6

Back in LA, I got back to the business at hand. With the new position as collector and distributor of major crews and keeping my own crews on top, my hands were full. But I had to also stay on top of my other businesses: the dry cleaners, the club, and the hair store. Thankfully, nothing was suffering, and business was booming at all of them. But it kept me active. Sitting at my desk going over the numbers at the club, I had no doubt that in a year they would be double. I credited a lot of the revenue to the Happy Hour I had started some time ago. Not to mention the new drinks that Sharita had come up with were a hit.

The crowd was pouring in every night we were open, and I had one of the hottest DJs in the city. But recently I had been thinking of new ways to the keep crowd coming. Because I understood the key to a successful business was to never get comfortable or content. Change was always good in a thriving business.

I looked up and said come in to answer the tap on the door. "She's here." Sharita held my office door open and slid her head inside without coming all the way in.

"Cool. I'll be right up." I logged off my computer to secure it while I stepped out for this meeting. This young chick from around the way had been stopping in for months trying to get me to hire her as a club promoter. I had been a bit reluctant, but I had finally decided to give her an interview to see what she had to offer.

The club was still closed, but would be opening up for Happy Hour soon. The only person on deck was Sharita, she would be serving up the drinks since this was her shift. I made my way towards the front. I could see the young lady who had been introducing herself as Shasha sitting at the bar. Sharita slid what looked like a sprite across to her.

I eased down at the bar next to her. She crossed her legs and looked at me. "Precious, thank you so much for finally agreeing to interview me." She beamed but appeared a bit anxious.

"Welp, I think your constant presence wore me down." I gave a chuckle. She had low-key annoyed me. But consistency was always good if you had a goal.

"I'm sorry to be a pest."

"Well, you here now, so tell me what it is you can do for this establishment, this club?"

She sighed, lifted her shoulders, and took a deep breath. She still seemed a bit nervous, but she shook it off. "Listen, I have been grinding all over this city of LA to get my name out there. For the past three years, I have been promoting people's parties, whether it be a house party, bowling party, club party, you name it, I promoted. All that to set myself up as a brand." For a minute I thought she might not take a breath.

"Okay. Sounds like you got a work history." What she had just spilled sounded good but that was one thing. I needed to know what she could do for this club in particular. "What are you trying to do different here?"

"Well, now I want to add club promoter strictly to my resume. I want to put all my energy into that. And I know

I could do this if I had the chance. If you gave me the opportunity."

"This club already has a reputation," I had to remind her. "We pack the place five days a week. We have Happy Hour, and three nights a week, we pull crowds just to party with us. VIP is always booked. What can you contribute that we don't already have?"

"Well, I've been grinding like I said. I've made some important contacts with a lot of local artists, some who have a hundred thousand or more followers on Instagram, Twitter, you name it. Meaning they have the potential to blow up and have a good following. I'm looking to bring those type of people in to perform and of course, their followers will come." She was really trying to sell me. But I wasn't all the way convinced yet.

"You've been doing your homework, that is a start," was my nonchalant response. For a minute she looked confused. I think she thought her mention of bringing in her contacts would seal the deal. I could see her brain turning.

"So . . . umm, I also see you are hiring for a part-time bartender. I'm great at mixing drinks. I have my license to do so. With that being said, I would also like to apply for that position." This time I was the one shocked. She really was shooting her shot to get in the doors and was determined not to be told no. And to be honest I really needed another part-time bartender. This could kill two birds with one stone. This time my brain was the one turning.

"I tell you what. I will give you the job as a part-time bartender. If you can bring in and promote some good clients that bring in good revenue, I will consider hiring you as a full-time club promoter, maybe." The alarm on my phone beeped. The time I had to spare for this meeting was up. I had another engagement, so I wrapped this up.

Shasha nearly jumped out of her seat; she was so happy I had agreed.

"Thank you so much for the opportunity. I promise you will not be disappointed." Her cheeks stretched out from her huge grin.

"I guess time will tell." I stood up. "Listen, I have to get going. But I need you to get started as a bartender this week. So, like ASAP. I'm going to leave you with Sharita. She is my top employee and in charge when I'm out. Sharita will finish up this interview with you and have you mix some drinks to make sure you are official. I know you say you have a license and whatnot, but the proof is in the pudding." I kept it real.

"Hey, whatever you want me to do." Shasha was still giddy.

Sharita had walked down to the other end of the bar where she was making sure the ice was stocked.

"How'd it go?" she asked as I approached her.

"Okay, I guess. I have to go. I want you to finish up the interview for me. She is applying for the part-time bartender position too. Have her mix some drinks ask a few more questions and report back."

"Bartender huh?" Sharita gawked at her. "Yeah, I guess." She seemed to read Shasha for clues. I giggled at her. Sharita had made it clear she wanted me to hire a guy for the bartending position. A fine one as she had put it to me.

I giggled as I walked away.

Chapter 7

"Can you give me a stop stick?" I asked the girl who passed me my cup of coffee out of the drive through window at the Dunkin' on Crenshaw. Her long orange nails with diamond studded decorations nearly blinded me as the sun hit them. But they were cute though.

"We out." She said so fast I thought she might be lying. I knew how lazy some of the workers could be. I nearly rolled my eyes from frustration. Stop sticks were important when people were driving. Just in case the hot coffee decided to spill over and burn the driver. I remembered hearing somewhere some coffee company had been sued for that exact same thing. If memory served me right, it was McDonalds. Clearly Dunkin' Donuts had not gotten the memo. "Can I get you anything else?" she asked as if she was in a hurry for me to move, tapping her long nails on the windowsill.

"No thank you. But let your manager know stop sticks are important, they were made for a reason. Google it." I added as a side note. Then I pulled out of the parking lot and out into the oncoming traffic. As usual, I noticed a few people hanging out, some attempting to sell things, others panhandling, and others telling anyone who would listen about their long-forgotten dreams. It was simply another normal day. But in Crenshaw you always kept your eyes open—it could jump off at any moment. And the last thing you wanted to be was the prey.

I was in the area to meet up with Mob. He had called me an hour ago and asked me to meet up at a spot we had in the neighborhood. But I was craving coffee something bad, so I had to make this pit stop.

"Precious, you really need to talk to the vendor." Promise was on the other end of the phone. Just that quick I had forgotten while trying to get my stop stick. Our ombre-colored, twenty-four-inch hair order had been delayed twice.

"I will handle it." I gripped my hot coffee cup, thanking God I didn't just waste it. "I'm on way to a meeting, but I'll hit Sarah up when I'm done." I placed the coffee in the cup holder as I slowed at a red light.

"Please and tell her we can send a courier to Miami if need be. But we must have that hair." Promise sighed. She was frustrated and so was I. But I was ready to make other moves on our hair orders.

"I told you we need to go over to Spain and cut a deal with the distributor. Cut the middleman out, it's the American way."

"Shi'ddd we need to do something, or risk getting jumped about this hair. These females ain't playing about their inches," Promise added. She was serious but it was funny.

"I have the solution to that though. Stay locked up behind closed doors until the hair is delivered Then they can't jump you. Now I gotta run." I was tickled about her summation of how it would go down if we did not cough up that hair.

I pulled up to the spot and put my Mercedes in park, turned off the ignition, and climbed out. It was an old house that we kept utilities on year round. Inside, Rob and Mob greeted me. They sat around a table that was in the middle of the living room of the house. Something was up because this was an emergency meeting.

I pulled out a chair, eased down. "Since I know this is not a social call let's not waste time on preliminaries." I cut straight to the chase. Getting unexpected news was a given in the game. But there was never a good time to receive it.

Mob had been relaxed in his chair, but he sat straight up. "Rolla's spot need to be shut down immediately." Mob's tone was matter of fact. "There was a shootout in one of his territories a few hours ago . . . an eight-year-old girl was shot and killed."

"Damn." Jumped out of my mouth. People being killed was one thing but a child being killed was another matter. A horrible one. No part of the game would ever make me used to that type of senseless killing. "Didn't I tell him to get that shit under control? That block been hot."

"Shit been crawling wit' cops, like flies to shit. Now babies' bodies poppin' up. That shit gone be full of Feds," Rob added. "Another dollar won't be made up that motherfucker, no time soon, they presence gone be so tight."

"Them hot headed ass niggas he got on his team. They tryna still make a name for they self. Gotta cut they ass off at the neck," Mob barked.

"A'ight. Make that shit happen, tonight. Hit Rolla up and meet with him. He is not to move shit in that territory past tonight. He needs to move that supply to one of his other territories. And have the customers move with the work. Have Don P watch to be sure that he follows orders to shut down that territory and that it stays closed. Nothing else happens there until I give the word."

"Done." Mob said. "I got a mind to merc the trigger

finger eight-year-old killer my damn self." Mob eyes were red with anger. He looked at me. "But I know the rules."

I didn't have to say anything because he said it. Sometimes we had to chill. But I agreed with him one hundred percent. A child killer didn't deserve to be walking around after stealing a life. I too had to remember the rules and why they were in place.

"And while I got you here, just a heads up. I need everybody's payment in two days. Every dime they owe. Anybody short, you know what to do." I had to head to Miami in two days to see El Guapo and bring him his money. So there was no time for games. Rent was due and there were no exceptions. Anybody who couldn't meet their obligations had bodily injury to death consequences depending on the shortage. It was simple, you got to pay to play. It was business, never pleasure.

"Let's get to work." Rob glanced at Mob. With that the meeting was over.

Now I had to get on the horn and let Marlo know what was going on. Since we were both in charge of both areas, we had to keep each other in the loop. We both trusted each other to make the right decisions on what we called minor matters. But if it was something we weren't sure about we would hit each other up. But there were certain matters that we had to speak about and agree on before acting. Like any successful business, we had protocol.

Chapter 8

"**W**ake up, sleepy head." I reluctantly rolled over and forced my eyes open. Promise had bounced down on the bed and startled me awake. I could not even remember when I had finally dozed off to sleep the night before. I had went straight home after meeting up with Mob and Rob, but I couldn't shake that bad news out of my head of the eight-year-old girl being killed. I felt so bad for her family, and what they were probably going through. After taking a shower, I had attempted to watch a movie on TV, but I couldn't focus. Eventually, I had poured myself a glass of Patron and mixed it with Cranberry. When the first glass didn't work, I had tried another.

I remembered feeling sleepy but had no idea when I had dozed off. But thankfully the Patron had done its job. Now the sun was shining bright through my windows, and Promise had popped up. But I was still sleepy and not in the mood to be woken up yet.

"Why are you up, out, and bouncing on my bed this early in the morning?" I placed my face downward into my Versace sheet set. It felt like silk rubbing into my face. "Did you not feel like sleeping in?" I pouted.

"Nope. Believe it or not I could not sleep. Trust me I tried, but no matter what I did sleep just wouldn't claim me. So, in the midst of my dismay I got out of bed at five o'clock and hit the gym." That made me turn over to face her. Promise never worked out without me all but dragging her.

"You went to the gym without me forcing you? And why didn't you wake me?"

Promise grinned. "I knew you would ask that. But yes, my dear sister, I found the courage to work out alone. And I worked out on the all the machines you have forced me to. And no, I did not skimp on the time." She was always trying to cheat on the routine. If I told her run on the elliptical for twenty minutes, she tried to run for ten. If I said do thirty squats, she tried to do fifteen. "I decided to not wake you since I know you don't get enough rest, and need to reset."

"Ha," I sang. "You didn't have any problem waking me just now. Bouncing in my bed like a crazy person. What about that reset you said I needed?"

"Oh, stop your whining." She reached for my covers and snatched them back. The cold chill in the room instantly turned to chill bumps on my skin. "Now get outta this bed and get in to gear. Rosa downstairs whipping up French toast and some juicy slices of bacon that she dipped in some maple, and it smells so good, Precious." She licked her lips. "I'm so glad I been to the gym already. Them calories already burned."

"You are silly." I smiled. "But I'm wit' all that. Now get off my bed. I'll meet you downstairs in a minute." I smiled and started to scoot to the edge of the bed. The sleep feeling was still weighing me down, but now my stomach was showing signs of being empty. And the announcement of Rosa's breakfast was more than enough encouragement to snatch me out of bed. I headed for the bathroom to brush my teeth and wash my face.

"Rosa what would I do without you? This food smells so good." I said as I entered the kitchen. The bacon smell was just purely divine. I could not wait to get that greasy, salty taste in my mouth. "I'm gaining weight just thinking about stuffing my face."

Rosa pulled plates from the cabinet. Promise filled two glasses with Tropicana orange juice. I walked over to the counter and stood next to Rosa, she handed me a platter with bacon. "Set this on the table. I'll scoop you both this hot French toast off the griddle." I set the warm platter in the center of the table and placed my body in a chair. Promise sat a glass of orange juice in front of me.

"I'm so glad I came here this morning. Rosa, you have her so spoiled."

"Don't she," I agreed, then reached for some bacon, I could feel the grease on my fingers, this was going to be good. I bit off my first piece and closed my eyes and chewed the goodness.

Rosa smiled. "Eat plenty and get full, señorita. You too, Promise. You both skin and bones."

"We are not." Promise and I said in unison while we grinned and chewed. Rosa always accused us of being too thin. She would feed us cornbread and flour tortillas everyday if we let her.

"I feed you until you get fat. American girls want to be skinny, nothing wrong with a little meat covering those bones." She laughed and exited the kitchen.

"Hey, if I get to eat this good every day, I'll welcome the fat." Promise drowned her French toast with Mrs. Butterworth's Light syrup.

"I know, right and save me some of that syrup. Dang,

you gone eat it all." I picked up my glass of orange juice. "So, why can't you sleep?" I pried. I knew it had to be deep if Promise was waking up hitting the gym.

"Who knows." She hunched her shoulders and passed me the syrup bottle. "Maybe I ate too late before laying down?" Pressing the fork down into her French toast she pulled off a piece and slid it into her mouth. "Mmmm," she moaned.

"You so greedy," I teased. "But real talk that could be why you couldn't sleep." I decided eating before bed was a good reason for sleep to elude someone. At least that is what I had heard many times in my life. "Are you going in at the salon today?"

Promise was chewing, she finished up then swallowed. "Yeah, around noon. I got two clients and some paper-work to handle."

"Did you make it over to the hair store to pick up those deposits?"

"Taken care of."

"Cool. I haven't been able to get over there. I spoke with Sarah last night and the hair will be here tomorrow. But I got to get over to the store and place some more or-ders. I just have been too busy. I leave for Miami in a few days, so I gotta get it done."

"Speaking of Miami, I've been talking to that guy, Money. He asked me to fly out."

"Fly out?" I repeated her words from shock.

Promise set her fork on the edge of her plate. "Why you say it like that? All suspicious like."

"Isn't it obvious? Why would he ask you that? You don't know him." I looked her in the eyes and forked some more of my French toast. I didn't want it to get cold.

She clasped her hands together and laughed. "Hence

why we have been talking on the phone. There is a reason people do that, you know." She teased me.

"Whatever, do what you want. But please . . . don't make me merc the dude." I tried to give a serious look but we both burst out laughing. But even still I was serious and she knew it.

Chapter 9

Today I really had a full plate of things I must cross off my to-do list. And I intended to do that no matter what tried to intervene. Which normally in the day and life of me could be just about anything. First, I was supposed to meet up with some painters over at Dad's house. They were giving me a quote for the inside of his garage, and the attic that I was having repainted. It had been a long time since those were touched up and it was time. The paint was peeling, cracking, you name it.

But once again, other emergencies were trying to derail my plans. One of the pressers at the cleaners was acting up again. Katrina had called me before she closed last night to let me know. I could hear the frustration in her tone. She remembered when Dad was having trouble with the pressers back when he was alive. But his finances had been so bad that he couldn't afford to have them fixed. And they were so old he couldn't insure them. The ones I had were new, purchased when the dry cleaners had been re-modeled. So, I was not sure what was going on, but I had to get the company on the phone where I had a contract, so they could get a technician out as soon as possible. To do that I had to be at the dry cleaners because there were specific ID numbers they required you to have off the machine when you called in, and I still had not gotten around to adding Katrina to the list of people they could speak with. I had been meaning for the past year to get that done. But for some reason or another I still had not. However, I would be making that change as soon as I was on the phone with them, this day.

"Hey Regina," I spoke, as soon as I opened the door and stepped inside the dry cleaners. She was turned around, her back to the entrance, sorting some safety pins in a container we kept on the back counter. They were normally stuck together so I knew she was trying to spread them apart, which could be a daunting task. I used to spend hours doing that when I worked my shifts and I hated it.

"What's up, Precious." Regina turned to around. "Please tell me you are here about that big presser. It has been giving me the blues this morning. I just been running orders on the small one."

"I'm so sick of that machine. I swear for all the money I paid for it . . . but yeah I'm going to call them now." I stepped behind the counter. "Where Katrina at? I thought she would be here this morning?" I was surprised Regina was behind the counter. I had been expecting Katrina. She was always here at this time, and she never called out. I could set my watch to Katrina's shifts; she was that dependable.

"She should be here soon." Regina glanced up at the clock on the wall. "She called me this morning to fill in for her." The door opened and a middle-aged Hispanic woman strolled inside. She had what looked to be a few pairs of slacks thrown over her right arm.

"Hello," Regina and I both said in unison. Regina stepped up to the counter. The dry cleaners' phone rang.

"I'll get that." I walked over to the cordless phone at

the far end of the back counter and picked it up out of its cradle. The caller wanted to check their order. After doing so I proceeded to the back office where I put in a call to the presser company called Pressers and Straights. Almost thirty minutes later and after talking to two different reps I was done with the call. And I made it clear, either I get a working presser, or my lawyer would be contacting them. They had been out three times and still the machine was not working right. This was a business and if my pressers did not work, I lost business and that was it, period. But once I mentioned my lawyer and identified him by name the debate ended.

Katrina arrived just as I made my way back to the front area. "Hey, Precious?" Her tone was upbeat but right away I could tell something was amiss. The smile on her face could not have been more forced or painted on. I had been knowing Katrina for a long time back when I was still in high school. I couldn't know her any better if she was my blood sister. Her moods, her likes, and dislikes, I knew them better than anyone who was close to her. "I'm sorry I wasn't here when you got here. I just could not drag myself from that bed this morning, trust me I tried. But I just don't feel well at all." I considered her excuse.

"Maybe you need to see a doctor if you are sick," I suggested. But somehow, I didn't think she was ill at all. Something else was eating at her. The gaze on her face wasn't illness, it was distress, and to me, they were not one and the same.

The hesitation that appeared on her face next told me she knew I wasn't buying her story. "Nah, I'll be fine, I think I feel better already, all I needed was a little extra rest this morning. Besides, Kenneth got my car, and I ain't catching no bus." There was that name again, Kenneth. Lalah's dad who had appeared out of thin air and was clearly a problem. I was sure my facial expression said it all. I was not good at hiding my feelings, and in this case, I wasn't sure I wanted to.

"He got your car?" My eyes darted towards the big windows where I could see outside. Not that I didn't believe her but for some reason I needed confirmation that her vehicle, that she herself needed for transportation, was not outside. And just as she said, her car was nowhere in sight, the spot where she normally parked it was empty.

"Yeah, I let him use it. He's been staying at the house with us." My eyes left the outside view and fell back onto her. She was smacking me with shocking news with every word she said. "He has been trying to find work, so of course he got to have transportation because you know the city buses suck. You could be on there all day. Besides, we trying to see where this goes. Us in this relationship slash family thing," She added to be more specific, and I had heard her loud and clear.

I had to close my mouth which was a bit open from the shock of it all. "Oh, for real, a relationship, huh? Welp, I gotta say, I'm bit surprised. Because I remember you telling my dad the guy was crazy. Did he change?" Dad was under the impression she was terribly afraid of him and was glad when he had gone away. Now he was back, living in her home, driving her car, and they were working on a relationship.

She gave me a grin, but it came off a bit embarrassed. Then I remembered we were not alone, I had all but forgotten Regina was standing there with us. But it was too late to take anything back, I had said what I said. "I will just say we were both young back then, learning about life, that almost seems like a lifetime ago. We are both older now, more mature, and we understand what's more important. And besides, Lalah loves him being around. You should see how she lights up when she's around him. And he's good with her, he missed being in her life. I think

I owe giving us a chance even if only for her sake." She stated it all like it was a case that she was presenting.

That was enough for me with the mention of Lalah wanting her dad around. I knew what it was like not to have a parent around, craving their presence, their love. And maybe the guy had changed, sometimes people did, but I knew only time would tell. And for that we would have to just be patient. I decided to drop it. So this time, I gave her a forced smile and moved on to another subject. Regina busied herself adding up the receipts that were attached to the tickets that needed to be calculated before she could close her shift.

"Welp, I think you both will be glad to know they are bringing us a new presser as of tomorrow. I just got off a long unnecessary call with them. But it is handled." I was glad to swipe that thorn in my side off my list so I could tackle the next.

"It's about time they stop tripping. Coming out here wasting our time only for us to still have to call them." Katrina huffed then smiled.

"Owee, I can't wait." Regina added, not missing a button on the adding machine. The girl's fingers were fast and on point.

"I know right. I had to threaten them with my lawyer to get their attention. But I am not playing with their asses. The contract clearly states if they cannot fix a machine, they will replace it. No if's and's or butts. Hell, those machines cost too much money and I refuse to lose another dollar messing around with their bullshit."

"Don't forget to put in the insurance claim to get reimbursed for the business we lost yesterday, what we will lose today, and let's be honest, what we'll lose tomorrow. Because you know they won't show up until late, probably an hour before we close acting like they on time," Katrina said.

"Yes, I put that on my calendar to do tonight when I get home. Listen, I will be out of town for the next few days. But if for some reason they don't show up tomorrow or they show up and on any bullshit, call me right away."

"Oh, trust me I will. That you ain't gotta tell me twice." Katrina screwed up her face with annoyance and rolled her eyes. She was fed up with them and I hoped they didn't show up tripping because she would probably let them have it once and for all.

With that I was out, I had managed to convince the painters to move their appointments around, so they could stop by the house in an hour. But I wanted to get there early so I could have the attic and the garage open so they could look inside with no hassle. But I wasn't halfway finished with my to-do list. I still had to make a run by the hair store to cover for a couple hours. Then be at the club to receive an order. Lastly, I still needed to pack for Miami. The last thing I needed to do was miss my flight because if I did I'd be beyond pissed. But my mind was made up on one thing. Soon as I got home the first thing I would do was take a Hennessey shot. Hell, maybe two.

Chapter 10

I found Miami alive and well when my flight touched down and taxied down the runway, rushing for a complete stop. I was not excited as usual about meeting up with El Guapo but it was a part of my duties, so I shook it off. Sometimes I just wished I was in town on pleasure instead of business but unfortunately my position only gave me the business option. I was always aware of the tourists when I came to Miami, especially at the airport. They were all happy jumping around and summing up the final plan of to-dos for their trip. I could hear in almost every conversation someone was excited about the beach.

Me, I just pulled my Louis Vuitton luggage through the airport and did my best to dodge little kids who were not paying attention, running, jumping up and down with excitement. And hoping no one stepped on my feet. Unlike them, I did not wear a huge grin on my face. Because for me it was work, work, work.

I had rented a Range Rover for my choice of vehicle. I jumped on the interstate and headed straight for Marlo's place. He was all but standing in the door when I pulled up. One of his maids normally answered the door but today he was playing doorman.

After hugging me tight he ran his lips up and down the side of my neck. Then he snatched up my luggage and led me inside. I really did not like staying at his house and I still was not sure why I had given in this time, but I did. I still insisted he let me sleep in a guest room when at first he tried to convince me to sleep in his, but I had stuck to my guns. Inside my room I told him to leave my luggage by the closet. Every room in his house was big enough to fit another room in it. I walked over towards the bed, and he was on my heels towering over me when I turned around. I would have loved to play hard to get but I was not in the mood. I had to have him.

Pulling him into me, I could not resist. I unbuckled his pants with so much force, I could feel the air swoosh by my hand. I pushed his pants down with one thrust and he stood at full attention. I licked my lips with satisfaction. I couldn't wait to have him inside of me. I'm not sure how, but he relieved me of my pants and shirt without my knowledge. He lifted me up and my legs instantly wrapped around him, and I slid down on him and moaned out from ecstasy. Two hours later we had snatched, pulled, and rode each other until we were laid out in the bed out of breath. We had dozed off and woke up. I laid in his arms and we both stared up at the ceiling.

"So, I found a new underground warehouse," he shared.

"That was quick." I replied. We had just talked about this on my last visit. I knew he was serious, but I had no idea he would find a place so quick.

"I know. It kind of came by me on accident. But I want you to look at it while you are here. I have not made a final decision if it will be the spot yet. I wanted your opinion. Will you take a ride wit' me?"

"Sure, can you give me a minute to shower?"

"That depends. Can I join you?" He leaned down and rubbed his lips across my face. It tickled.

I giggled. "I don't know, what you are giving me in return?" I teased him.

"Hmmm. Let me see." He slid his face down towards mine again and we started kissing. I opened to him without any hesitation. The shower and warehouse had to wait.

We arrived at the warehouse almost four hours later, and I was liking what I saw. The location itself was perfect. It was about an hour out of the city in a kind of country but suburban area which I could appreciate.

"What do you think?" he asked as we walked around.

I nodded in agreement. "I think it could work. The space is great. With double the supply, we will need this space. I'm sure every inch will be used. And you know I'm feeling this out of the way location."

"My thoughts exactly. Then in three months, we can decide if we need another location."

"Yeah, we definitely should know the numbers by then. And I think we need to move on that Palm Beach scene. That's gone be a major score."

"I'm on it. I will send Phil down, he knows how to lay low and move lots of work. I had a meeting with him two days ago. So, the word is final. I got a little meeting set up so he can meet with both you and I tomorrow."

I nodded my agreement. After leaving the warehouse we hit the interstate and before long we were pulling up in front of Pablo and Penelope's house. Sitting in the car we both could only look up at the mansion, in silence for a few minutes.

"It looks so quiet." I felt strange just gazing at the house with no activity. And knowing that Pablo and Penelope were not inside and would never return. We would never have another meeting or party with them at this spot. Just still unbelievable.

"Pablo put this house in my name years ago. I think when I was about twelve years old to be exact. That's how long they owned the property." I looked over at him as I could hear the sadness in his tone. That same sadness was etched on his calm face. I felt bad for him. Even though Pablo was a notorious man, he was still Marlo's father. And even though it was complicated, I understood the love and understanding they shared with one another. "He always said if something were to happen to him and Penelope, he wanted me to have this house. But I'm so conflicted and unsure what to do with it. So I drive over and sit out here, hoping I will get the answer. But I never go inside. I will never live in it. Of that much, I'm sure. I have no desire to."

That was something else I understood all too well from when my dad died. The only difference was, the house was where I currently lived so I could not escape it. But I had never considered selling his house. I can remember when he died, and they sent a letter to foreclose on the property. I had received the money from his insurance and with the dry cleaners also going under I had a choice to make on which had to go. Even though the dry cleaners was my father's legacy and his first love, so was the house and I had grown up there, it was my history, and I felt his presence all around. In the end I chose the house. While Marlo didn't grow up living in Pablo and Penelope's house, he was a constant visitor, and I was sure there were plenty of memories inside.

"You really never go inside?"

"Nope. Not once. Just can't bring myself to do it yet."

"The house is probably really lonely."

"Nah, I still have the cleaners on staff. They are here

daily. I pay them well, so they be here eight hours or longer every day. Trust, this house gets plenty of company."

I was glad to hear he was maintaining the upkeep on the house. Pablo and Penelope would expect no less. "Listen, you just need time and that is natural. Time to adjust to the loss and the gain of the house. It'll all come to you, and you will know when you can do it."

"I know. He also left me all of his money."

"Really? He didn't have any family?"

"None that he was close with. He has a brother that lives down in Texas, but he is estranged. Penelope had more family members. She left money to them."

"Wow. I never knew she had family."

"Yeah, a lot of them live in Mexico, she only really dealt with her sister and an aunt. But they never came here, she always visited them. She pretty much bought them an island over in Mexico. They set up good. And if she left them money like Pablo left me, they should never want for anything. I also thought about giving them this house to live in." Again, his eyes fell on the house and the sadness was heavy. "What do you think?"

"That's a hard one. I think you should do what's in your heart to do. Whatever you think Pablo might be happy with."

"Hmmph, he would tell me 'I give you this house, you give it away, hell no, what were you thinking of?'" Marlo tried to mock Pablo's accent, but his country tone was too powerful. It was funny. We both laughed for a minute but stopped as we continued to gaze at the house we both used to love to attend for fun but probably never would again. I hated the sad feeling we both had sitting outside of it. I was more than glad when he started up the Porsche and drove away.

Chapter 11

"You ready to do this?" Marlo asked as we pulled into El Guapo's spot out in Malibu. This was one of what I was sure was many spots he had in Miami. It was beautiful. With the view of the ocean, it was picture perfect, but that was not to forget the torture that someone could probably meet on the property.

"You already know my answer." I slowly opened my door and climbed out. Two of El Guapo's henchman came to the car. Marlo pointed to the trunk of his Lamborghini that was left unlocked for them. Another henchman led us inside as the other two retrieved the six duffel bags full of money that we had brought along. Those bags of money would cover three weeks of supply that amounted to six million dollars of hard-earned cash.

Inside we were led to the living room where El Guapo was leaned back, comfortable as shit on a sofa. That I was sure was custom made from somewhere foreign. A muscle built male henchman patted Marlo down. Then a tall, chocolate, super thin female who looked like she stepped off the cover of *Vogue* patted me down. Once it was clear that we didn't have any weapons on us El Guapo spoke to us as if it was a normal day in the neighborhood.

"Listen, mane, they can chill wit' all that." Marlo barked; he was not feeling the pat down. Nor was I.

"Come on Marlo, you know it's just business. Never personal." El Guapo's eyes were watching the duffel bags as they were being brought in. The one henchman who patted Marlo nodded to him, signaling all the money was there. "You all delivered, and I expected nothing less. We should all be happy. Now, I'm boosting your supply starting a week from today."

My head almost spun around on my shoulders he had to be kidding. Shit, we was already crazy busy, pushing weight like mad people. And more than enough: quick cash was coming in. We had just delivered the insane man six million dollars in the span of three weeks' worth of work.

"Why?" Jumped outta my mouth and there was nothing I could do to control it. "We still getting our blend just right working with the Crew, making sure shit tighter than ever. I ain't sayin' we can't handle the supply. But we already breakin' down and bringing in top dollar in crazy time. We some Weight Pushin' Motherfuckers." Everything I said was facts. The evidence was sitting in his face.

"Dead ass facts." Marlo co-signed. "And a few bodies done popped up. Few leaders had to be shift around." Marlo added more facts.

"All that, and I got six million dollars in front of me in three weeks. Make no mistake about it. I know who I got on my team. Precious and Marlo. Enough said." He stated our names like it was lit up in Gold Bars. Everything we had said only gave him encouragement that he was on the right track. He said nothing else, and it was clear he did not want to hear anything else from us. And just like that, the meeting was done. Marlo and I gazed at each other, turned on our heels, and put one foot in front of the other. In a week we would receive enough product to bring in close to sixteen million dollars in four weeks' time. No questions asked. Like I said, we were some Weight Pushin' Motherfuckers. Top stock for sure.

Chapter 12

I rang Promise's doorbell three times before she finally opened it. In a pair of silk pink boy shorts and a wife-beater she was breathing hard as though she had run to the door. I pulled off my Burberry sunglasses and gazed at her.

"What took you so long? I was about to karate kick this damn door down."

"Well, you could have tried. But I doubt them Louboutins was gone do the trick." She glanced down at my red Christian Louboutin pointed-toe heels I was rocking. "I was just getting out the shower. I dang near broke my neck getting to this door. I should have figured it wasn't nobody but you out here ringing my doorbell like the police."

"My bad." I stepped inside past her. "Thought I'd come by. I've been back from Miami for three full days, and I haven't heard from you until this morning."

"I been at the salon, it's been stupid busy around there. I have no free time to make a call. By the time I get here I fall into bed." That sounded much like my life, too busy. The only thing I did besides work was sleep when I could.

But I would not go into that, she had heard that story before.

"What's with that text you sent me about that dude Money being in LA?"

"Yep, he got in this morning." Her response was a bit too casual for me. I'm sure my facial expression said as much. And she had totally ignored the fact that I called him a dude. Normally, she would have asked me why I had called him that.

"Why is he here? To visit you or just to sightsee in LA?" My tone matched my questions.

"To see LA?" She chuckled as if my question was funny. "To see me. What you think? Pfft." She sucked her teeth then folded her arms across her chest and twisted her lips at the edge in a sarcastic gesture. "He was trying to get me to come to Miami remember, I told you about that. But I told him to come here first. Cause I could tell you wasn't feeling that. You know that look you had on your face. Kinda like the one you have now." She smiled, but I did not return it.

Instead, I replied, "I gotta say, he know he is forcing his way in. Who comes all the way to LA for someone they met for five minutes?" I tapped my right Louboutin to show my slight apprehension at the whole idea.

"What's so wrong wit' that? Them five minutes must have been enough to tell him everything he needed to know." Her smile never faded. I knew she thought I was overreacting, so she taunted me on purpose.

But in that moment, I could see that her smile was not just a smile. She was happy. I stopped tapping my foot. "Nothing I suppose. I guess you can bring him by the club while he in town. My new club promoter got some local celebrities coming through. So the club will be on fire."

"Shi'dd your club always on fire." This time I smiled.

She was right about that. There was never a dull night when the club was open. My cell started to ring. I recognized Mob's number right away.

"There goes your hotline." Promise sat down on her couch.

"What's up." I answered.

"We got a problem. Rolla on that shit and not following orders to shut that shit down." Mob's tone was matter-of-fact and not at ease. He didn't take disrespect easy. Rolla refusing to shut down was exactly that. In the past, the old Mob probably would have shot him first then called me after he got rid of the body.

"Get him on the phone and set up a meeting asap." I ended the call, there was nothing else to say. Rolla needed my special attention, that much was clear. I understood having a new boss was sometimes a challenge just like on a regular job. But this was not a regular job, we didn't report to the IRS. And the termination process was a whole lot different.

"Is everything okay?" Promise asked right away. She knew from my tone and body language something was up.

"These niggas want to test me today, it's all good, though. But I gotta be out." Promise got back to her feet. "I'll hit you up later though." I smiled to ease whatever she thought might be amiss with that call. I knew sometimes she worried about me, but I tried to reassure her as much as possible that I had this. By the time I was in my Range Rover truck Mob hit me up to let me know it was set. It would take me close to an hour to hit the meeting spot, so I hit the gas.

Don P greeted me at the door, and we walked to the meeting room together. Case and Mob were seated. I knew Mob didn't come to the door because he wanted to keep an eye on Rolla, who was seated at the table among them.

Along with two of his henchmen. Mob was giving him the death-eye, which was so convincing I shivered.

I pulled my seat out and sat down. I counted to ten in my head. I wanted to remain calm so that my delivery could be well received. Reluctantly, I turned my attention to Rolla who I too wanted to choke. I cleared my throat as a test run of my tone. "Let me make two things clear and simple." Rolla and everyone in the room's eyes were fixated on me. "This here is a single table, and everybody come here to eat. But when just one leg breaks from underneath it . . . it fucks it up on all ends."

I intertwined my fingers together and placed my elbows on the table, my eyes still never leaving Rolla. And the urge to jump across the table and squeeze his neck did, in fact, intensify. "You are one, nigga. And when you fuck up—" I stopped talking and sat back in my seat. My blood was boiling.

To my pure agitation, Rolla's voice came across the table. "Look, I need my block running. Without that one territory, I am missing major money and losing loyal customers. That situation with the little girl, that shit been died down. And . . ." Before he could utter another word, I pulled out my Ruger from under the table and pointed between his eyes. My forefinger was locked on the trigger.

His words about the little girl stung deep. His voice was crawling under my skin. The one thing I hate is for a jabber jaws who don't say shit, to say nothing. "Shut down the spot or the next time you see my aim it will bust red from that brain that you don't use to think. And have some FUCKING RESPECT . . . FOR A LITTLE GIRL WHO LOST HER LIFE, IGNORANT ASS NIGGA!" Spit flew outta my mouth I was so pissed. I eased the gun down, laid it on the table and stood up. "This shit is done." I turned and exited the room.

How dare he sit in my face and reduce a child losing their life to "that shit died down," all the while disobeying my direct orders. Honestly, had El Guapo not had a huge sum of money tied up in him, I would have blown his brains out myself no sooner than those words came out of his yuck mouth.

Chapter 13

The club was always packed on its opening nights Thursday, Friday, and Saturday. But it was a Sunday night, and the line was still hanging off the property line. It was clear Shasha's latest promotion for a local celebrity performance was going to be a hit. As usual when I knew I was going to be lit I rented a driver to pick me up and bring me home. My driver pulled up to the front of the club to let me out, security opened the door for me. Anytime it was packed they were on point for my arrival until I left the building.

Lil Wayne's "Lollipop" blasted out of the speakers as I made my way to the bar. It was an old song, but I did not see one person who wasn't singing along, and the dance floor was full.

Sharita as usual was all dolled up and serving up the drinks. The people loved her. The nights she took off the regulars would ask about her. She was popular in the club. The girl raked in at least twenty-five hundred in the three nights we were open during the week. A night like tonight would just be the extra icing on the cake. She might rack in twenty-five hundred in tips tonight alone. She smiled when she saw me. "I guess your girl really bringing them in with her promotions. It has been non-stop since I got here. And it's a Sunday night."

"No doubt, the line is around the building," I replied. From the bar I looked out and viewed the club. It was indeed packed. Soon they would be turning people away at the door. And they were going to be pissed. But we had no choice. There was no way I would risk the Fire Department coming in to shut us down because we were over the maximum occupancy limit.

"Umm, are all VIP rooms stocked and taken care of?"

"Of course, and there are two servers to a room. We gone get this bag tonight." She grinned, while mixing a drink.

"Facts," I chirped. Sharita was always on top of it. She was much more than a bartender. Honestly, she was like my assistant at the club, just not with the title yet. The girl was definitely keeper material.

"What's up Precious? Hey Sharita, girl." Regina bounced on stool at the bar in front of us. We both said hey. "Can I get a vodka shot?" She looked over her shoulder.

"Coming up." Sharita turned to do her thing.

"Hey, you know you are on the VIP list." I reminded her.

Turning her attention back to me she grinned. "I know, I'm just working the crowd for a minute. Ran into an old cutie." I should have guessed that is why her lips were stretched from cheek bone to cheek bone.

"Okay. Well, I'll catch up to you later." I exited the bar just as Sharita slid her the vodka. They started chatting and giggling. No doubt Regina was filling her in on more detail about that cutie she had referred to.

Security fell in line behind me as I left the bar. He kind of stepped to the side of me to make sure I had passing room. I gazed up towards the VIP rooms, I could see Shasha in one of them. I could tell she was checking on the guests.

A part of her job, besides bartending and promoting, was to work the crowd to be sure everyone was good. She really seemed to be good at it.

I spotted Toya right away as I stepped in my designated VIP. I saw Quavo, one of the crew leaders who now served under us in her face, and Toya was just like Regina. All tooth and gum.

I sought out a drink. "Precious." Stylz G approached me before I could get my hand on that much-craved drink. Stylz G, also one of our crew leaders, was known as a somewhat of a pretty boy. He was hazel skin toned and kept a curly flat top. But his hustle spoke for itself. He kept his traps tight, made the dough, and kept the drama out of his territory. "Aye, your spot on hit. I fuck wit' this the strong way. My first time up in here, but it won't be the last," he complimented.

"Yep, come through," was all I had. One of his home-boys stood behind him. And two females were on his hip like a baby ready to breastfeed. He introduced them both as his girlfriends. I wrote them both off for being stupid groupies. And told them all to drink up and turn up before I walked off. I needed that drink.

I signaled one of the servers over and told her to grab me a shot of Apple Crown Royal. Promise was in my face in a New York minute, I didn't even notice her approach. Right away I noticed Money on her heels. I remembered his face well from when we met in Miami. "Sister, it is off the hook up in here." She was hype.

"You know how we do, I'm glad you could take time out of your busy schedule to be here." I teased her. Promise didn't miss no special events at the club. And she didn't miss too many Saturday nights if she could help it either. If she did miss it, she had to be dog tired or sick.

"I wanted to be here an hour ago, but I was late getting

out of the salon." Money stepped to her right side, I guessed he was ready to be acknowledged. "You remember Money." She looked over at him and gave him a reassuring smile. "And Money this is my heart in life form, my sister, Precious." She introduced us as if we had not been introduced before.

"How can I forget such a beautiful face." He tried to lay the charm on before I could respond. Promise should have told him that shit would not work with me though. He would learn that really quick.

"Glad you could make it to LA." I tried to be hospitable.

"Shi'dd if this how y'all do. I'm all the way in. Your club is HOT!"

"Thanks, business is normally good and with the help of my new part-time club promoter it's only getting hotter." I gave Shasha some credit, she would have been glad to hear it herself.

I watched Promise's eyebrows stretch to the ceiling. "I need to meet ol' girl. This club promoter." She bobbed her head to Beyoncé's "Ego" as it blasted out of the speakers. I had not had a chance to tell her about Shasha. I had planned to but so far time had just not permitted.

"You will," I assured her just as Toya walked up and Prel, along with Regina, joined. They all eyed Money. Promise wasted no time introducing him. Money spoke then excused himself to go to the bathroom.

"Promise, that Money is fine as hell." Toya could not wait until he was out of ear shot, to boast her opinion.

"No lies. He is," Prel added her two cents. "Does he have a brother? Cause you know I'm single." They all burst out laughing. I didn't join in on it though. Instead, I used that time to down my shot the waitress had delivered me.

No sooner than my drink wet my throat was Quavo in my face. "What's up, Precious?" He spoke to me but the entire time he was eyeing Toya. I spoke back but it was clear he only came over to get another look at Toya. Which was fine but why must he be so obvious?

"Okay ol' boy just came over and spoke to my dear sister but Toya it's clear he got eyes for you. And please don't try to deny it. I done already seen him all in yo' face when I got up in here." Promise made it clear she had facts. The protest that Toya was brewing chilled.

"Yo, that is fine ass Quavo from around the way, if y'all don't know. He got the bag, but he a player too," Regina stated.

"I only just met him tonight. But I figured that. He looks like the player type," Toya said.

I just stood back and listened and downed my second Apple Crown Royal shot the waitress had delivered me. I was starting to feel good, and Moneybagg Yo's "Time Today" blasted out the speakers at the right time.

"That's my slap." I chanted and started singing along.

Promise started twerking. "Aye," she sang. We all joined her dancing after that we danced back-to-back on a few more tracks. After the third song I was determined to sit down for a bit and Promise joined me. Money was sitting down on one of the couches chilling.

"You good?" Promise asked him over the music as she sat down next to him.

He sat up, cradling a cup of what looked like Hennessey, he replied. "I'm enjoying myself."

"I told you it's always popping up in here." Promise leaned over and kissed him smack on the lips.

"See I told you I could bring the city out." Shasha approached and stood standing over me.

"It's a start," I said loudly enough so she could hear me over the music. That was all the credit I was willing to give her in person. Like I said, the club was always packed. She would have to show me this on a consistent basis.

Promise snatched her attention from Money and cued in on Shasha and my conversation. "So, you are the new club promoter? What's your name?"

"I'm Shasha," Shasha replied but her eyes were glued to Money.

"Shasha," I said her name to grab her attention and eyes away from Money. I could not believe how hard she had stared at him. "This is my sister, Promise, and her friend Money."

"Hey," Shasha's lips moved but her eyes again briefly landed back on Money.

Promise grabbed Money by his right hand. "Actually, Money is my man."

A smile spread across Shasha's face. Her eyes this time landed on Promise. "Well, I hope you both have a good time tonight. And Precious, thank you for this opportunity I promise you this is only the beginning."

"Well, you get back to work and have yourself a good night." Promise said before I could say anything else. Her tone and statement were dismissive. A stunned looked crossed Shasha's face; she looked at me as if to be saved but I said nothing. Appearing a bit dumbfounded she left.

I gazed at Promise and almost laughed out loud. She had hoe'd Shasha and sent her packing with a few words.

Money scooted to the edge of his seat. The mood between Shasha and Promise was clear. "I'ma go catch a server and grab me some Don Julio shots." He stood up and flexed away.

I could no longer hold it in. I laughed out long and hard. "Promise, your ass is crazy as shit."

Promise rolled her eyes then smirked. "Lil disrespectful bitch . . . where you find her at anyway? COMPTON HOES BOULEVARD?!"

I could not stop laughing. I had to catch my breath and breathe slowly to control it. "I didn't, she found me." I finally was able to release my breath. "I think she got your message loud and clear."

"She better, next time I'ma smack a muzzle on her lil hood ass." I laughed some more. I needed a good laugh. These young girls were bold these days.

Chapter 14

"Hel . . . lo." I could barely get the words straight. I was so sleepy I didn't even pick the cell phone up. Laying in the bed above my head between my disheveled pillows I just located it and touched the screen to answer. I noticed the time and it was only 3:46 AM. I had just got home and literally fallen into the bed at 3:00 AM. I hadn't even been asleep long enough for the crust to form between my eyes.

"We need to meet." Mob's voice came through the phone.

I wanted to scream at him I was so damn tired. I had just gotten home from the club, and I was wiped out. Shasha's party promoter event had been a hit. Mad money was made, and plenty of fun was had, now I needed at least four hours of shuteye. "A'ight I'll hit you with the location." I ended the call. Reluctantly, I slowly pulled my body up and sat up in the bed. It really crossed my mind to throw my phone on the floor and stomp on it until it was dead and gone. Instead, I got up, threw on a black and white Nike sweat suit, with some black Air Max with the white Nike sign and bounced.

I slid into the booth next to Don P, who was sitting

across from Mob. I had told them to meet me at a low-key all-night diner from the old neighborhood where I grew up. For one I needed some coffee to work on this hangover and to wake me up. And two, I knew it would be quiet and virtually empty. Soon as I sat down a waitress approached, and I ordered accordingly.

"This shit had better be good," I mouthed soon as the waitress was out of earshot.

Mob shook his head then rubbed his forehead. I knew he was irritated. "That nigga Rolla had that spot open again tonight. Some of them same lil niggas I was talkin' about earlier was out. Cops rode down on them about an hour ago and arrested them."

The words out of his mouth made me so angry instantly my right eye began to twitch, and I tightened my fist. I was so full of frustration. The waitress approached with my coffee and exited our table.

"Them niggas tried to be discreet. But I saw they slimy asses just as I went to hit up Mob, the shit went down." Don P filled me in on the details.

. "Where Rolla at?" I asked.

"He at a strip club down in Compton? I got eyes on him."

I picked up my coffee and took two swigs. It wasn't enough to do the job, but it would have to do. I pulled a hundred-dollar bill out of my pocket sat it on the table. "Let's ride." I stood up and exited with my henchman in tow.

I pulled in behind Mob and Don P at the stank strip club Rolla was allegedly at probably catching some disease. Shit was so ratchet I thought I might catch something just going inside. But I followed Mob and Don P who led me straight to the VIP area he was held up in. Bodyguards stood outside the door ready to deny entrance to any unwanted party. Mob and Don P both stepped to the side so my presence was clear. The bodyguards no doubt recognized me and moved to the side so that I could enter.

I stepped inside to find five strippers all but fighting to get to Rolla so they could make the money. Meanwhile, two of his boys laid back on a couch close by watching the action but getting no play. Sleeze, one of his henchmen, stood in a corner by the bar. Between the gap of two of the busted-up looking strippers, Rolla caught a glimpse of me standing still in the middle of his VIP. The look on his face read surprise. He motioned for the strippers to get off and told them to give him a minute. They quickly reached down and start grabbing at the money and scrambled out of the room.

"Precious," my name slid off his tongue. "I always thought a woman boss would never come down here to Compton." He chuckled, but it was kinda an uneasy one.

I say nothing. There is nothing for me to say. The sight of him made my right eye twitch again. The intentional disrespect was too much. I gazed at Mob and Don P. I noticed that one of his boys seemed stiff. The other one who went by the name Goose sucked his teeth. Goose liked to play tuff in the streets. Particularly in gunplay, but usually it was someone who was disrespecting. He made it clear, don't fuck wit' it if you couldn't hold up.

"So, what do I owe the pleasure this time?" Again, Rolla tried to speak, and once again I said nothing. This time the sweat beads that had formed on his forehead were clear. The nigga was dead nervous. And he had good reason to be.

"LOOK, I RUN MY SHIT, THEY MY BLOCKS, MY BUSINESS!" His voice boomed. "Pablo never came down here and try to FUCK me out my territory. And I ain't . . ." I was done listening to his bark. There was no bite in it.

I pulled my nine-millimeter, equipped with a silencer, from the back of my sweatpants and shot him twice in the chest. His eyes bucked as he jerked forward and looked down at the bullet holes, as the blood started filling his shirt. He raised his right hand to touch it but suddenly his eyes fell back to me. I thought he looked pitiful. I pulled the trigger once more and watched as it landed between his eyes.

Sleeze and the unknown guy pulled out guns, but Don P and Mob shot them dead on sight. Goose didn't twitch, he just sat there, unmoved. I eased my gun back into my sweatpants.

"You are the new leader of this crew," I laid out to Goose in no uncertain terms. I knew his reputation and he was ready to lead, that I was sure of. "You report directly to me. The money for all sales is due in two days. And reup in three. Mob will hit you wit' the details. And don't fucking shoot nobody."

"Boss, day two, and three. Lay off the trigger. Got it." Goose confirmed he was on point.

I turned to Mob and Don P who stood by waiting for my orders. "Take care of this scene." With that I stepped out of VIP. One of the two bodyguards outside the door, along with Rob who had been Mob's eyes, escorted me to my car. That business was handled. Not the outcome everyone wanted. But business was business.

I made it home and fell onto the sofa in my den. There was no way I was going to take another step. I had to have rest. But once again my nagging cell phone was disturbing my sleep. "HELLO!" I answered it this time with attitude. My eyes opened wide, from the throbbing my head felt from the strength I put into yelling into the phone. I realized that it was now actually daylight outside.

"Umm . . . why you are yelling at me?" Promise asked from the other end of the call.

"My bad." I sat up slowly. "This damn thing just won't stop ringing and I need some sleep."

"Hung over huh? I told you about that Apple Crown. It may taste like candy but strong like that Don and sneaks up on that ass."

How I wished what she said was not true, but I would only be fooling myself that Apple Crown was a beast. It snuck up on me every time just like she said. "It's kicking my ass," I admitted, I squinched my eyes at the sunlight coming through the window. It was not matching my hangover.

"Well, I would come over and pat your head and burp you." She teased me. "But instead, I'm just going to advise you to take some pain meds. I am on my way to the airport with Money. We are about to catch a flight out back to Miami."

Shocked from what she had just said, my headache almost cleared up until I went to scoot to the edge of the couch and the pounding stabbed my brain. I eased on back to a relaxing pose. "You going to Miami today? Right now?" I kept my voice soft and low as to not tempt the pain.

"Yep, I'll be back in a few days."

"What about the salon?"

"Toya is going to be in charge making sure the clients are taken care of and keeping everything on point. But can you handle the deposits for me?"

"Sure," was all I could say. To be honest my head was hurting so bad I couldn't do nothing else but wish for some Extra Strength Excedrin. And as soon as I ended the call with Promise, I made that my mission. Every painful step of the way.

Chapter 15

"She's been in Miami for two weeks now." I sat in my Range Rover outside the dry cleaners. I was on the phone Facetiming with Marlo. We had discussed a little business in code of course since we were on the phone. Then I decided to tell him about Promise and her trip out to Miami. I still could not believe she was out there.

"Aww, you miss your twin huh?" He teased me.

"Of course I miss her."

"Listen, she couldn't help herself it's hard to resist coming to the three oh five."

"If you say so." I rolled my eyes at him but smiled.

"Aye, why don't you fly out tonight? Stay a few days, see your sister. See me."

I knew he would add that. His eyes smiled at me. I wanted to scream yes. I'm on the next flight. Instead, I gave him reality. "You know I can't do that. Too much business to attend to. But I'll still be out in a few weeks as planned."

"Always the business huh?" He played disappointed. "So, how did the collect and reup go with that new situation?" I knew he was referring to Goose being appointed new Crew Leader.

"Everything was a go." I was not surprised that Goose had stepped up in his position, he had an in-charge personality. In just a few weeks he had gotten everyone on his team in gear. He rearranged the crew, dropped some dead weight, appointed his right hand, and was tightening territories, in ways Rolla never had. My decision had been the right one, not that I had ever doubted it.

"No doubt. A'ight. I got to handle this business over here in less than an hour. I'll hit you up, though."

"Yep." I said then ended the call on my end. I headed inside the dry cleaners.

"Hey, Precious." Regina was sweeping around the front area. And once again I was surprised to find her instead of Katrina.

"What's up, K in the back?" I asked but knew the answer. While sitting outside I had noticed her car was not in sight, but I figured her baby daddy had dropped her off again. Regina's car was in the shop parking space, so I wasn't looking for it.

"Nah, she asked me to open the store for her yesterday and today. Said she couldn't make it in."

"Two days in a row?" I had to be sure.

"Yep."

"Is she sick?"

"Actually, she never said. I was about to ask her this morning when she called to be sure everything was going okay, but she said she had to go. She didn't sound like she was sick though." Regina hunched her shoulders and continued to sweep.

"Hmmph, okay. Are the deposits ready?"

"You already know it. In the back waiting on your arrival, I got you. Katrina would slash me otherwise." She joked with a smile while adjusting her AirPod in her right ear with her free left hand. She still gripped the broom with her right hand.

I drove to the bank with Katrina on my mind. I tried to shake her, but as I stood online at the bank to make my deposit, I concluded something just was not right. It was eating at me so to be sure I drove to Katrina's house, soon as I left the bank. My hand balled into a fist; I went in for the fourth knock before Kenneth opened the door.

His face didn't say hello, and his stance was not a welcome one. He eyed me hard. For a moment I thought he was working on intimidation, but I shrugged that off. Because I was sure he did not want my smoke. Trust I was strapped; I didn't leave home without it. That was one of the first things DaVon made sure I understood.

"Where's Katrina?" I asked with no hesitation. This time I eyed him hard. Two could play that gangster game.

He glanced over my shoulder as if he saw someone, then looked back at me. "She asleep." He gripped the doorknob and leaned more on his right side to keep me from seeing inside.

He was rude and it was irritating me. "Can you go wake her up? I need to see her on some business that can't wait."

He let out a low grunt from his throat. "Katrina don't need to be bothered on no matters right now." His energy was in defense mode, and clearly testing me. He gripped the doorknob more aggressively.

I gazed behind me because I needed to count to ten to remain calm. I turned back to him. "Hey, what's your name again? Kenneth is it?" He just stared at me. I decided to make myself clear. "Listen, Katrina is like a sister to me. Trust me, she wants to see me."

His lips moved and he opened them, but just before a

word could escape his mouth Katrina popped out from behind him. Right away I couldn't deny something was up.
Katrina slowly made steps in my direction. She looked at
me but did not invite me inside. I thought that was strange
of Katrina. We were like family, her inviting me in was
natural.

"Regina says you've been off for two days. I wanted to
come over and check on you, are you okay?"

"Yeah, yeah." She waved her hand casually and breathed
a loud sigh then ran her right hand through disheveled hair.
That too was odd. Katrina always kept her hair done. "I
haven't been feeling too well." It was a bit dark on the inside, but she was close enough that the light from outside
was shining inside, and I thought I noticed the right side of
her face looked a bit swollen. I tried to focus in on it, but
it was also clear she had tried to put makeup on. If there
was a bruise, the makeup was hiding it.

Over her shoulder I looked past her at Kenneth who
still had suspicious eyes on us. His watchdog tactic was
bound to be making me angry. I put my focus back to
Katrina. "Why didn't you call me? I could have filled in
for you at the dry cleaners."

"No, it was cool. Regina didn't mind filling in. We had
the shifts at the new location covered so it was all good. I
know how busy you are. Besides, Regina does well holding it down when I'm not in."

I nodded to agree with her. I was aware that Regina was
doing her thing. She was learning a lot working so close
with Katrina. I was paying attention and her hard work
was not going unnoticed. "A'ight. Where is Lalah?"

"She's at Mom's house with her cousins, you know how
she love to play with Mika's kids." She chuckled, but it
was as fake as the smile she followed it up with. But I was
aware Lalah enjoyed her cousins. Mika was one of Katrina's

sisters. She had two kids and a deadbeat boyfriend that stole her money all the time. "But I'm good . . . I'll be back in tomorrow."

I was just not feeling good about Katrina's demeanor. She was trying too hard to convince me she was good. This was not the Katrina I was used to. I held my head down and counted to ten. Kenneth's presence was not helping the situation. His gawking was really getting to me. I contemplated shooting him in the knee or possibly his big toe. The counting to ten gave me time to reconsider. I chilled.

"Okay . . ." I thought once more. "Listen, if you need anything, no matter the hour, you hit me up. No matter what," I said, with my eyes on Kenneth.

I watched as he took a few steps and landed beside Katrina. Looking me in the face he said, "Precious, huh?" He said my name as a question as if he was tasting it for the first time. He slid his right hand into his pocket. "Yeah, I know you DaVon's lady." A weird, yet odd smirk spread on his face.

I wasn't sure what he was trying to accomplish but I decided to share some important information with him. Information he would do well to abide by. "You should be careful about who you think you know. And whatever problem Katrina has is a personal problem of mine." With that I turned and left the premises. The guy was a slimy piece of gunk on the bottom of my shoe. And I would scrape it off if he did not tread his step. And I meant lightly.

Chapter 16

Today was deposit day for Promise, so I made it the first stop on my list for the day. Toya had been doing a good job holding the salon down with its day-to-day operations. I stopped by three days during the week to grab the money. But I had been there for Toya to do my hair and Reese hooked up my makeup.

"Precious, when you think Promise gone be back? I thought she'd be back by now it's been two weeks." Reese sat down at her booth and pulled the lid off her coffee and added more cream. According to her, Starbucks never quite got that right, so she always asked them to give her extra on the side in another cup.

Toya wiped down her station even though she had done it the night before she left. The girl was a classic case of OCD. "I know right . . . I thought she would be too. But I ain't hating, because each time I've spoken with her she sounds like she is having a ball."

I stood at Promise's booth. I sat the deposit bag down for a minute to check my eyelid, it felt like something was in my eye. I plucked the hair out of my eyelid and got fast relief from it. I turned back to the girls. "Yeah, I guess she is having fun, but I spoke with her last night. She says she'll be home in the next couple of days."

"I sure hate I missed her new man Money when he was here. He must be some kind of fine the way he got Promise all on his top. Jumping up leaving with her man in the heat of the night," Reese said with a huge grin then sipped her coffee.

"Girl, I told you he was that fine," Toya confirmed. "Ain't he, Precious?"

As much as I did not want to discuss Money, I could not help but smile and be honest. "He is cute." I still downplayed it. I was not about to call him fine.

"Told you." Toya folded her arms across her chest and shook her head with a grin.

"But like I said, Promise will be back in a couple of days. Oh, before I forget, Toya, can you squeeze me in in the morning for my hair? I'm going to the gym later so it will need to be touched up." Unless I had braids, I normally got my hair done once a week. If I had a sew in, I was in getting it curled or straightened. No matter what I had I was getting it touched up especially after the gym, it always got frazzled.

"You know I got you, can't have you out here looking crazy." Toya did not hesitate. Her phone rung but she quickly picked it up and hit ignore.

"Who is that you trying to ignore?" Reese teased with her coffee cup cradled at her mouth.

Toya playfully rolled her eyes. "I swear you so nosey. But girl, that fine ass Quavo." She smiled and was giddy.

"Quavo . . ." Reese said his name, her eyebrows raised. "Oh, the one that came by here yesterday, to see you? Yeah, he definitely fine, and I love those white teeth he kept advertising, every time he said something."

I looked at them both. For one, I was surprised to hear his name brought up and to learn that he had been to the shop. I know I had seen them talking at the club, but I did not know they had exchanged info. Toya hadn't said anything about him. "Quavo been by here?" I asked, even though I just heard Reese confirm it mere seconds before.

"Yeah, he just stopped in trying to convince me to go on another date with him." Toya tried to sound all casual but the twinkle in her eyes said it all.

And that statement about him trying to take her on another date dropped my jaws. "Damn you two dating?"

"No not really, I wouldn't call it that. We did meet up for drinks though, but he has been asking for a date." She shrugged nonchalantly. "I ain't really trying to go there."

Reese sucked her teeth. "She thinks everybody Dell's sorry ass. Girl, you better not miss out on no nigga thinking about that bomb."

Reese was exactly right. Dell had been a horrible boyfriend to Toya. And ever since she had broken up with him, she had taken herself out of the dating game. No one could blame her. I knew of Quavo from the game. As far as his hustler rep, he was on top his business. He pulled in good dough and had a loyal mentality towards the game. Now as far his rep went with the women, I had heard he was somewhat of a player like Regina had said. But I had no facts to prove that. The way I saw it was simply gossip, until I saw some proof. So, I had no comment on that matter.

Toya gazed at Reese and smiled then turned to me. "Precious, don't Reese sound more and more like Dee every day? I swear she does."

I couldn't help but laugh out loud. I looked at Reese and thought of words of philosophy. "Aye, you do kinda . . ." I was about to say more but my ringing cell phone cut me off. "Hello," I answered the call. I could hear Toya and Reese's voices in the background as they continued to talk.

"So, this is a gang up?" Reese asked Toya. They both laughed lightly.

I recognized the voice on the other end as Phil. My heart instantly sped up. Phil had never called me before. The words outta his mouth stung. Marlo had been shot.

Chapter 17

All flights going to Miami were booked. The only thing I could catch was a red-eye. I was not trying to wait that long. I made some calls and chartered a private plane which took me straight to Miami. I normally chartered private flights when I was carrying large amounts of cash and I always booked in advance. But money talks so I had no problems getting one at a moment's notice.

While on the way to the airport I had booked a rental, so everything was in place for me when I touched down. I went straight from the airport to the hospital. I noticed in the waiting area some of Marlo's henchmen. A nurse sitting at one of the nurses' stations gave me the room number. I opened the door to his room slowly, full of apprehension of what I would see. All I could think of was my dad when I found him shot to death at the dry cleaners. That image would never leave my mind. But I had somehow placed that in a corner of my mind where I could survive daily without the torture of revisiting it every day when I opened my eyes.

Phil sat in a chair across from Marlo with his head

buried in his hands. Reluctantly, I laid my eyes on Marlo. At first my feet were frozen but slowly I made strides towards him. His eyes were closed, and they had him hooked up to IV's. I wasn't sure at first, but I thought I had not seen a life support machine. Again, I used my eyes to quickly search the area. I calmed down as I realized he was indeed not hooked up to a life support machine. I breathed a sigh of relief just as Phil looked up to find me standing over Marlo.

"Yo', Phil, what the fuck happened to him? Is he going to be okay?" I threw questions at him. The look in Phil eyes read tired, and weary. Marlo was his guy. They ran the streets tough together, hustled together, murdered together, and had each other's backs no matter what. And that's why the henchmen were in the waiting room, they were the muscle if anything jumped off at the hospital.

"He gone be straight. He was hit in the side. The bullet went straight through . . . We was at the club though when it happened. We had partied and was on our way to the car when another car pulled up, and shots rang out. A bullet grazed me. Marlo and two of our guys were hit."

It was crazier than I thought. A drive by. At best I figured Marlo was face-to-face and someone pulled a gun. But a drive by was considered a sneak and more dangerous. "Do any of you know who responsible, yet?"

"Damn right we do. And trust, them niggas over TOMORROW!" he barked. He had been trying to keep his voice down. But on this he couldn't hold it. The boom in his voice had woken Marlo.

Marlo's eyes fell from Phil to me. His lips moved. "Precious." He said my name low; his tone was groggy. He tried to clear his throat, but I could tell it was a struggle. "Nah, Nobody." He coughed.

I was already close to him, but I separated any distance

and leaned down. "Marlo, don't talk." I hoped he listened to me, but I doubted it.

Marlo's lips formed into a smile. "See, I knew you loved me."

"Oh, shut up." I said playfully.

Marlo turned his attention to Phil. "I want the word on the street . . . Nobody is to touch the dead men walking."

Phil nodded his head right off. No hesitation. Marlo's word was law. "I got to bounce but I'ma leave two guys on guard. I'll hit you later." Marlo nodded, and with that Phil stood, said goodbye, and exited.

I leaned back down into Marlo's space again. I looked him in the eyes. Now that his eyes were opened, I could tell he was good. He had his color in his face, since he had been talking that groggy, dry tone had cleared up.

"You got here quick." Again, he smiled at me. He was loving my presence; he was energized off the fact that now he knew I cared, no matter how nonchalantly I acted. "Listen, I'm good. The doctor said they are just keeping me to keep watch on my vitals for a while as a standard practice. I will be released first thing in the morning." That was good news to hear.

"They might decide to keep you for a few days to adjust the way you move." I teased him.

"Nah, I'll break up outta here. I hate hospitals." He chuckled. But I knew that was a typical thing for a man to say. "But nah, on some real shit. I got a meeting in the AM with the leaders for collection."

"You don't have to worry about that. I'll handle that. I know you good, but you need to get some rest. It's okay to take a day off, ain't no need to be going to a meeting bandaged and bleeding." I was being dramatic on purpose.

"I hear all that but I'm showing up to my meeting." He was being stubborn. And I expected no less.

"Look, I know you the Incredible Hulk. And I ain't trying to block that. But take my advice and just chill and heal. I'm your partner and I'm telling you I got this."

He looked at me and I could tell he wanted to fight my request and be combative. But he also knew I was not going to give in, either. We both could be stubborn. Finally, he agreed if only to shut me up. Either way I was satisfied with the answer.

Chapter 18

Phil had texted me the address to meet up for collections. I was still getting familiar with the spots Marlo had set up in the city. I had only been to a few so far but I had plans to know them all and soon. I was a bit tired because I hadn't had any sleep since I left LA. I had sat up most of the night. I talked to Marlo in spurts, when he would wake up from the pain after the pain meds wore off. Other than that, my mind raced over so many different things that I could not even keep track. I was relieved when morning rolled around, and the sunlight crept through the window. It gave me a boost of energy that I needed to get me going. But now my mood was once again turning bleak, and the bullshit of the game was guilty.

"Ayeee. Just last night shit got stupid. I found out one of my block boyz been stealin' . . ." Crush, one of the Crew Leaders was sitting before Phil and me with a short payment and story to tell. His southern drawl was thick, and he seemed to be dragging his words. "I had to body him and another one for loss of product."

"Tell me this." I sat up in my seat and placed both my

hands on the table, with my eyes on Crush. "Why are you here? Why you show up today?"

"For reup." He had the nerve to sound confused with my question. "Shi'dd I need to reup so I can double up and get my money back." I could not believe his response. And the look on his face told me he was serious. My chair seemed to shrink and turn into brick I was so dumbfounded.

"Are you smokin' that coke you SUPPLYIN!" I barked at him. "Clearly you a high nigga comin' up in here talking dumb shit. Bring yo' RICH ass up in here without my money. Nigga, if two runners and a hit stop yo' show, you a fucking peon. Now get yo' ass up and outta here . . ." Crush slid his chair back and stood up. But I was not done. "You a dead man walking until five o'clock today. And all yo' blocks are hungry as of this second. Maybe a hype will put a bullet in you before I do." With that I turned my attention to the next man with my money. Crush exited. I handled that business and headed back to Marlo's crib. He had been released first thing this morning before the meeting.

No sooner than I got in and prepared to have a drink, Promise arrived. She had called me early that morning and told me she would visit since she was still in Miami. I was as glad to see her as she was to see me. We hugged tight. We headed to one of Marlo's bar rooms. He had two in his mansion is what I called it. My house was huge but his was even bigger.

"What you drinkin'?" I stepped behind the bar.

"Oh, please give me a shot of Hennessey. Put a little Coke in so it's not too strong. I don't want to be lit too early in the day."

"Sounds good to me. And I'll pour myself the same. Welp, minus the Coke, I need it strong." I grinned. But if I was being honest what I really needed was a Don Julio shot. Dealing with assholes like Crush you need a strong drink to remain sane.

"Sister, I can't blame you. How is Marlo doing? I really wanted to come to the hospital last night. But it was so late, and Money and I were just too tired."

"It's cool. Marlo understands. He's asleep now, he all doped up, on those good drugs the doctor prescribed."

"For a bullet wound they give you the top of the line high." Promise joked. I laughed and agreed, just as I looked at her and noticed how much smaller she had gotten. Her face and arms seemed thin.

"You look like you shed some pounds. Are you eating?" Now I sounded just like Rosa. She would be really tripping if she seen Promise.

Promise looked down at herself then back to me. "Hell yes, I eat. That's all we do." She followed up with a chuckle.

But that wasn't all I noticed; her eyes seemed a little dark as if she wasn't getting any sleep. "I know you said you were tired but are you getting any sleep?"

"I sleep some. But they party hard out here in Miami. And I, sister dear, haven't said no to a good time yet. I just been going and going."

"Well, I don't won't try to stop your fun, but you need to catch sleep, or it will catch you. And you need to get back to LA, to the salon. Everybody miss your big head self." I chuckled.

"Yeah, I know. Toya told me to get my ass back ASAP or else. So, I plan to be back in two days. Right after Money's birthday, though."

"Good. Everybody will be pleased to hear you coming home. I'm leaving out tomorrow. Gotta get back to business, I kinda ran off at the last minute."

"Wait how you gone just fly out like that? Don't you

have to stay here and nurse your man back to good and stable health?" She laughed then passed me her shot glass for a refill.

"Haha. You are so funny." I stood up and grabbed the Hennessey bottle off the bar. "Marlo is not my man." I said his name so I could be clear on my stance. I filled her glass but this time I didn't put in no Coke. "We are just cool, friends and all that."

With her lips twisted, Promise sighed. "Here we go." She always did that anytime I disputed my attachment to Marlo. Never did she want to hear we were only friends. She really believed we were a lot more. There was no telling her different.

"I know you find this so hard to believe. But Marlo and I are only partners in crime." It's how I described us. "We work well together. We vibe in the working aspect." I shut up because no way that I tried to describe it did it sound any better.

She laughed with her shot glass at the tip of her bottom lip. "I bet." She turned up her shot glass, downed it. Stood and placed it on the bar. Then she rushed off.

"Where are you going?" I called after.

She turned to face me before exiting the room. "I left Money out in the car, he has a meeting at the club. Bye, Mrs. Marlo." She teased me and ducked off. I could only shake my head and smile. My sister was a trip.

I took one more shot which turned out to be my third one and I was feeling it. And it felt good. I headed for Marlo's room to check on him and fill him in. Upon entering the huge room, I noticed Marlo was not in the bed, just as I wondered where he might have snuck off to, he came out of the bathroom.

"There you are, I was wondering where you had dipped off too. 'Cause I know you can't do right."

"Nah, I'm obeying your rules." He chuckled. "Nature calls, though." He slowly continued to the bed. "Actually, I was about to hit you up."

"I was downstairs. Promise was here, she just left."

"Dang I missed her? Why didn't you bring her up?"

"I told her you were sleeping, and before you ask, no I was not about to wake you up. You need your rest, so you can heal up fast."

"I guess some might say so, or maybe just you, the boss." He smiled at me. He eased down on the bed and got comfortable. "So how were the collections?" It was time to fill him in.

I sighed with frustration. Just the thought of Crush bothered me. "This idiot, Crush, brought his punk ass up in there short. Talkin' about one of his block boys was stealin' and another one lost some product."

"Lost some product." Marlo repeated with a slight chuckle. "These pussy ass niggas still wake up every day living a TV series. Creating Superman characters."

"That they do now, but I promise they will learn. The hard way don't never die out." I shook my head with disappointment. I just couldn't understand the way some people processed life. And played with their own. "All other collections were good though. And reup complete. Phil and I delivered the money to the cleaners to be counted, stacked, and banned for cleanup." Marlo nodded to show his appreciation. "Oh, and Crush got until five o'clock to deliver the cash. And once payment is received Phil got orders to finish him on sight. Tomorrow you can name his successor."

"Done." Marlo mouthed.

Just like that, we were done with that situation. Crush had to go, simple as that. The stunt he pulled was immature to be sure, but a dumb mistake that would cost him his life. Marlo and I were new successors, which meant we still had the seal on us, which meant we were going to be tested. And that is exactly what Crush set out to prove: he could test us and pass. But he was wrong, and he had failed, miserably. He and others who wished to try us with foolish stunts in the future would know in a few hours, the penalty for failure was eternity.

Chapter 19

I was glad to be back on my stomping grounds, but I had been busy non-stop since I stepped off the plane. I was barely making time to eat on a daily basis, all I seemed to do was drink coffee to stay woke. But finally, I had made it home early enough for a hot cooked meal. Rosa had thrown together some Mexican food before she left, so I fixed myself a nice plate, sat on the couch in the den, and stuffed my face. I was so content with my full belly, before long I had drifted off into a peaceful sleep.

Suddenly my eyes popped open. The television was still going. I had been watching the first season of *Downton* on Prime and it was still in full swing. I lay there now realizing that my father had been in my dream. I could see his face very clearly. His lips were moving, and I knew he was talking to me. I could not hear the words and I wasn't able to make out what he was saying. But he has this huge grin on his face and that was enough for me. I figured whatever he had to say was amusing to us both. My yawn turned to a smile. I looked at my plate still sitting on the ottoman in front of me. Since I had been sleeping so comfortably on the sofa, I didn't see any need to transfer to the bed. But taking my plate to the kitchen was a must, then I could grab me a throw blanket to cover up with.

Just as I attempted to sit up, my cell phone rang. My head turned towards the cable box so I could see the time, it read two-thirty. This was the time everyone seemed to decide to call me. "Hello," I answered. Since I had woken up on my own, my tone was pleasant.

"AGGHH! I KILLED HIM! HE'S DEAD!" Katrina screamed over the phone. The trauma in her voice shook me for a second.

"Killed who?" I asked her but knew the answer before I asked. Katrina did not respond. "Listen to me good. Do not touch anything else in that house. Nothing," I stressed. "I'm on my way. Am I the only person you called?"

All I could her was sniffing and sobbing. "Yyy . . . yes," she finally was able to say with trembling words.

"Keep it that way." I ended the call and wasted no time getting out the door. The plate going to the kitchen, my throw blanket, and the rest of my sleep would have to wait. Katrina needed me ASAP. I figured there might be some unwanted drama with her and Kenneth eventually that might need my attention. Like maybe I would be the one killing him or having him killed. But never did I think I'd get this type of call from her that she had finished the job. This had to be handled quickly and correctly. Katrina had to raise Lalah. But I would need some assistance, so I got Rob on the phone and told him to meet at Katrina's address and to bring Case. Mob was on another assignment, so I did not disturb him.

I tapped lightly on Katrina's front door. I did not want to call her again; we had done enough discussing this situation over the phone. She opened the door slowly and shocked ripped at my stomach. Rage rushed through me. Katrina did not look like Katrina. Her face was swollen on both sides, it was clear she had been punched repeatedly. Especially on the left side. Her cheek bone did not seem to exist in that area at the moment, her face was so swollen. Her top lip was busted and blood in the right corner and blood under her left nostril.

She stepped back so I could enter. She started crying as she shut the door behind us, then flew into my arms. I allowed her to cry for only a minute. We had to handle this business first. Tears filled my eye sockets, but I fought them back. I did not have time to cry, no mistakes could be made here. This was a crime scene it had to be handled as such.

I released her. And looked her in the eyes. "It's going to be okay, alright? I'm going to handle this. You have nothing to worry about." She was still crying and sniffing she shook her head that she understood. "Where is he?"

"He's in my room."

"I need to see him." She led the way through the house. Her entire body seemed to be shaking. I knew she was in shock.

We reached her room, and there that asshole was laying on the floor flat on his back a bullet in his heart. Blood had flowed down both sides of his mouth and onto Katrina's carpeted floor. His eyes were wide open, and I could see the evil in them. Both his knuckles on his hands were scuffed from where he had been hitting Katrina. But he also had scratches on his face where she had put up a fight. I rooted for her all the way. If I could wake his ass up and blow his brains out I would. Too bad the asshole didn't have nine lives.

"Where is Lalah?" I suddenly realized she was not in the house. On the ride over I had wondered if she were home. And if so, I had hoped she had not seen him dead, even though he had deserved the bullet he got and earned more. He was her father and as a child she did not need to lay eyes on his bloody dead body. It might be something she may never forget, and I did not want that for her.

Katrina stood close to me with her arms folded across her chest. She had on some pink fluffy Ugg house slippers, and I could see blood on them. I then noticed the gun on the floor where she had either dropped or laid it.

"She is at Mom's house. Lately things had been crazy around here with Kenneth and I arguing and fighting. I could not get him to leave, and I didn't want Lalah around it, or him for that matter. So, I've been leaving her over there." Katrina choked up and started to cry again, this time uncontrollably and shaking more violently.

I grabbed her hands and gave her eye contact. "Aye, I need you to calm down. You are in shock right now and that is normal. But I need you to take a deep breath, then slow breathe. Okay? It's going to be okay alright? I promise."

"I hated him for the way he treated me. But I didn't want to kill him. But he just wouldn't stop hitting on me . . . beating me, Precious. I warned him to please stop. And just finally I couldn't take it anymore. I got my gun out, he didn't even know I had a gun. And I did it. I pulled the trigger . . . I PULLED THE FUCKIN' TRIG-GER!" She yelled. "Then it stopped . . . he stopped . . ."

"Listen, you did what had to be done. Nobody would blame you for that. And nobody will because this never happened. Remember that." She nodded slowly.

Katrina knew who I was, she knew my lifestyle. She understood what I was saying. My cell phone rang. The call was my cue that Rob and Case were there so I could answer the door. Katrina followed behind me to the door, I knew she didn't want to be left alone with Kenneth's body.

I opened the door and let them inside. Katrina was quiet as a mouse. I told Case and Rob to follow us. Katrina once again led us to the room. This time Rob and Case witnessed what I already had. I told Katrina to make sure the house was secured as far as windows and everything. With no questions she raced off to do as she was told.

Rob moved in close and glared down at Kenneth's body. "Mane, I know this punk ass nigga. He used to mess with my cousin some years back. Used to beat her up till she was black and blue. But she kept that a secret by hiding from us. By the time we found out I think he had disappeared, we couldn't find him nowhere. And nobody ain't seen his ass on the block since. Nigga woulda been dead before tonight, otherwise."

"Yeah, that's probably when he was locked up. He's been in lockdown for some years," I shared.

Rob stepped even closer to the dead body kneeled down and barked at him. "Look at yo' punk ass now. Layin' up stanky. Ain't karma a bitch." Case busted out laughing.

I grinned. They were funny. "I got to get her up outta here. Ya'll know what to do with this mess. Carpet and everything replaced, same material. Handle it and let me know when all is clear."

"Shi'dd we got you without a doubt. It's an honor to take out this trash." Rob gritted his teeth. The pleasure was all over his face.

"Fo'sho," Case co-signed.

I told Katrina we had to get going. I instructed her not to take anything. I didn't want us carrying bags out of the house in case some nosey neighbor caught a glimpse of us. I knew Rob and Case would handle the body and get the place cleaned up and carpet changed out with the same person we always used. And they would make their activity scarce, so that people didn't notice anything out of the ordinary. I took Katrina back to my house and called up a medical doctor that I could use for house calls that I paid good money for no questions to be asked. Like I had assured her, everything would be okay. Katrina had gotten rid of a monster, and we would handle the rest.

Chapter 20

It had been a few days since the incident at Katrina's house had transpired. She was still at my house recovering. The doctor had prescribed some Tylenol for the pain from the injuries she had received courtesy of Kenneth, and encouraged rest, which had been getting plenty of. She really didn't have an appetite, but I had been picking her up takeout every day, just in case. Rosa had also made her a homemade pot of broccoli cheddar soup which was her favorite if she decided to eat.

I was just glad she was away from Kenneth for good. My dad didn't like him, and I should have known there was a good reason why. And for more than him just being a creep. No, Dad had known that he was capable of the harm he had brought on Katrina. But now he would have twenty-four-hour company with dirt and worms. That suited me just fine. I just hoped Katrina really would be able to get over what had happened. Killing someone could be a torment. Taking a life was never no easy thing no matter how many times you did it. Some simply couldn't handle it. I had hoped every day since the incident she wasn't that person. Because she had been in a situation that was simple. Him or her. Live or die. The choice should have been easy.

I would support her though and keep reminding her the meaning to the ends if need be. Today she was looking at peace sitting in the den watching television with a bowl of Blue Bell French vanilla ice cream in hand. Finally, she was eating. I joined her, but only for a minute. I had errands as usual.

"What's up?" I sat down on the sofa next to her.

"Nothin' just enjoying this good creamy ice cream. Blue Bell got the best."

"Why do you think I buy it?" I smiled. "Two o'clock in the morning that's my go to snack. I add in some pecans and fudge or caramel. Umm delicious. Rocks me right back to sleep." Now I was craving a bowl but didn't have time to eat it. But it would be the first thing I do when I get in from making my rounds.

"Dang I should have put some of that fudge on mine. Oh well, it will be in the next bowl. You better pick up another gallon, on your way home tonight."

"No doubt. I got it."

She spooned another bite, swallowed, looked at the spoon. "Look, I really want to thank you again for coming out to help me the other night. You were the only one I knew I could call."

"You already know there is no reason to thank me. I'm glad you called me. I would not have it any other way. But I gotta ask, why? Why didn't you come to me for help when he started in on you?"

"That's a good question." She rested the bowl in her lap. "Honestly, this might sound stupid or dumb . . . but I thought he might have changed from the first time. He said he had. And more than that I wanted . . . no I prayed that it would work out for Lalah's sake. Precious, I really wanted her to have her dad in her life." A tear escaped her right eye. She wiped at it.

That statement I understood because I could relate. Not having my mother was a big wound. A wound I had that probably would never completely heal. Having Promise though made it bearable. Having my sister was like having a piece of my mother. "I understand that. I know what that is like, as you know. But you remember this, ain't nothing worth abuse. And know this also before you even think of having regrets. You and you alone saved your own life. There was a choice to be made and you made it."

Katrina eyes cast down on her bowl of ice cream. "I know." She raised her eyes back to me. And I could see the relief in her eyes. It assured me she would be okay. "I do wish though that I had not allowed him back into my life. This could have all been avoided. And maybe still Lalah could have him in her life."

"Remember, no regrets." I repeated. "Just get on with your life. Choose that chapter whatever you wish for it to be. That situation is handled."

She breathed in and I heard her release a sigh of relief. "I can't wait to see Lalah in a few days once this swelling has gone down. And the bruises as you can see have started to disappear. A little makeup will handle the rest. I miss my baby so much. Oh, and I can't wait to get back to work."

"Listen, I can pick Lalah up and bring her here in a few days and both you guys can stay as long as you want. But you already know that. This is always your home if you need it. And please stop worrying about work. It's handled."

"I swear you are so good to me. But I do miss work, I love being a working woman." She lifted her bowl from her lap, prepared to devour the rest.

"You are so stubborn." I stood just as the doorbell rang.

I opened the front door and welcomed Case in. He had stopped by at my request to pick up a package. "What's up." I ushered him in.

"Nothin' mane, it's so far out here. You gone have to give a brother some gas money? I need a straight up fill up." He joked. I only allowed Mob, Rob, and Case in my house. Don P had been here only once. But they all knew they could only stop by at my request, I would never open my door to anyone who had not been invited, not even them. And they knew I kept my handguns, rifles, grenades, you name it, on hand at all times.

"Put it on my tab." I always said to their gas jokes. "Come on, you can join Katrina in the den while I get that." I led him towards the den where Katrina had continued her ice cream. She seemed startled when Case entered.

Case seemed surprised to see her sitting there as well. "What's up Katrina?"

"Hey," she returned. She'd had one of her legs folded under her on the couch, but she stood just a little to release her leg and sat completely on her butt.

"K, keep him busy and watch him closely or he will eat your ice cream." I teased and left the room.

It took me about a minute to grab the package because the painter who was working at dad's house called. I made it back to the den and just as I entered the room, I noticed Case and Katrina chatting and they both looked really comfortable. I walked over to where Case was now seated on the other end of the couch from Katrina. He stood up once he seen the package in my hand. He bid Katrina bye as we exited the room. We walked towards the door as I explained some things about the package. It basically was just money that I needed him to deliver to the painters. I had to be at the dry cleaners and then I had to go by the club and hair store. So I didn't have time to stop by and pay the guys but Case like all my guys were always willing to help out.

I noticed as I reached for the door, he was smiling ear to ear, and I knew it wasn't because of my package. He skipped off and I shut the door behind him. I went back to the den to find Katrina also staring at the television and she too was wearing a grin. And I knew the Lifetime movie she was watching was not the cause.

"Why y'all so happy? Both of you smiling like you hit the lottery."

"Oh, he asked me for my number. And I actually gave it to him." She shrugged her shoulders.

"Oh, really," was all I could say to that. What had I missed? Something told me now was not the time to ask.

Katrina stood up and the grin on her face had grown wider. "Hell, I need someone to put a smile on my face. I been in hell for a few months. It is time the sun shined."

That part of her statement I could not dispute. And who was I to say it might be too soon? So, I didn't. But I did have this to say. "I swear you and Toya infiltrating the squad." I chuckled. First Toya and Quavo. Now Katrina and Case. Who would be next? I wondered to myself laughing inside. Katrina looked at me confused. I smiled and said, "I gotta go."

Chapter 21

I left my house and went straight to the hair store first. I had to check on an order that had come in. And I needed to check the sales numbers to be sure they were matching up to my report and I ran the day before.

"Hey you." I spoke to Promise as she strolled through the door. She had told me she would be stopping by to pick up some hair for two of her clients. I was so glad to have her back in town. Things felt normal again. When she was in Miami, I always felt like something was missing but I could never put my finger on it. That something was my other half. My sister who was also my best friend.

"Nothing, ready for this day to be over so I can go home and get some much-needed rest." I could tell that she was tired.

"I thought you were getting some rest. I haven't talked to you as much as I would like. You actually been pretty quiet since you got back." I had noticed she wasn't calling as much as usual but I'm always so busy myself, I hadn't made time to pester her about it.

"I know." She sighed. Then gave me those puppy dog eyes. "I've been so busy at the salon, with clients, ordering, payroll, and financial, coming over here helping out, you name it. But I have been meaning to thank you for handling the deposits while I was away. That was a huge help."

"You know I got you," I assured her. I picked up some hair on the counter and went through them to be sure they were the right matches for what was on the sheet next to them.

"I know you do. And Toya did a great job too. You know she has been stepping up around there. I'm really considering promoting her to manager. What do you think?"

"Hey, I think she is more than capable. There is nothing out of place or no customer left unhappy when she's in charge. She stayed over to be sure everything was handled and took care of your clients, that includes me. And I never heard her complain."

"Tell me about it. I get a lot of good feedback from the customers about her. She has that leader quality. Besides, I'm going to be spending a lot of time in Miami. I will need the help."

"Damn, it's that serious?" I had to ask. Miami was once again the topic. "You are making future plans?"

"Precious, I really like Money. He's an interesting guy. He's funny, ambitious, warm, considerate, and more."

Now that was something I had never heard her say about any of the other guys she had entertained besides Clip. Clip she had loved, and she made that obvious in every way. I knew Clip personally, so I was familiar with his personality. He truly was a good guy, with a good heart. And he loved my sister as much as she loved him. Money, I didn't know, and I had not spent that much time with him to get to know him. But just by observing him nothing stood out to me that he was this interesting guy she had just described.

"Hey, just don't forget you are a business owner. It's

good to have management in place to help keep things abreast in your absence. But people depend on you . . . the owner."

"Absolutely. I get that. Right now, though, I'm just having a little fun, living a little."

"There is nothing wrong with any of that. Besides, I trust your judgement." I decided not to continue with the big sister squabble.

"How is Marlo? He on the mend?"

"He's cool, about to get his stiches out. I'm flying out there in a few days for a meeting."

"Dang, I hate I won't be there at the same time as you. We gotta get out there at the same time so we can shop together."

"I know we have so much fun. Listen, the way the numbers looking here at this hair store I was thinking maybe we should open one in Miami. Get some of the southern money."

"Yo, that sounds like an awesome idea, we could get paid for sure. And with you being out there and me planning on being out there more often it could work."

"My thoughts exactly, we just need a good location." We were both agreeing it was a good idea. When the thought had entered my mind I knew Promise would be on board. Both of our goals were to be successful business owners and to branch out. And we were well on track. "I think I'll get the ball going when I'm out in Miami. Marlo got connections out there that can put us in contact with realtors. He knows the area so he can help with the hot spots."

"Sounds like we got a plan, then. Next, we need a budget. Discuss layout, space etc."

"I'm thinking we try to stick to something about this same square footage. We don't want it to look like a hair warehouse. That's when it starts looking cheap and basic, we ain't coming from LA to do basic. Nah, we keep it so-phisticated looking like we have here." Our brand was going to speak no matter the city, and its rep would remain top notch.

"My thoughts exactly. We will just do a different set up the interior design and all. Dang, I'm already excited." Promise was giddy.

"A'ight I'll get the ball rolling when I'm out in Miami in a few days." It was time for execution, something we both proved to be good at. I had business school behind me, and Promise had her knowledge. But sometimes I simply thought running a business was in our blood. Although Dad had faced financial issues when he was running the dry cleaners, he still had done a good job. It was his dream, his passion, and he built his businesses from nothing to what it became and for many years it was successful. I would say we came by our skills naturally. I was proud of our family.

Chapter 22

As always, Miami welcomed me back like the prodigal daughter, and I obliged. I hit the town already with a full agenda. First up on that list was viewing potential properties for the hair store. I had already told Marlo about our intentions. And since I would have a few hours downtime, he wasted no time contacting one of the top realtors in the city: David Newman. He came highly recommended, and Marlo also used him. We balled down the interstate in his all-black Bentley Continental GT headed for the second spot I would be looking at for the day.

"You sure you feel okay?" I glanced over at him from the passenger seat. If I had not known he had been shot, I would never guess, because he played the unbroken solider well. He kept a straight stance and never showed any sign of pain. While I knew he was much better I also knew he was not one hundred percent healed on the inside. A bullet had ripped through him, but he never winced.

He kept his eyes on the interstate but smirked. "I'm good. Even better now that you are back in my city. And close to my side. A dose of you can always make me better." He loved to talk like that, but I never gave that fuel any igniting. Now my eyes were glued to the highway to pretend to be uninterested in his flirting.

"How long before we reach the next location?" I asked to change the subject.

"Should be there soon. I think you will like this one better. David is the best so either way he got you." We veered onto the next exit to get off the interstate. We then drove for another ten minutes before he pulled into the parking lot. David was already inside.

Once inside I was feeling the place right off. The space was already equipped with the counter space and shelves in the back storage area where we could store the hair. According to David the electrical system had been updated in the building in the last two years. I took pictures so I could send them to Promise, so she could give her thoughts. But I could already see the plans we had discussed coming alive in the space.

"All the businesses in this area have high revenue, respected brands, and good traffic flow. Most of them have been here over ten years all with a rise in equity and revenue every year they have remained." David shared valuable information with me. He wanted me to know as a realtor he had done his homework.

"I like the sound of that. What about crime?" That was a top priority to me as well.

"No crime has been reported within twenty miles of this area in the last seventeen years." That turned my head on my shoulders. No crime in seventeen years in anyplace in Florida. Hmmph.

"That's a plus." I shook my head with approval of that fact. I slowly started walking around again, reviewing some the spots I had already seen. Marlo stood back and spoke with David. I could hear Marlo ask him about his wife having the baby. After taking a few more pictures I rejoined them.

"What do you think?" Marlo asked.

"This is definitely a workable space."

"Sounds good. Well, I can line up some more properties by tomorrow afternoon? If you need to see a few more."

"Tell you what, I will let you know something later today."

"Sounds good. It was really nice meeting you, Precious." David smiled, he was nice looking, he appeared to be about twenty-six or so but younger than thirty. Marlo said he was cool guy; his father was a big shot lawyer who had represented Penelope and Pablo for many years. And that his wife Tangela was a black super model who worked a lot in Europe, they had just had their first baby a daughter Melanie Grace two months prior.

"You want to grab something to eat?" Marlo asked as he started up the Bentley. I was about to answer just as his cell phone interrupted me.

Marlo shook his head as if whoever he was speaking with could see him through the phone. He simply replied to them to hang tight. He ended the call and put the whip in drive. "I'ma drop you back at the crib but I'll be back to scoop you, soon as I'm done," he said as he entered traffic, turning block after block with focus to get back to the interstate. He looked calm but his body language read something different, like aggression. Something was up.

"What's up with the call, is it business?" I asked him straight out. The light in front of us was yellow. He slowed and then made a complete stop as it turned red.

Marlo gazed out the window to the left of him and gripped the wheel, then looked back at the light. "That was Phil. He got the sucka ass nigga who tried to body me in eyesight at the barbershop with two of his fuckboys and his old lady."

Now it made perfect sense. The focus, the aggression. But he wanted to go handle that business and seat me in the protection room until he was done.

"Hmph," I replied out loud. Now I had a bit of aggression. "You never told me who was responsible." I didn't like the fact that he had not voluntarily shared the information with me yet. But I knew he had been in pain and trying to heal so I had tried to give him time.

Marlo took off soon as the light turned green. He eyeballed traffic, sucked his teeth, and said, "It ain't shit. The nigga a fake ass boss wannabe in Miami . . . he go by Maurice. Word on the streets he been trying to get next to El Guapo but El Guapo ain't fuckin' wit' him."

"So, he a hater. Okay." I looked out the window my mind was made up regardless of why he had violated but I had to make myself clear. "I ain't going to the house to be a sitting duck. We partners, remember? I think I proved that shit when we first met, if I need to jog your memory." I was referring to when not long after Penelope and Pablo thrown us together. He had taken me along for a ride wearing a long hot ass red coat in the dead heat wave of a Miami summer. And unbeknownst to me it was on some settle the score shit. So, I think I had made my point. I looked over at him, he took his eyes from the street and glanced at me. "I won't be caught not having your back." And I meant that.

I could see the stubborn set of Marlo shoulders. "Nah, this my beef. I ain't trying to involve you."

I ignored him. "Where the guns at, Marlo? This ain't no debate." I uttered just as he veered back onto the interstate.

Again, he gripped the stirring wheel tight with his left

hand then gazed at me. "My shit in the trunk. Don't leave home without it."

"Point this car to the exit that takes us to that barbershop." My tone was matter of fact. He knew I was beyond convincing otherwise.

We arrived and with no words soon as the Bentley halted, we both jumped out. I stood by the edge of the trunk while Marlo popped it open. I gazed around the scenery. Not being from Miami I didn't know the area, so I had no idea what it should look like. But there were people jumping out vehicles going into shops on both sides of the streets. It was a normal hot day in the three o five.

I stepped around the trunk and stood next to Marlo and their lay out as if they were waiting to be picked over was gun heaven. I reached in and grabbed a short Uzi for the muscle. Then I grabbed a nine-millimeter complete with a silencer and placed it in my hand and held it close to my side, pointed towards the ground. Marlo held two of the same nine millimeters as I did.

Marlo shut the trunk and took the lead we and quickly made our way inside. He pushed the door open and right away I noticed two of Marlo's guys standing post with guns on two unknown dudes. It didn't take a genius to know they were with Maurice, who I quickly understood was the guy Phil was guarding.

Phil wasn't holding a gun, but his stance was clear. Maurice sat glued to the barber's chair. Dark skinned, with a stocky muscle build, he looked like if he stood, he would be every bit of six-five in height. His body language read bully. But his bald head and goatee made him a very attractive man. I was sure he was a player for the bitches in the streets. Damn shame he was on his last day. I noticed his "old lady" as she had been called, sitting in the corner off towards the right. Her eyes were glued on us, she looked unbothered by our presence. She was a pretty girl with big eyes, clear skin, but one look at her and I could see the street in her, she looked me up and down.

The dumb look on Maurice's face when he caught sight of Marlo turned anxious. He chuckled lightly and tried to give a stupid smile. The sight of his gold-plated teeth and a few diamonds told me he was definitely from the south. "Aye mane . . . I'm glad you here . . . maybe you can figure out why yo' man here violating me and my crew." His eyes were on Marlo, but he quickly turned them back to Phil. He was trying to keep his eyes on them both, but his nervousness could not be hidden. He was a pussy at the moment.

I could see Phil's face twisted up he looked like he might explode. "Marlo, can I please dead this sucka ass nigga?" He barked; his body moved from side to side. He was ready to buck.

A calm look was embedded on Marlo's face. "A sucka ass pussy nigga to be sure." His words were harsh, but his tone was calm. I watched both his hands as they slowly raised in the air, yielding a nine-millimeter in both. Maurice's eyebrows seemed to raise in slow motion as he laid eyes on each gun. "Lights out nigga." Marlo squeezed one bullet from each gun hitting him twice in the chest. Maurice's body bucked forward as he tried to stand. Just as he did, I see his woman pull up a Ruger like I said I could tell she was from the streets. But I was prepared, I squeezed a round off and hit her between the eyes.

Maurice's body was slumped back in the barber's chair. The chair swayed a bit to the right then stopped. Marlo stepped over and shot him in his upper skull. He watched as Maurice's brains filled the back of the chair then the floor beneath it. Marlo turned and faced Maurice's flunkies.

"Damn, y'all gotta die for this weak ass nigga." He sucked his teeth as if in thought. "A damn shame." Again, both his guns go up one pointed at each; a bullet released from each chamber at the same time. Both shot in the head. Dead.

"Take care of this." He instructed Phil, his demeanor still calm. He then faced the owner who he addressed as Ray. "This shit will be cleaned up in a minute."

"No problem." Ray said. Phil picked up a duffel bag that was next to his feet and told Ray it was his. Ray had been the connection to Maurice. And for that he was paid nicely, but everything came at a cost. Ray's life was also no longer his. Any suspicion that he had ran his mouth, him and his family would be six feet, no hesitation, no questions asked. That was the true price of the duffel bag full of green dreams. Either way Marlo and I were done. We exited the barber shop.

I was relieved when we made it back to Marlo's house. "I'm going to take a shower," I told him soon as were inside. The sticky Miami heat was too much for me. I shed myself of my clothes no sooner than I stepped in the bathroom. I turned on the hot water and stepped inside. I placed my face under the warm water. It felt so good to my skin I could have screamed out from pleasure of the shower's soothing feeling.

Reluctantly I released my face from the water so I wouldn't drown. I held my head back and let the water cascade down my neck and breasts and let the warmth from the steam relax me. I slowly opened my eyes and glanced off to the left of me. Marlo stood on the other side of the glass. Even through steam I could see he was naked. He pulled the glass door open and stepped inside. The look in his eyes as he ate me up with them was full of lust. I matched his look. The boy was so fine.

"Partners, huh? Are we only partners in crime?" He leaned down closer to my still damp face. I was on complete fire for him. My face was not the only thing wet; I was so ready for him. I reached up and placed my hand behind his head and pulled his luscious lips into mine. We kissed so long and deep. He wrapped his free right hand around my waist and pulled me into him so tight. He felt so good. Suddenly I remembered his wound and slightly eased back.

I looked down at the area of the scar tissue where he had been stitched and noticed it was barely visible down there. "Is this okay? I don't want to hurt you." I looked into his eyes.

With no answer Marlo lifted me up and I straddled him, with the water running down his back I rode him, as he guided me, until we both moaned out in ecstasy. Talk about soaked and wet.

Chapter 23

Miami was becoming my second home all over again. All the constant trips out here were starting to remind me of when Pablo had me and my crew heading up his territories. Not that I minded coming to Miami, but LA was home and sometimes I felt like I had attachment issues to my hometown. But with Promise spending so much time in Miami visiting Money, I didn't mind so much.

This time she had been out here for three weeks, and I missed her and couldn't wait to see her. And we were in for a good time because I had flown Toya and Reese down for the party Money was having at his club. I had booked us a President Suite at the Ritz and they were hype about staying there.

"Oh shit, I can't believe we up in Gucci." Reese said in a whisper holding on to my arm. Toya was walking on my heels, her eyes as big as flying saucers. They both were in awe of the place.

"Pinch me, Precious." Toya finally made her way to my side. "This place is bananas."

I grinned. "Aye, look over there." I pointed towards Promise in the shoe section talking to the saleslady. One thing I could count on, my sister not being late to shop. Promise was a shopaholic and I always allowed her to go crazy.

"Promise." Toya almost leaped in the direction but kept her cool. Promise looked up and saw us and excused herself from the saleslady and skipped towards us.

Toya reached her first and they hugged. Then Promise raced over to me and we hugged. "Aww, Precious, I missed you." She held on tight before letting go.

"You sure?" I teased her. Reese stepped around and hugged Promise.

"I'm so glad you guys are here. We are going to have so much fun. We gone tear these Miami streets up." She eyed Reese and Toya. "Precious, where's K, I thought she was coming?" She referred to Katrina.

"Nope, I tried to get her to come but she wanted to hang back."

The saleslady approached. "Hi ladies, I'm Marsha. I will be attending you today. Can I get you a bottle of white wine while you relax?"

"Yes, please." Promise smiled and winked at Toya and Reese. "First class, right?"

"For real. This here is the life." Toya grinned.

"So, what have you guys been up to since I been gone? Catch me up with the juicy," Promise inquired.

"Quavo asked me to go to Puerto Rico with him," Toya revealed abruptly. "What y'all think about that?" She asked. Her eyes seemed to land on each of us individually. Marsha approached us with a tray that held four glasses and a bottle of wine. She popped the cork then filled a glass for each one of us.

I took a sip of my wine right away. Then I was ready to give Toya an answer to her question. "You have to make that choice." I know my answer was simple and probably not the response Toya was seeking. But it was a real one.

"I agree with Precious. Because if we tell you not to go then you gone be trippin' on us if you find out he took another chick, on that free trip." Promise teased.

"Yeah, I might be." Toya smiled. "And not for nothing, I think I'm starting to like him but I'm also afraid . . . Dell put me through so much."

"Oh, hell NOOO!" Promise squeezed up her face with disdain. "Please don't tell me you gone let that sorry, good for nothing determine the rest of your life." She still looked agitated from the thought of Dell.

"Fuck Dell! With his punk ass." Reese gripped her wine glass and twisted her lips. There was no secret that none of us cared for him.

Toya smiled; she was not surprised by their reaction to him. "That's what I keep telling myself, whenever he pops in mind. But . . ."

"You got a passport?" Promise asked cutting her off.

"Yep." Toya replied but looked curious at Promise question.

"Then that's yo' answer to your question. Fuck Dell!" Promise rolled her eyes.

Toya turned to me. I had nothing different to say when it came to Dell. "Aye, you heard Promise." I threw my hands up. "Now stop talking about Dell and pick some out of this Gucci so we can hit up Chanel."

Toya and Reese both look at each other and said, "Chanel." They hugged and jumped up and down.

The plan was to spoil them rotten while they were in Miami. There was no budget. They could have all the Gucci and Chanel they liked. And they weren't shy about grabbing what they liked either. I dropped sixty thousand in Gucci and eighty thousand in Chanel and didn't blink. And it was worth it, we were going to look good at the party.

Toya eyes rolled with her head as she glared around

Money's strip club. The dancers were climbing poles and doing tricks that looked to be almost like magic. It brought back memories from the first night Promise and I had attended. "They bad, right?" I chuckled. "But you ain't seen nothin' yet. Wait until you see the baddest bitch they call Taste."

"Well, if she better than what I see now, I'll be here until the doors shut." Toya eyes were lit up with excitement.

"And I'll be with you. I'm about to spend all of my money up in here tonight." Reese followed up. She too was so impressed at first her mouth had just hung wide open from disbelief. She finally closed it so she could speak.

I shook my head with laughter and continued towards the VIP lounge. Guys all but groped us with their stares as we made our way through the club. Reese was behind me and leaned over my shoulder, enough so I could hear her. "These guys fine as hell up here. I might need to go jump on one of these poles."

"I know right," Toya added with a chuckle. I laughed and kept on to our destination.

Promise's face lit up at the sight of us as we stepped inside the VIP lounge. A few people were in the room standing around in a group involved in a conversation. I didn't notice Money, but I was sure he was about the club somewhere or in his office, conducting business.

"Aye, the turn up just arrived." Promise scurried over to us.

"A bet. And I'm all sorts of ready for it too." Reese started swaying her hips and bobbing her head to Cardi B and Bruno Mars's "Finesse."

"Ya'll lookin' good in that Chanel and Gucci," Promise complimented Toya and Reese. Toya had on a bodycon dress that cut off at the thighs by Gucci with some bad pink Gucci pumps to match. Reese was killin' a pair of white Channel pants with the Channel belt wrapped perfectly around her waist, and wife beater type top by Channel that look like it had been painted on.

"I feel like money right now. Can't NO BITCH TELL ME NOTHIN'!" Toya tugged at her dress as if it was trying to rise above her butt. I could only smile.

"Y'all some bad bitches for real though," I complimented them. "We about to get this party started tonight, ain't no limits." I boasted, then turned to Promise. "I hope you told your man. We got this tonight," I added. One of the bodyguards that had been at the door when we came in approached us.

"Marlo" was what he leaned over and said in my ear then handed me a Louis Vuitton bag which I already knew was full of money. Marlo had wanted to be sure we enjoyed ourselves to the full extent and supported the young ladies that were on the poles doing their thing.

Toya and Reese were still dancing with each other. I stepped closer to them as they watched the bag in my hand. "Like I said ladies, we got this. With this bag we gone make sure these females' bills are paid for a couple months. A trip to Chanel might be possible as well." I grinned, as I unzipped the bag and allowed them to see the bills inside. It was no less than sixty thousand dollars in the bag. "Be generous."

Toya's hands went to her mouth from the shock of seeing all the money.

"DAMN!" Reese released, then stuck her hand in the bag to touch the money. Excited, Toya and Promise followed suit just as our personal dancers hit the room. We danced, drank, threw money, and was having a good time. Money had joined us, he wanted to be sure we were having a good time. He danced with Promise then hung out with some guys that I assumed were his associates of sorts. Marlo had a few of his bodyguards outside the VIP for our protection, he did not want me to be out in the city in a club alone. As he had put it to me, some people knew who I was. So he wanted me protected in a closed in space where my guard might be down a little. But the Lambskin Chanel Bag on my shoulder was not just for show. I had a Ruger inside locked, loaded, and ready to adjust any situation I saw fit. My guard was never completely down.

By the time Marlo arrived I was having so much fun dancing I didn't even see him enter as he came up from behind me. He wrapped his arms around me, and I noticed another duffel bag full of money in his left hand. "I see your girls are having mad fun. And you, too."

"Yes, we are." I turned to face him and released myself from his embrace at the same time. "More cash?" I smirked.

"Yep. Gotta support the ladies who don't make it inside VIP."

"I thought about them and I knew you would deliver." I smiled.

Marlo ate me up with his stares, his eyes that told me he approved of me in every way. "Damn, Precious. You look so sexy." He came closer, leaned down, and put his face in the crease of my neck. He allowed his lips to caress that spot gently. Then stepped back. He knew how I felt about public affection. I was his partner, and I never wanted people to get the wrong idea. Like maybe I was a woman and for that reason I was weak. I looked around him as he stepped back. Then focused on him.

"Not here, okay?" I said.

"I know, I know. I just couldn't help myself, you are so delicious. And if I could eat you alive I would." He grinned.

"No you would not because I ain't food." I playfully rolled my eyes.

He took a step closer probably about to try to kiss me quickly but was interrupted. "What's up Marlo." Money approached him and grabbed his attention away from me. They started chopping it up. Promise scooped in and snatched me up so we could dance. I then reached back quickly, grabbed the bag full of money Marlo had sitting at his feet, and we three ladies went out to the main floor and made it rain on the dancers. The ladies made sure they earned it, too. They turned up the heat on the tricks as the fifty-dollar bills started flooding all over them. And there was plenty to go around so they all got major paid.

Tired, we made it back to VIP to finish off the night which was going good. Standing next to Marlo and Toya, Reese danced all over some guy she had met. My eyes roamed the scene and landed on Money. Sitting with his crew and Promise right next to him, I watched him dip his head into a platter that he held with one side of his nose, then carefully snort a line of coke. Casually and calmly he lifted the platter from the table and passed it off to Promise. My whole body felt as if it heated up by a blow-torch, I could feel the blood rush to my head, and ooze out through my nostrils. "Give me your gun?" I turned to Marlo. A confused look sunk in his brow. "NOW!" This time I yelled. Without asking a second time he passed the gun over. I did not have time to explain to him. I was strapped with my own gun but Marlo as I figured carried a nine-millimeter, and it would do a better job because of the weight of the gun for what I planned.

I glided across the room so fast and steady one would think I slid across on frozen ice. The nine-millimeter in my hand connected with Money jaw intentionally drawing blood from the first blow. Promise screamed in horror, as I landed my second blow. Ignoring her pleas for me to stop I placed the gun to his head.

Promise jumped up screaming and tried to pull me away. Pissed, I pushed her off. I needed space. "Nigga that's what you think?" I pressed the gun to his head with more force. "You gone turn my sister into hype?" I held a grip on the gun so tight my hand started to sweat as I cocked the gun. Money's eyes darted from me then to the gun. Perspiration popped out of his pores. He was nervous as shit. "I'll end yo' pussy ass right here." Again, I pressed the head of the gun hard against his head.

Marlo gently placed his hands on both my shoulders. "Come on babe. Give me the gun," he whispered in my right ear. All eyes in the room were locked on me, everyone who had been sitting in that circle ready to get their chance at snorting the coke had scattered.

I could still hear Promise in the background crying. Slowly, I released the gun from his head and handed it back to Marlo. I took a step backwards, my eyes still clawing him apart. Money stood slowly as his eyes held an unsure gaze. Promise ducked around me and ran to him asking if he was okay.

"PROMISE, LET'S GO!" I screamed at her.

"I ain't leaving yet." She turned to me with a face full of tears. I couldn't believe she was crying for that loser. But I wasn't giving her no choice. And now was not the time for her to try me.

I stepped back over closer to her and Money, closing the gap between us. I looked in her distraught eyes. My lips barely moved, but the words flowed easily. "Promise, if you don't leave this place with me right now I will shut this bitch down and somebody gone be leaving in a body bag. And that is my solemn vow." My eyes fell to Money. If he had guessed who was leaving in that body bag, he had guessed right. Him.

Promise knew me enough to know I was not playing, and I didn't say shit just to be talking. She was well aware of the Precious Cummings who could and would take a life. Her eyes were full of tears, they constantly cascaded down her face leaving her skin soaked. Reluctantly, she allowed her hands to slowly release from Money, so upset that she brushed past with so much force I felt the cold wind. She headed for the VIP lounge exit. I looked at Money and stared him down before finally I turned and walked away. With all eyes on me.

Chapter 24

Promise had come home from the club and pretty much locked herself in Toya's room, still crying, angry and upset with me. But I was equally upset, and I knew we needed to talk sooner than later. I had to make some things clear. I was not concerned about Money and what he did with his own life. He could jump off the Golden Gate Bridge and I would not blink. But my sister was a whole other matter. And no, I was not sorry for cracking his jaw with Marlo's nine-millimeter, nor did I regret it. Promise would have to get over that. Because that was the least harm I would do to him. I was capable of so much more and he almost found out firsthand.

The drinking I had done at the club had put me down not long after we had arrived back at the Ritz to our presidential suite. And I welcomed the rest. But speaking to her was what I had planned to first thing in the morning. My eyes popped open suddenly and I realized it was a new day and I welcomed it. My bladder was so full I bolted out of the bed to my private bathroom. Flushing the toilet, I walked over to the sink and stared in the mirror at myself. My face was still red from the night before. Despair was still on my face. The thought of my sister getting hooked on drugs was just something I could not handle or would not handle well. Hell, I didn't even want to think about it.

Reaching for the faucet, I started the water then reached for my toothbrush, then a hand towel to wash my face. I allowed the water to soak the towel. The hot towel on my face woke me up and rejuvenated me a bit, and I was glad of that. Back in my room I picked my phone and to my surprise it was one o'clock in the afternoon. I could not believe I had slept that long with no interruption. I opened the door to my suite to find Toya and Reese in the kitchen.

Both holding a glass in their hand I could tell they were drinking mimosas. The solemn look on their faces told me something was up.

"Good morning," they both said as if it was rehearsed. And I instantly did not like the sound of that. Something was definitely amiss.

I looked around I but didn't see no sign of Promise. I understood she was still upset and probably still hiding out in Toya's room. And I did not want to impose on her space. "What's up. Promise still asleep?" I still asked to check on her well-being.

Toya looked at Reese. Reese looked at Toya. "What?" I stopped walking and stared at them.

"Umm. Promise is gone. She left first thing this morning. But she also left you this note." Toya picked up an envelope off the counter and held it in my direction as I walked over to retrieve it. The apprehensive looks they both wore on their faces told me they already knew what was inside.

Listen I know you will be pissed but I went to check on Money. I had to. Please don't worry about me I promise I am fine. I will be home in the next few days.

My face was once again flushed red because I was hot. She was damn right when she assumed I would be pissed.

How could she sneak out when I was asleep, knowing how much I wanted to speak with her? I said nothing to Toya or Reese. Instead, I turned around and went back to my room to retrieve my cell phone. I hit Promise's name on my phone and it went straight to voicemail. I tried it for the second time and got the same annoying result, voicemail. It was clear she had her phone off because she knew I would call.

I showered, dressed, threw Toya and Reese ten stacks, gave them the information to call the driver who would take them anywhere they wished to go in Miami. I headed straight for Marlo's crib.

"Good morning, Ms. Precious." One of Marlo housekeepers answered the door all chipper. Unfortunately, I was not in the same mood.

"Marlo, in?" I asked, my tone dry. It didn't dawn on me until that moment that I had not called Marlo before coming over and had no idea if he was home. My mind was so full of Promise, I had not bothered to find out. In my haste I had just drove until I arrived at his front door.

"Yes, I think he's still in bed though." She stepped aside, so I could come inside.

"Okay, thank you." I tried to sound a bit less dry. All his workers were always nice to me. I didn't want them to start thinking I was a rude bitch. I headed up the stairs and straight where I knew he would be. I opened the door to his massive room. And there he was arms under his pillow and his head snuggled on top of it. He was sleeping so peacefully; I did not want to wake him up. I strolled over and sat down on the edge of his bed. I rested there in silence as minutes passed. I was in such deep thought Marlo startled me when he moved. I turned to see him as he rolled over to face me.

"What time is it?" He looked at me his eyes open but still half closed.

"It's almost three o'clock." I revealed.

His eyes popped all the way open, at the knowledge of the time. He sat up on his elbows and chuckled. "Mane once again . . . too many of them damn Don Julio shots fo'sho." He pushed the covers back. "What's wrong?" He knew something was up with me. And I'm sure he knew it was about Promise.

"Woke up to find out Promise had dipped out on me. She gone over to check on Money's bitch ass . . . I knew that nigga wasn't shit." I balled my right fist up. I was so full of anger. "He out here getting her addicted to drugs. I just can't believe what I saw." My head moved from side to side. I was so full of disappointment. "What should I do?" I turned and looked Marlo in the eyes.

"Well, it's lots we can do. We can dead that nigga. And to be honest, that might be the easiest, fastest, solution to the problem."

I loved Marlo's idea. Here was my go-to answer to put an end to the situation. But as much as I hated to admit it to myself it would hurt my sister. And that was something I never wanted to do. "I thought of that . . ." I bit my tongue because I hated the rest of what I had to say. "But clearly, she like that rat nigga. And I can't let him come between me and my sister. That I'm not willing to chance."

Marlo went silent when I said that. "Welp, you can give it sometime. Promise is good people, she smart . . . she'll come around."

Marlo was right. She was good people and smart. I wanted to believe those two things would kick in, as her rational thoughts. "Yeah, but drugs we both know are a different ball game. Especially when it comes to being smart because that shit chew up and spit out good and smart people." I had to keep it real. "She claims she has it under control and that that was the first time she was going to try it. But to be honest, I doubt that is true. You know something just seems different about her since she has been coming out here." My gut had a strange feeling just speaking on it.

"Maybe." I could feel Marlo's warm body get closer to mine. He wrapped his arms around me. "Lay with me for a while." All of sudden I felt weak and defeated. Marlo's arms were a comfort I could not resist. I let myself go and slid into his arms my face to his chest.

"This is where you should have been since you touched down in Miami. Instead of the Ritz," he said.

I knew he had wanted me to stay with him. "Nah, I could not this time. I wanted to stay close to my girls. We had plans, remember. Besides, I can't be staying with you every time I'm out here. People talk." Again, I had to remind him of us being discreet.

"Well, would they be lying?" he asked. I sighed and pushed myself deeper into his strong embrace. It felt so good, and I was in complete comfort. I was glad I had come to him, being with him at the moment was what I needed. It calmed and cooled me at the same time.

Chapter 25

"Can we get the thirty-piece wings? Make them half lemon pepper, the other hot, fries, and carrots. And we'll both take Lime Margaritas with a splash of vodka." Promise ordered for the both of us. We were at one of our favorite wing spots. We had been back in LA for almost two weeks, but this was the first time we'd had time to meet up to talk. She had done my hair a few days prior, but we didn't have any privacy at the salon, so we didn't talk about the recent incident. "I am so hungry I could eat a whole pig," Promise said soon as the waitress walked away.

"Me too. I skipped breakfast this morning since we were having lunch. I haven't been to the gym in almost two weeks, nor have I had time to go running. I have got to watch these calories though."

"I know. Let's run tomorrow morning. Five miles."

My eyes widened and I tightened my lips to show my shock. "Oh shit, you want to run the full five. Remember this is your suggestion."

"Yep, let's get it. I haven't been exercising either." Not that she needed it, she was so thin.

"Alright, I'ma hold you too it. My house, seven AM, and I do mean sharp." I said it as if it was law but expecting her to show up late either way. I grinned.

"Bet." The waitress sat our margaritas in front of us. I took a sip right away. "So, listen, I know we haven't had a chance to catch up since Miami. I know you've been worried about me."

"Worried I think that would be to put it mildly. And I think I have good reason to be. Coke. Promise . . . not cool."

"And I know that. And that's why you don't have to worry. I ain't messing around wit' that. In addition, Money says he is going to stop doing it. You know he spend so much time in that club it's his life. Nothing but party, night in and out. Said before he knew it being in that constant nightlife, he kinda fell into it. Getting high was just a part of it."

I had to fight not to roll my eyes. Money's so-called words sounded like a cop out and excuses to me. And that's why I didn't believe for a minute he would stop it. If anything he would get worse. And I was about to say as much but I chilled. Promise wasn't ready to hear it, she would believe Money no matter what. Because that was what she wanted to hear to put her at ease. But time would reveal all, so his lies would surface nonetheless. Until then I would keep a close eye out on him.

I soon changed the subject. There were more pleasant things I would love to chat about. I was just glad to have my sister back at home. And I would keep working on her, talking to her. And hoping she come around. We ate our wings, fries, and carrots. Drank two margaritas and I was feeling great. The bartender had clearly put extra tequila in our drinks, but they were so good, it was worth it.

I left the restaurant and headed straight for the dry cleaners, I had to go by both. I went to the new one first then the old one. Katrina was on cloud nine as I strolled through the door standing at the counter, she was all tooth and gum. It had been two full weeks since she had left my house and returned home. I had tried to get her to stay with me or go to my dad's old house for a little longer. But she told me that she was good, and nothing was going to keep her out of her home where she paid good money to live. I thought she had a good point.

"How is everything at the house?" I asked.

"Good, Case took me to the gun range to brush up on my shooting. He also purchased me a new gun with a better safe deposit box or should I say a safer safe deposit box to be sure Lalah can't get into it."

"Okay, that's what's up. You and Case have been spending a lot of time together," I pointed out. A few times when we had spoken on the phone she was out with him.

Katrina smiled. "Actually, we have. He's a sweet guy."

"Yeah, I think he is cool. I never seen him disrespect a female before," I added.

"Yes. I'm glad we met." She looked down at the order list in front of her, but I could tell she was not reading it. "Let me ask you something?" Suddenly her eyes were back on me. "I know we don't talk about your life. What you do . . . but you know that I know." She was right. We never discussed my lifestyle. But Katrina knew of DaVon from the streets. And it was no secret he was my boyfriend. And without words she understood from the streets who I had become, but she had never attempted to question me. What was understood did not need to be explained. "I know before you became who you are, you were with DaVon, as his girl. What I need to know is, is it safe to be around Case? To be honest with you I like him a lot already. But I have Lalah to think about."

These were questions I was not prepared to answer. I hated that she was asking me this, but I comprehended why. "Look, Katrina. Like you said I learned this life from DaVon before I ever knew what it meant. You been knowing me way before there was a DaVon in the picture. You are well aware how I was raised. So, you know I knew nothing of the streets in depth. Then I wake up one day and go searching for the street life. But to be honest with you, I kinda flocked to DaVon out of anger at my dad. But when I fell in love with him, I never once gave the life he lived a second thought. Was I safe? I don't know. Will you be safe? Will Lalah? I cannot say. Should you be afraid? Maybe, maybe not. The best answer I can give you is . . . only time will tell. You must figure out the moves as they come your way, keep your eyes and ears open wide. Let all that be your guide. That and your instincts will keep Lalah safe. And know I always got your back. No matter what."

Chapter 26

"What would you like to drink?" Shasha asked me. She was behind the bar mixing drinks. She bartended part-time when she was not hosting parties. She was actually pretty good at it. Tonight, was one of our weekly Happy Hour nights.

"Make it simple. Sprite, light vodka, a lime and two olives."

"That's plain enough." She teased with a big grin etched on her face. The club vibe was kind of mellow. I had arrived early so people had not started coming in yet. She poured up my drink, mixed it, dropped the lime in it, then a straw with two olives embedded on the edge of the glass just as I requested.

"Thank you." I accepted the drink she passed to me. I knew she wanted to talk; she had texted me the day before saying she had a new idea to pitch to me. The girl was ambitious.

"Sooo." She entangled her hands together than looked at me. "I really would like to throw a big bash for this new R&B artist. He goes by Freeway. He from Arizona but he's coming in town to meet with A&R over at Elektra, they just signed him a few weeks ago."

"Really? That's dope." I loved to hear positive things like that, people living out their dreams.

"Yeah, the boy bad. Mad vocals. He's been a YouTube sensation for a while now and got almost five hundred thousand Instagram followers. That's how he got discovered."

"Hey, say no more. Freeway is more than welcome to showcase his talents up in here. Do what you do to make it happen."

"I'm already on that, just needed your blessing first, one of the reps over at Elektra told me that they wanted to rent out all our available VIP areas, spending a hefty sum on the bar etc."

"All sounds good, but you have to get with Sharita to book the VIP areas to get those dates locked in. At the same time let her know about the drinks so the order will be on point. She'll get all that info to me for final numbers."

"Bet."

I tasted my drink as a customer approached the bar and put in an order for two drinks.

"Hey, Precious." A regular walked by and spoke. I wasn't sure of her name, if I had to guess I would say it was Yolanda, but she used to attend back when Keisha was the owner. And soon as I had opened the doors back, she was inside. On opening night, she had approached me and thanked me personally for reopening one of the hottest clubs in LA.

"Soo . . ." Shasha slid back over to where I was still holding post at the bar. "I heard your sister Promise had one the hottest salons in the city?" I wasn't expecting her to bring up Promise, let alone her salon.

"That's a fact." I sipped my drink.

"If that's the case you think you can hook me up?" I almost spit my drink out I laughed so hard. Had she forgot her and Promise's introduction? I had not.

"Are you sure you want Promise in your head?" I teased.

Shasha stood back and put her right hand on her hip. "What? I got green money. Are you saying your sister ain't feelin' me?"

"Nah, I'm just teasing you. But for real though, like you said it is one of the hottest salons in the LA area. With that being said they don't take new clients, haven't in a long time. Besides, Promise only has a few selected clients that she services, personally."

"Okay, I can understand that. But what about the other stylists up in there?"

"Honestly, they all have a clientele list of people that are like grandfathered in, seriously."

"Really, see that's why I got to get up in there. I would love to be a part of an exclusive salon; you know it's like having VIP access. Please, please, Precious, can't you talk to Promise and get me hooked up?" She begged. "They the baddest and the owner is your sister." I wondered how she had even found out about Promise's salon. Maybe now she wished she had not stared at Money too long.

"I'll see what I can do. But I can't make you any promises. Okay?" I laughed. She was persistent.

"Okay, okay. Oh, thank you so much, Precious."

"Girl, you are always trying to talk yourself into something. The gift of gab." I shook my head and smiled. "Now stop worrying about hair appointments and serve up these drinks. Hell, you on the clock." I stood, grabbed my drink, and headed off towards my office. The crowd had started to come in. I would use this time to look over the books and relax.

Chapter 27

"I'm so glad you are finally here. I'm so hungry." Promise reached for the top platter in my hand that held a fifty-piece wing. I also had a platter with carrots, which all the girls liked. I had dropped by the salon with lunch for everyone. "Did you get blue cheese and ranch?" Promise asked going through the bag.

"Yes, I did. No worries. It's in the bag with the veggies." I sat the platter of veggies on the counter next to the wings. Promise had already pulled off the top and was digging in. She filled her plate, and I handed her a container of ranch dressing once I opened the bag.

Promise sat down in her seat, bit a wing, and chewed vigorously. "Precious, dear sister this tastes so good. I swear I'm starving and tired."

Toya now stood over the wings fixing a plate. "Her clients are so glad she is back they have been booking her every two days for a fresh look. They scared she might sneak off again."

Promise rolled her eyes and bit off a celery stick. "That is no lies." She talked with her mouth full. "I've been doing them so much I haven't had time to get myself all dolled up. I look a mess," she exaggerated. I smiled.

"You do not look a mess." I reached for a plate so I too could join in the smacking of good wings and carrots. The lemon pepper wings smelled so good; I craved my first bite.

"My sister is so modest, she thinks I look good even when my hair is flying the coop." She chuckled. "But Reese, can you please do my eyebrows later before you head out."

"Yes, I got you." Reese stood next to me putting carrots and celery on her plate.

"Speaking of you being busy. My club promoter Shasha was wondering if you can do her hair. She has found out that you are one of the hottest stylists LA got going." I grinned so hard my jaws ached. I bit a carrot and waited.

Promise eyes went downward and she sat up in her chair and gazed at me. "You mean that bootleg, scullery snot you hired? Hmmph, I'll do her hair a'ight. Lil heifer know she rude, with no home training." Promise eased back into her chair and reached for another wing. I laughed.

"What she do?" Toya asked. "I remember that chick getting on the mic that night at the club talking about her name Shasha. Ghetto name to be sure."

"I know right?" Promise agreed right away. "And she stared at my man a little too long, that night at the club." She tossed at Toya. "Anyway, Precious, don't she know this is a five-star salon? Ain't no walk-ins."

"I tried to tell her that."

"Why she want to come here anyway? Plenty salons down in Compton, for the likes of her." We all laughed at Promise's antics. We knew she was just teasing.

"Hey, say what you want. She is determined to get her

hair done here. She even asked if one of you ladies could do her." I nodded at Toya and Reese with a smirk.

"Nah, I can't do it. I'm booked for the next six months." Toya chimed in.

"Welp, I tried." I threw up both my hands, my plate was leveled in my lap.

Promise sighed and rolled her eyes again. "On the other hand, I am in the mood to do a good deed. Tell Ms. Thang, I'll fit her in . . ." She picked up a wing. "Sometime this year or next," she added. We all busted out laughing.

Toya stood up with her empty plate in hand. "I gotta go." She was still laughing. "I'm going out to this fancy restaurant with Quavo."

"What's up with Puerto Rico?" Reese asked.

"Oh, yeah, that. I told him maybe in the future but I'm not ready for that now."

"I swear you are procrastinating." Promise added in. "Tell the brother I'll go. Shit I ain't never too busy for a free vacation. And I do mean never."

"Me three." Reese raised her right hand to the heavens. "Currently, seeking my next contributor. Until then, I'm hitting the gym on the regular to keep this body tight so when the opportunity presents, I'm beach ready. Aye." She chanted and stood up and twerked holding her plate in her hand.

"Ya'll a mess. Bye." Toya exited towards the back where she could discard her plate first before leaving.

"Reese, you are hanging around Promise way too much. She is changing you." They both were laughing. Promise shook her head in agreement. "I gotta go too." I stood up, still grinning. I was enjoying myself with them and hated I had to leave but as usual I had a meeting with the crew.

"Aww, don't go," Reese said with her lips in a pout.

"I don't want to, but I got to bounce. But I swear y'all so crazy." I waved off. "Oh Promise, don't forget we are hanging out at Dad's tomorrow night. I'll have the chef come over and cook dinner and do some desserts. Unless you volunteering to get in the kitchen and shake it up."

"Umm, tell the chef I want cheesecake minis with thick strawberry sauce." That was her answer to her volunteering to cook.

"I will let him know because I was craving those too. And guess what, we are running five miles the morning after those cheesecake minis. So don't forget the work out gear."

"Always trying to take me on a run. Why can't I eat my sweets and be happy?"

"Bye." I smiled and threw up the piece sign. My fun time was over, it was back to business. The grind.

Chapter 28

"Precious, it is so cold in here," Promise complained. We were at Dad's for our sleepover. I had just gotten out of the shower and put on my pajamas. "Can't you please adjust that thermostat to some warmth. Or are you trying to torment me?" she whined.

"Promise, you have on a wife beater and boy shorts." I described her pajama outfit to clarify why she might be feeling the chill.

"What's your point? I'm still freezing." She continued to pout and bounced down on the sofa with her legs folded under her and her arms crossed. It looked as if she was fighting the cold in a standoff.

"Welp, just maybe if you added some clothes to the naked parts of your body, you might not be as cold." I teased her.

"That is a thought but that would be too much like right. Besides, I like this outfit, I look cute and comfy in it. Who wants to look warm and comfy?"

I laughed and shook my head at her philosophy. "Such a baby, I'll adjust the thermostat and grab one of those nice throw blankets I brought for you." I spoiled her as usual.

"Dang I always forget about those. Thanks, sissy." She smiled. I went into the room that had been designated as hers, opened her closet door, and reached onto the shelf for her Chanel throw blanket. I went into my room and retrieved my Ralph Lauren throw. I wasn't freezing but I did want to get comfortable on the sofa. Plus, we would be in the den most of the night and would probably fall asleep in there like we normally did.

"Aww, this feels so good to my skin. Yesss, comfort," Promise sang and snuggled under her throw no sooner than I passed it off to her.

I bounced down on the sofa next to her. We had already had dinner. Now we were going to watch movies, drink champagne, eat desserts, and chat until we passed out. Our first movie was going to be *Boyz n the Hood*. I popped the champagne bottle and poured us both up our first glass.

Promise gripped her glass and took her first drink. "Ahh, this some good bubbly. Just what I need."

I followed suit. And she was right. I got that tingly feeling in top of my throat. "Yep, good stuff."

"You know as many times as we come over here and spend nights, I still sometimes get that odd feeling." Promise looked around the den as if she was unfamiliar with her surroundings.

"What type of odd feeling?" I inquired with concern.

"I don't know. That maybe I don't belong. I know you always are trying to make me feel comfortable. Like I'm a part of this house, its history, like this is my legacy too. But . . ."

"That's because it is a part of your legacy . . . you do belong here. At this point there should be no question about that. Dad made that clear in that letter we found. Remember?"

Promise looked away. Tears filled her eyes. I see she was trying to hide them from me.

"Wait . . . what's wit' the tears?"

Promise sniffed and took in a deep breath. "Nothin' I'm just being silly, soft, and emotional." She wiped her eyes and tried to chuckle. "It's just sometimes when I come here, I think I miss Mom just that much more. I think of the memories she had here, ones that she probably did not share with me. And I think about when she and I were all alone. Just us. Then she was gone, so suddenly. And I was alone. No one to love me . . . no one who really cared. Then I think about the love that I feel I was cheated out of from Dad . . . at least the love from him that I could see . . . touch . . . feel." I instantly felt all of her pain and hurt from her words, thoughts, and the hurt on her face.

"Aww . . . Promise." I scooted to her end of the couch, and we hugged. I wished I could hug her pain away, we both had so much pain from our pasts. Slowly we let go. "Listen, we both missed out on a lot. I know I don't have a house that Mom owned that I can go sit in and know that she was there. But I have you . . . and I used to look at you and regret with my whole heart on what I missed out on. But I have given that up. All I know now is that we belong to each other. And no past will destroy that, we can't allow that to happen. This house is yours just as much as it is mine. You belong. You are loved."

"And you are loved." She smiled at me. We hugged again. She scooted back on the couch and sniffed again. "Now I'm done being silly, all these dumb tears. Tell me something good, what's up with the business, the new position and all that?"

"Ah, that. Good at least as far as the eye can see. That's all you can ever say in the game." I kept it real. "Seizing power, comes with a lot . . . jealousy, hate, betrayal, and of course probably one of the worst. ENVY!" I sucked on that word with a lot of emotion. Envy had brought the end to a lot of street hustlers. And I knew one firsthand DaVon. Keisha and Quincy envied his power, his respect that he had in the streets, and his wealth. In the end the only way they saw to measure up was to murder him and take his spot. Envy was a dangerous plight.

"Are you worried about anything, or should I say anyone in particular?"

"Nah, nothing in particular." I kept that short. I really tried to never go deep into the business with her. Mostly for her own protection. I wanted to keep her involvement at a minimum. The less she knew the better. I knew she understood the streets and hustling were not the safest place for me to be. And she understood my position put me at risk. Simply, she was no fool about the game. But I kept the killing, especially as of late, from her because although it had been a lot, it had been necessary. Quite of few people had put Marlo and I to the test recently causing us to prove to them the truth. That disrespect of any kind could not and would not be tolerated.

But I did have reason to worry, and she should know. "I am worried about someone though." I realized.

"Aye, look I know Marlo being shot got you shook. And I know how much you care about him." My eyes fluttered. I was a bit surprised that she pulled Marlo being shot out of her bag of answers.

I could only smile. She loved to talk about Marlo. She was determined to break the case wide open to prove my feelings for him. I was convinced she would stop at nothing. "I do believe you must be Marlo's biggest cheerleader and doubt he would appreciate it. Yes . . . I was concerned about him, when he was shot." I was prepared to downplay the Marlo conversation as I always done. I continued. "But Marlo is on the mend. A fast one I might add. And I never expected less."

Promise chuckled. She shook her head at me, reached for the Champagne and refilled her glass. "Sister dear, you can continue to play like you have Marlo replete and I will fake like I believe you." She smirked, then sipped from her glass.

"Anyway." I sighed then drank down the rest of the champagne in my glass. "If you are done, we can get to the person I'm really worried about. Which happens to be you." I was matter of fact in that last part.

Promised allowed her lips to fly apart in attempt to be shocked at what I said. "Me. Why? I told you I am fine."

Once again, her face carried a sincere look, and I wanted to believe more than anything that she was okay. But I had to be honest with myself, ever since she had been home her energy seemed off. But the last thing I wanted to do was argue with her or accuse her of being untruthful. I needed a different approach. Maybe understanding. "Well, I heard you when you said you were fine, and I try to stop worrying." I tried to sound upbeat. "Listen, I want you to be happy. I hope that you know that. Just the right kind of happy . . . and sometimes lately I just get the feeling that you are not."

"Ahh, no. I'm happy. As happy as a girl can be right now. With Money by my side everything is refreshing. I love his energy, it revitalizes me." She broke it down to me so I could feel her emotions.

"Okay, okay I get it . . . I'll relax."

"In fact, I'm headed back to Miami for a few days, but I won't be gone long." She revealed too soon. I could not have hidden the apprehensive look on my face if I wanted. So, I quickly reached for the champagne bottle and filled it to the rim and prayed that I could keep my mouth shut.

Chapter 29

There you go telling me no again. There you go . . .

I sang along with Keith Sweat so loud and filled with emotion since I was in my car alone. I loved old school music and listened to it sometimes as I bended corners in the LA streets headed to my destination. Today I pulled up to my club. I had a few things to check on; it was happy hour so as I expected a bit of a crowd inside. I shut off the engine and climbed out of the Range Rover and hit the alarm.

"Hey boss lady." One of my bouncers Chris spoke to me at the door as I made my way inside. I spoke back and kept it pushing.

I stalled for a brief second as I caught the sight of what I believed to be Black sitting at the bar. I found my footing and continued in the direction of the bar, and the closer I got it was clear his black ass was sitting in my club at the bar, as if he owned it. Two of his peons were hanging off his coat tails. Sharita passed him a drink. I stepped behind the bar and made my presence known.

"Well, well, Precious." I hated the way my name sounded coming out of his mouth. He tried to smile but, he was so ugly he was not in my opinion successful at his attempt. "My favorite LA Boss." He crooned.

I could never fake with him he always rubbed me the wrong way with the shit he babbled so I responded. "Black, the blackest nigga I know." He knew me well enough to know what might come outta my mouth. And I was sure he wished to slap the shit out of me for my cruel words. But really what could the nigga do. He could try but he knew my gangster was always ready to match his. Anytime. In other words, I dared him.

He did only what he could do to address the bitch that he thought I was. He laughed showing his white teeth that he paid a pretty good penny for. That too I was sure of. "I set myself up for that one." That was all he had better have said.

"You are sitting at my bar, so I expect you are cashing out." He knew exactly what I meant. If he was at my bar, he had better spend no less than two thousand dollars. I would have preferred if none of my liquor ever slid down his rusty ass throat. But since he was here, he had better make it worth my club's while.

"No doubt . . . you know that." He sat a stack on the counter that now belonged to my club. "I really like the vibe up in here. One can't pay enough for this type of atmosphere, cool, and calm."

"That's because we are professionals. Enjoy your drink." Before walking away, I gestured for Sharita to get the stack off the counter. Rolled up and wrapped in a rubber band. It was probably about five thousand easy. I would give Sharita the whole stack of whatever was in the rubber band. Serving him, she had more than deserved it.

In my office I sat at my desk and pondered over Black's presence in my club. This had to be the first time since I had opened the doors he had ever been inside. I also had caught that statement about murder he was shooting his mouth off to his peons about when I approached. I waved that off though. Whatever he was gossiping about I knew better than anyone. Black had a big mouth and was messy like a bitch.

The knock on my office door grabbed my attention. "Come in." I had my hand on the nine-millimeter placed under my desk. Ready to end whatever or whoever thought about getting a start.

Sharita peeked her head in the door then stepped in and shut the door behind her. "Here you go." She handed me the band of money. I didn't reach for it, so she sat it on the desk.

"Those pussies. Ugh. They are worse than females." I told her.

"He gave up the rack when you came in."

"You keep it." My eyes feel to the stack on my desk. Sharita's eyes bulged. "You earned it."

"Really?" She stared at the stack sitting in front of her.

"Yep. Take it."

She picked it up. "You sure? This like seven thousand dollars. I counted it."

"Yep. All yours. Aye and why are you not at the bar?" I asked.

"Oh, it's fine Shasha is up there now. She just got in."

"She good up there? That rusty nigga and his boys probably bothering her." I speculated.

"Oh no, she familiar with them. They been comin' in here about two months now, on a regular. And while Black is not easy on the eyes, he is normally a good tipper. Well not as good as he was today. I had no idea you knew him." She smiled, gazing at the money in her hand.

While the money was mesmerizing Sharita, the statement she made about him coming in my club for two months was roaming around in my brain like bad gas. How in the hell had this snake been in my club and I had never seen him? I always stopped in during happy hour. Unless I had been out of town, or he came in before or once I left. Either way the snake had slipped me. But I would be watching for his ass from now on.

"Precious," Sharita said my name and snatched me away from my thoughts. The look on her face told me she must have called my name more than once. "You good?" She looked concerned.

"Oh, yeah, just a long day, a bit worn out. What's good?"

"I kinda wanted to bring to your attention that Shasha has not shown up for her last two happy hour shifts. Nor did she call up in here to say she would not be coming in."

"Really, why didn't you call me?"

"Well, I thought you she might have called you or something but when you didn't mention it by now, I believed maybe you didn't know . . . Anywho, I just covered the shifts. Besides, I didn't want to make a big deal out of it. It was only four hours each time. But what bothers me is the way she rolled up in here today like everything fine and dandy. Like she ain't missed two of her scheduled shifts. And frankly she irks my nerve with her crass, sometimes entitled attitude. It's something about that girl. She always trying to take over when she is here and then be trying to boss me around like she knows everything. Oh, and the rearranging shit, like someone asked her to do it." Sharita went on and on once she started spilling her concerns to me. No longer smiling about the cash, she gripped it tight in her balled-up hand. She appeared annoyed at first then pissed. Sharita had had it.

Sharita being upset was new to me. Never since she had been working for me had I seen her upset or vent about another employee. And once again I realized Shasha was on the bad end of someone's thoughts of her. It was becoming clear that she was racking up more enemies than allies. Promise was not a fan of hers, now Sharita. I felt bad for Sharita because she seemed really angry with Shasha, but on the inside I could not help but laugh.

"Sharita, you know I appreciate all you do here at the club, you go above and beyond in your duties without ever being asked. Not to mention you are reliable, you are re-sourceful. So, I take your grievance serious. I will have a talk with Shasha today. But in the future, if something is out of whack like someone not meeting their shift, please let me know right away. I'm here to help you. I never want you feel bound or stuck to deal with any issue alone."

"I know you wouldn't, I just didn't want to burden you. But the next time I will let you know. And again, thank you so much for this stack. Whew. You have made my day." She bounced on her toes to her feet.

"Aye, from Black's hands to yours. Run up a bag." I chuckled. She nodded her head in agreement then raced out of my office.

Chapter 30

Promise had been gone to Miami for over a month now on her latest getaway. Once again, she had asked me to drop in at the salon and deliver the deposits to the bank. While I had no problem helping her out and she knew that, my biggest question was when was she coming back to LA? I didn't feel good knowing she was getting so comfortable being in Miami. I was in her office sitting at her desk and going over the deposits. Everything was correct down to the penny and all the paperwork matched up. Toya always did a good job with that as she did with everything else. I logged into the computer and updated the numbers and everything else was ready to go.

I looked over the order that Toya had put in and drew down the payment to place the order so product would arrive on time. I headed out to the booth areas.

"Precious seriously, when is Promise coming back? She was supposed to be here two weeks ago." Toya pouted. Reese stood at her booth mixing up some concoction she would put on her client's head.

"Soon." I sat down in the chair for a second, the

deposit bag was gripped in my hand. "I just drew down the payment for your order. The supplies should arrive tomorrow."

"What the budget for next week's order?"

"I emailed that to you. The numbers as usual look good."

"We making it happen for sure. All the clients just miss Promise being here. So do we." Reese frowned. "Me and Toya thinking about getting us a ticket out to Miami and kidnapping her back to her home."

"Aye, I'm down to help, just let me know." I said.

"Cool we leave tomorrow." Toya smiled. "You need to wear all black." We all laughed.

"Nah, on some real stuff though. I'm doing a wedding party and I really need her help." Reese looked disappointed.

"Yeah, I'm going to help out but we gotta have Promise. Only she can provide her special touch." Toya added. They were all top notch, but their work complemented each other's. "Her calls have been few and far between. I tried texting her the other day, but she didn't respond. Guess we just gotta hope she'll be back before the wedding." Toya didn't sound optimistic.

"She'll be back. She got y'all." I tried to assure them. But to be honest I had the same concerns if she would actually be back as she had said. Her calls to me had been few and far in between as well, but she called me when she needed me. I chalked it up to the fact that she was enjoying her man.

"I will hope for the best, but that nigga Money got her love drunk." Reese chuckled.

"Nah, I doubt that. This is Promise we are talking about. We all know she chew them up and spit them out, on a regular." I grinned. I was still in denial but maybe my sister was in love. I had hoped not to no avail. "I gotta bounce ladies, got more deposits to pick up before I head to the bank. Hit me if you need anything."

"Bring bagels next time you come and make sure cinnamon crunch is included." Toya shouted as I rounded the corner towards my destination, the entrance doors. I smiled. I had them spoiled.

Chapter 31

Another week had passed since Toya and Reese had expressed their concerns about Promise returning and we had joked about kidnapping her. And still she had not returned. But today when the plane touched down, I had made Promise my destination. Nothing in Miami at the moment mattered more to me. We had planned to meet for lunch, and I headed straight for the restaurant no sooner than I was on the ground. I needed to lay my eyes on my sister, not speak to her over the phone or Facetime which we never did anymore.

I sat down at the table and ordered a margarita. We were at a Mexican restaurant, but I really didn't have an appetite. My main goal was to see her. Already she was running fifteen minutes late and I felt apprehensive. I was more of the late one not her, but I also knew Miami traffic was shit and could make even the promptest person late. So, I relaxed and waited. I took a sip from my glass and my drink was just right.

I caught a glimpse of Promise as she made her way towards our table, and I suddenly became overwhelmed at the site of my mirror image, my twin. Noticeably thinner than she had ever been before as far as my knowledge. The sunglasses she wore seem to wear her. My legs seemed a bit weak all of a sudden, but I managed to bend them to stand up.

I reached for her and wrapped my arms around her, but she was light as a feather I was scared to squeeze for fear she might break.

"I missed you," escaped from her lips as we parted. Tongue-tied I watched as she pulled out a chair and sat down. I followed suit.

One look at her fingers and my first thought was that they were frail, skinny fingers, on a hand attached to a skinny arm. Why was my sister so small? Bones at best. Rosa would freak at the sight of her.

"Don't stare too hard, I might turn to stone." She tried to joke followed up with a light laugh. Clearly my stares had not gone unnoticed. "But really what's with the stares? Something wrong? I got boogers hanging from my nose?" She still tried to joke but nothing was funny.

"Are you eating? What's wrong?" I just couldn't hide my concern, unease.

"Of course I eat. Hell, I eat everything that's not nailed down." That was a lie if I had ever heard one. She must have thought I was blind. She had no meat attached to her bones.

"If you eat so much tell me why you are so small? So thin?" I was not hearing the bullshit today. The gloves were coming off. No more lies and her ducking and dodging. "Are you on that shit? COKE?" I accused her straight out.

Promise's shoulders tightened, and her eyeballs bulged. "I'm not doing drugs; you are jumping to conclusions again. Assuming and thinking the worst of me." She was defensive as I expected her to be but was calm.

"Look, I'm not stupid. Stop sitting in my face and telling me bold-faced lies. I expect more from you, Promise."

I paused and rubbed my forehead. I was more than agitated. "Pack your shit tonight. You are going back to LA with me," I demanded not asked.

Again, her eyes bulged but her look said she was remaining calm. "I . . . I can't, not now."

"Oh, you can't huh? Well, why not? And please don't say nothing about that nigga. Spare me that cock and bull." I spat. "FUCK MONEY!" I was clear on my stance before she even tried it.

"Why, Precious? Huh? Why must you always take everything out on him? He keeps me sane . . . he . . . he helps me, not stress, or think . . ." She stopped talking her eyes darted across the restaurant. I wondered why she stopped talking I was anxious for her to finish her statement. She licked her lips then looked at me. "Look I don't want to bring this up. Actually, I thought I could handle it. But I can't. I have been battling depression since the kidnapping. And I can't seem to get it out of my head."

The mention of the kidnapping shocked me and for a moment I felt my heart had stopped. My breathing became a bit shallow. I could not speak, I had to take a few breaths. I looked at my sister. Why had I not known? Why had I not seen any sign? Why had I not asked? Why had she not said anything? How had I been so blind? I closed my eyes and swallowed the knot in my throat that was sure to choke me. My airways narrowed.

"Umm." I stopped to find my voice which seemed to have buried itself somewhere within' my vocal cords. I cleared my throat and tried again. "Why didn't you say something to me? Why didn't you let me be there for you? I would have."

"I know you would have been there, okay?" A tear slid down her cheek and she wiped it. Both my cheeks were wet, but my hands would not move to my face. "I just didn't want to worry you. You have so much on your plate. And when it comes to me you drop everything. I couldn't have you do that. Not again."

"I'm your sister, Promise. If not me who?" My hands finally mobilized, I picked up the napkin and wiped my face.

"I know. But . . ."

"There are no buts . . . Listen, I know you like it here, but I need you to come back to LA with me. I can get you in with one of the best therapists in town."

She shook her head as if she agreed with me. "Thank you and I know you think that is best. But right now, Money is good therapy for me. I need him." I cringed at the sound of his name. "I know you don't won't to hear that." She had the nerve to analyze my thoughts. That aggravated me even more.

"First off that is bullshit, so stop ripping it off to me. That nigga gettin' you high ain't therapy. Wake the fuck up." My lips were tucked in so tight if they got any tighter, they would be sealed.

Promise face turned into a frown. "I'm not getting high. And I'm getting sick and tired of repeating and explaining that to you." She got an attitude. But I would not be deterred.

"Promise, give that lie up, okay? You are skin and fuckin' bones. Ray Charles could see that. You look like you ain't ate shit since you left LA," I accused.

That hurt her feelings. Her body swayed back, and her right hand went to her chest. This time it was Promise who tightened her lips. I could tell she was pissed and was ready to match me. "Like I said to you when clearly you were not listening to me. I'm depressed. Depressed." She repeated as if I was slow. "Because of that I do not have an appetite most days to eat. And what's more, I am a grown ass woman so you can stop drilling me like I'm some child under your tutelage. Because that shit won't change my mind."

I pondered over her bold approach to me and my wrath. "Grown, huh? Well, you are acting like a child. A spoiled one. Now go pack your shit for LA," I once again demanded. I was not ready to give up or in.

Promise's hand slamming the table caught me totally off guard, and shook the table at the same time. I didn't flinch outwardly but inwardly I did. "DAMMIT, PRE-CIOUS!" She all but yelled at me. "Can't you just lay off for fucking once? I am not leaving Miami. Not yet. I know you hate Money. You have made that more than clear. I get it. Okay. But I can't . . . no I won't be in LA right now. Not with the memories of the kidnapping. I just can't. I know you will not but try to understand." Her chair seemed to slide back on its on accord, and she was on her feet in a split second. She snatched her Chanel purse off the table and rushed out.

Chapter 32

The Miami trip had been nothing but overwhelming gloom. I stayed for two long agonizing days attending meetings with Marlo. I was supposed to look at some more properties for the hair store we had planned on opening up. But instead, I put the brakes on that project and had Marlo put the realtor on hold. I didn't know what I would do, if I would go ahead or not. That was one of the things I had planned for Promise and me to talk about when we had met up. I had wanted to invite her to look at two of the properties I had already seen. That plan derailed. But I had to stay on top of my other businesses as well as be sure Promise's business stayed on top. No matter what I had to be sure my sister's business thrived and with Toya's help I was confident we were good.

Back in LA, Marlo had come into to town the day before and we had attended meetings with the LA crew leaders. A few things had changed. Product was going out faster, as El Guapo had hoped. In light of that more shipment was needed at a much faster rate. Then there was the price which of course was on the rise. Marlo had picked up the cash and it was on the run back to El Guapo. The day had been busy, but we had got all that was planned handled. Today we were getting a bit of rain which was unusual for California. So, the bed was a good place to be.

"What do you think about being like this all the time?" Marlo snuggled up closer to me and bit on my ear.

I chuckled at the tingling feeling. "You know we can't." I gave him the exact same answer I always did when he sang that tune.

"Why not?" He had to ask the question that he already knew the answer to. Sometimes I was convinced he did that to drive me mad.

"Boy . . ." I play annoyed. "Because for the thousandth time businesses ain't to be made personal. Besides, I don't won't to ruin the friendship we have." I meant that part more than anything. I enjoyed our friendship; our vibe and work ethic were parallel. I missed that in a guy since DaVon. I didn't take it for granted.

"Oh, you actually consider me a friend. I guess I have moved up." I knew he was teasing.

"Don't be sarcastic. You know how I feel about our friendship." I had enough of this conversation. I did not like when he brought it up. My answer never changed because the situation never changed. It was a waste of time.

I changed the conversation. "I haven't spoken to Promise since I've been back in LA. That's been more than two weeks ago. I know she was upset with me but to not call in all this time? Now I'm starting to feel insulted, like maybe that asshole Money is keeping my sister away from me." I had my own assumption.

"Come on. Maybe it ain't like that." Marlo tried to play good cop in Money's defense.

"So, you think my sister just pissed at me? And is ignoring my presence?"

"I didn't say that. But maybe she does need a little space and she will come back to LA when she is ready. And don't worry, she will call you. I'm sure of it."

I wanted to believe him, and I know she wanted space and had said as much, but it was hard when I had no idea how she was doing. It was bad enough that I knew she wasn't eating, she even admitted it. And with us not talking I had no idea if anything else was wrong. I hated wondering or assuming.

"Well, I haven't called her. I'm trying to give her the room she needs to reboot. But it is hard. Every day I want to wage war. But for now, I will chill."

"I think that is a good idea. Now on another topic. El Guapo is coming to the states in a couple of months. He got business in Oakland with some major players. And will be stopping in LA for some fun times, of course."

"He chose right then. LA is hot on the party scene."

"Y'all a'ight. I mean it ain't the three o five but . . ." He joked.

"Oh, whatever, y'all country bumkins' ain't poppin'," I teased back.

"Haha." He laughed. "Since you got jokes I was thinkin' I'll bring in a celebrity act at your club for entertainment. If you cool wit' that?"

"Ah, yes that's cool. Who are you thinking about bringing?"

"Shi'dd now that I ain't sure about, just yet. I will get my people on it though. I know I can pull pretty much whoever, long as that money long enough."

"Right. What's the budget?" I asked and turned over my shoulder to gaze at him. But I knew the answer to that. Like me I knew that Marlo had millions, I was sure no less than sixty million. The boy was young, black, and rich. The same could be said for me but I was female.

"Precious Cummings. Stop playing wit' me." He chuckled. And I smiled. "You know I don't do budgets. The sky is the limit."

"I forget you a baller." I laughed. "But cool, I will make sure we have the club ready. We are at your disposal."

"Now that is what I like to hear." He kissed my shoulder then gently coaxed me on to my back with no rejection from me. We started kissing and my cell phone of course started to ring.

I tried to ease away but Marlo wouldn't let up. "Come on. Don't answer it." He begged.

"You know I got to answer my phone. No matter what." I smiled. He eased up and I reached for it. I noticed it was Sharita.

"Hello." I answered.

"Precious, the delivery truck never showed up with our order today. I've been here waiting for three hours." Sharita talked fast and was clearly upset.

I sighed with annoyance. All the money they charged for alcohol, and they couldn't show up on time. "Okay, stand by, I will find out what the holdup is."

"Cool, because we open in less than six hours, and we are all out of vodka and running quite low on cognac." She filled me in, and I knew right away those were some of our top sellers.

"Shit." I was pissed. "I'll handle it." I ended the call and sat up in bed. I had to get up in the rain and handle this bullshit. "This just ain't my week," I said. Soon as the words left my lips the sun outside shone through my window.

"Whatever happened must have made the sun come out." Marlo glared outside. "But what's up?" He was now sitting up next to me his chest exposed. I was holding the sheet up to my breasts.

"I didn't tell you yet, but I had a water main break at the new dry cleaners the other day. Now the driver with my alcohol for the club is ghost. And Sharita says we out of vodka and cognac, and that's some serious shit."

I dropped my grip on the sheet and scrolled through my phone contacts searching for the company that was in charge of my liquor shipment.

"Damn all that is fucked up. But let me know what you find out about the liquor. I know somebody in the city that can get you enough vodka and cognac to get you through the night and maybe a few days." Marlo tossed the cover back and stood up stark naked, heading for the bathroom. I was focused on the alcohol, but he was so fine I had to watch until he disappeared into the bathroom.

I found the number just as Marlo was coming out of the bathroom. He reached for his boxers and stepped inside them one long leg after the other. "Let me know," he said again.

"I swear you give me hope, the phone is still ringing though." I held the phone to my ear listening to the ringing.

"While you do that, I'll grab some of those tamales Rosa hooked up for us." Rosa had left hours ago but had told us but before she had left that she had made us something to eat.

"Oh yeah, bring me up some too." I loved Rosa's tamales. Marlo was starting to fall in love with Rosa's cooking but who could blame him. He had fallen in love with everything she had made so far. He teased me all the time that he was going to double her pay and take her back to Miami to cook for him. I told him that his chef might try to murder Rosa out of jealousy, so she was staying. We laughed. "Yes, I need to check on my delivery," I said through the phone soon as a rep answered. They had better have a good excuse or I would start off cursing them out until I ripped them a new one. They were playing with my money and even more, my reputation with my clients. I was about giving grand customer service. If I couldn't even supply my customer with the drink of their choice then I was failing as a business owner. And I would not allow them to drag me down to that. They had better get me my liquor and now. I made that clear as the rep assured me the driver was running behind because of unforeseen traffic and delays but was due to arrive in the next forty-five minutes.

I called and told Sharita, and she was beside herself with happiness. She said they were not going to mess up her tips. That she'd flatten the delivery man's tires the next time he showed up if he caused her to lose a dime. I laughed but somehow thought she might be serious. What I liked about Sharita, she was a go getter. A bonified hustler when it came to her money. If I didn't know her personally, I would gladly bring her on to be the first female hustler on my team. The girl hustled that hard for her coin.

Chapter 33

"Can I get you anything else?" the doorman asked. He had brought up the food and desert I had ordered. I was back in Miami on business. My day had been long and tiring. But I needed a break from talking numbers, new product, and shipments. Being back in my Presidential Suite at the Ritz was just the unwind I needed.

"No thank you." I handed him a one-hundred-dollar bill for his tip. He bid me a good day with a smile then left. Soon as he left, I raided the cart with the food on it. I had ordered everything like I was feeding an army: salmon, steak, shrimp, asparagus, you name it I had it. But what I really wanted was one of the slices of the cheesecake I had ordered. I stared at the choices in front of me, of salted caramel, strawberry, and plain, my mouth watered they all looked so delicious. I decided on the salted caramel, the drizzle of sweet caramel was a twinkle in my eye. I picked up the plate that held it, grabbed a fork, and dashed off towards my room.

I jumped in the king size bed that would be my chariot for the night and sat back with the dish in hand.

"What took you so long? I thought you had run off with the doorman." Marlo was sitting up in the bed flipping the tv channels.

"I thought about it and I'm sure he did too," I teased back. "But I needed to eat this cheesecake first." I slid in bed beside him and stuck the fork down into the cheesecake and prepared for my first taste. "Ummm, this is so rich and delicious." I talked and chewed at the same time. I then forked another piece and fed it to Marlo.

"Yeah, they got that shit right." He winked at me and chewed at the same time. We finished off that slice together in record time.

"Go grab the shrimp?" I urged him with the empty plate that had only moments ago held the cheesecake. He could put it back on the cart when he grabbed the shrimp.

"So, you want to eat dinner in bed?"

"Yep." I smiled.

"If that is your wish." He retrieved the plate from my hand then leaned over and kissed me on the nose. It tickled. I giggled out loud, he knew I was ticklish.

We sat in bed and ate the shrimp together, chatting, finally too full to do anything else. We both laid back down. I snuggled against him and tried to find sleep. But once I was relaxed my mind wouldn't stop running around, with Promise on it. The unrest was so annoying.

Ever since I had touched down, I had done everything to keep concerns about her at bay. It was the only way I wouldn't go insane. It was really hard too, knowing she was in the same city but not in contact with me. But I wanted to respect her wishes and give her the space she had asked for. Back home I had found a routine that didn't include my twin and made it work so I wouldn't be blowing up her phone with worries. I still played my part at the salon as she wished to make sure everything was taken care of, and I would continue to do that. And with Toya, Reese, and the other girls at the salon staying on top of their parts, her business was still thriving just as if she were there.

Going over all these things in my head gave me some comfort, so I was feeling good about things and my mind drifted to DaVon and I remembered his smile. Warm, inviting, and loving, he was really a good man. I gazed down at Marlo's face as it was so peaceful. For the first time I realized he and DaVon had a lot in common. Again, my mind drifted to gather all these goods they had in common.

I stirred and slowly opened my eyes as my body responded to my ringing cell phone. Unbeknownst to me I had fallen asleep. And the last thing I remembered was thinking of DaVon and Marlo. My phone seemed to be on the other side of the bed as I was snuggled under Marlo, like a part of the blanket. Slowly and reluctantly, I dragged my sleepy body over too it.

"Hello." I couldn't hide the grogginess in my voice.

"Precious." The low, nervous, clearly sobbing, voice said from the other end of the phone. My body nearly bolted up from the bed at the sound of my sister's voice.

"Promise, what's wrong? Why are you crying?" I was overly concerned.

"It's Money. He is here . . . hold . . ." She took a breath. "He has been holding me against my will for the past two days," she cried.

"What the fuck you mean, HOLDING YOU!" I barked into the phone. My entire body turned hot as a burning stove. I threw the covers away from me. Marlo scrambled straight up beside.

"Precious, listen to me . . . I want to get out of here. It is not right for me any longer. The drugs . . . any of it. But

Money has snapped out and he refuses to let me leave. He has finally gone to sleep after being up for two days straight doin' coke. I know you are in Miami. Can you please come and get me . . . he has me locked up."

"LOCKED UP!" I screamed through the phone. "Text me that nigga address I'm on my way." I ended the call.

"What's going on?" Marlo asked soon as I ended the call. I was out of the bed already sliding into some pants.

"We got to go, that stupid ass Money holding my sister hostage."

"The FUCK!" This time it was a shocked Marlo yelling. He was out of the bed in record time and dressed.

We headed to the address Promise had sent no sooner than the call had ended. I had tried call her back but received no answer. Marlo drove his Lambo like a bat out of hell, running stop lights, cutting people off, you name it. Neither one of us even thought of getting pulled over.

To our utter shock Money opened his front door looking like shit from the back of a monkey's ass before we could even knock.

"NIGGA WHERE THE FUCK MY SISTER AT?" I barked at him like a mad woman.

He had the nerve to stand in the door with a calm demeanor. "She is resting and don't feel like being bothered." His eyes blinked because he was lying.

"BITCH STEP YO' PUSSY ASS ASIDE!" I demanded, but Money only tried to push the door shut.

Marlo took two steps forward with so much force I felt his body heat. "FUCK NIGGA MOVE!" He barked in his face as he pushed the door away from Money's grip, then slammed him to the floor. He ushered me inside, and I stepped over Money's pitiful ass.

Inside it looked like a drug addict had been up for days on end the way it was tossed. And Promise was nowhere in plain eyesight. "Promise!" I yelled her name but received no response. "Promise," I tried again but still got nothing but silence. "Where the fuck is my sister?" I turned and screamed at Money as to where she was. Marlo had snatched him up off the floor and forced him on his feet.

"Bitch, find her yourself." He had the nerve to get gangster. Marlo took his pistol and slapped blood from his mouth. Money's body flew back against the wall, and he caught himself and staggered.

I found the stairs and raced up them, calling after Promise. Once at the top of the stairs I heard faint screams. I followed them to a room where they became clearer. They were Promise's cries. My sister was locked in what I was sure was the bathroom.

"Get back from the door if you are near it." I warned Promise because I was about to break it down. I raised my right leg and put my foot to the doorknob. The door flew open, but I didn't see Promise until I gazed over by the shower to find her clutched in the corner.

I reached for her. She cried out. "Aye, you good now. I got you." I tried to comfort her.

"Bitch, I'ma beat yo' ass when they leave. You just wait." Money's voice boomed. I looked up to see him standing outside the bathroom door. Marlo was behind him, the gun to his head. I couldn't believe he was threatening to hit my sister. Had he done that before?

"Hoe ass nigga, you been puttin' yo' hands on my sister." I gently let Promise go and eased my piece from the back of my pants. I moved across the floor at top speed and laid the steel so hard across Money's cheekbone his body dropped to the floor. It sounded like his cheekbone cracked, as blood flew out of his nose and mouth. He looked weak and defeated as he let out a weird laugh with blood running from his lips like wine.

"Mane FUCK THIS PUSSY!" Marlo stood in front of Money and shot him square between the eyes.

"AGH!" Promise screamed and then went silent. I ran back over to my sister to comfort her. She was safe now. I would always keep her safe. That she could count on.

Chapter 34

Two months later

"I went over the books this morning and the profits since last year has tripled. This hair selling like hot cakes at Cracker Barrel. I knew it would be a hot topic, but never did I think they would go crazy over this shit like this." Promise and I were at the hair store putting out a shipment and rearranging some things. We always did that together instead of having the workers do it. I had done it alone when she was spending all that time in Miami, and I hated it. But I had her back now and we both gladly jumped back into routine.

"This is LA, you know everyone here is about appearances. These females got to have they hair, no matter what. They will buy this weave before they eat. But what can I say, aye, I got to have mine too." Promise tossed her head full of ash brown weave and danced around.

"That's a fact." I agreed. "That ginger orange is runnin' off the shelf faster than we can stock it. There is a full box right behind us that just came in. I guarantee you in two days tops we won't have any."

Promise turned around and opened the box. "Oh yes, Toya just put some in her client's hair last night, it was bomb. I got to have it on my head. Maybe we both can get it?" Promise suggested, but I had other plans.

"I am feeling it, no doubt. But I really want you to put that honey blonde on my head at my next appointment."

"Oh, I got you. But real talk these colors are going to be hot at the Miami store. Especially like this Sky Blue. She pointed at another opened box off to the right of her. "They love that color and this pink. Are we still going forward with the store out there?"

I had forgot all about the Miami location. Hadn't thought about it in months with everything else that had transpired, so I was surprised that she was even thinking about it. Stocking it or otherwise. "Actually, I kinda put a halt on finding a location when shit was crazy." We both knew I was talking about Miami and the situation with Money. We hadn't talked about him but once since the night Marlo lit his ass up. Honestly, if I never heard his name again that would be too soon. But Promise had made it clear that he was a bastard and she only wanted to forget him because he was a weak moment in her life. And a reminder of what type of man not to meet. And I totally agreed. That was enough for me.

"Listen . . . I know we got off track, but it's cash to be made out in Miami. I still believe that. I mean we a million dollars ahead on revenue from just selling hair at this here hair store alone in LA. We open a store in Miami we will be the kings of hair. Selling that top of the line shit put us in a class all by ourselves. We ain't no ninety-nine-cent store."

I thought about what she said, and she was right. My goal was for us to have as many legit businesses as I could, and with my sister along for the ride was the icing on the cake. I would stay focused on that goal for us. "Hey, if you are up for it, we can do it. I will have Marlo get his realtor back on it as soon as him and his wife return from their trip around Europe."

"Say less."

"So, how are the therapy sessions coming along?" The therapist had come highly recommended but even I knew the proof was in the pudding. And I knew that Promise would be straight up about her sessions.

"Oh, Precious, this therapist is good. I'm glad you got her for me, it was one of the best ideas you could have had for me. I'm sleeping all night without taking any sleeping pills. I can breathe the air when I come outside, and not feel stifled by it. I don't feel like I'm being watched all the time, I'm not jumpy. I'm becoming me again. And I can't begin to explain how much I craved that feeling again."

My heart was so happy it could have jumped right out of my chest and landed in my hands. Nothing at the moment could bring me more joy than to hear my sister say she could sleep at night and breathe easier. To think that she was suffering the way she had been still tore at my soul. "Promise, I'm so glad to hear this. I would have done anything to have you be okay."

"Yep, there has never been any doubt that you would. I know you got me." She smiled. "Oh, speaking of the Miami location realtors and all. You do know that Christopher has his real estate license down in Miami? He is also expanding his businesses dealings down in Hawaii. Precious, he told me they got some hot properties down in Hawaii at good prices, he said right now it's open season for their market. I thought this was good news because remember we talked about possibly opening a business there someday. Right now, I'm thinkin' why wait? Maybe now is the time to just jump right in and invest."

"Really?" I started thinking. "Well, I do remember our

conversation and I would still love to expand out there. I'm thinking we start living bi-costal."

"Oh, I am so down with that Precious. I could use some of that sun glistening on my skin with the Hawaiian breeze soothing my lungs. Ahh." She breathed in and sighed.

I laughed at her dramatic demonstration of the air clearing her lungs. "I feel you, though, my lungs could use some of that breeze also." I imagined myself standing on a balcony with my head leaning back breathing something other than LA city air which was full of toxins of all sorts of only God knows what.

"Let's do it then. I've been really considering giving Toya and Reese full reign over the salon. They are more than up for the challenge. This way it will free up time so I can travel. And maybe even open up another salon location right here in LA. You know we get people up in the salon everyday trying to become a client, but we can't take on anyone else. So at another location I can hire more top-notch stylists, makeup artists, you know, a full team."

I nearly ran over and hugged her. My sister was back. She was thinking positive, with her future in mind and ready to execute. Just a few short months prior she could only think about getting to Miami to a trifling drug addict. I was overwhelmed with excitement for her.

"Sister dear, you are on a roll. Let's secure this location right now for the new salon and do this." I was hyped. "And speaking of Christopher when did you two reconnect or talk?" I was surprised to hear her mention him.

She grinned and I knew something was up. "Well, actually . . ." She dragged. "We never really stopped talking, or should I say lost touch." She admitted to my complete surprise. Which I'm sure my facial expression revealed as much.

"Oh." Was all I had.

"Yeah, even when I was in Miami with Money, Christopher persisted with calls, he would text to check on me. But the more he persisted the more I tried to push him away because he was a good guy. And I think I have proven more than once; I am allergic to good guys. But I draw to bad guys like a magnet."

I chuckled. "Well, you might not be alone there, sister. I think it's fair to say we both might be guilty of that. Falling for bad boys." We both laughed.

Regina startled me as she stepped in the back area where we were. She had been up front running the register. "Hey ladies, I'm locking up for the night. Time for me to get out in the night life."

"Dang it's that late?" Promise asked. In the back we could not see the outside so unless we were looking at our clock, we wouldn't know what time it was.

"Yep, closing time. I'll be back tomorrow afternoon to reopen."

"Cool, well enjoy your night, Regina," I said.

"Good night, Regina," Promise added.

Regina told us both goodnight, then bounced.

"I'm really thinking about making her the assistant manager here. If you are okay with it, of course? She has been working hard at the dry cleaners and has proved herself there. And she fills in here more often. She knows the product, she is dependable. And got a good rapport with the customers."

"Yeah, I've noticed that as well. I been seeing her when I'm in the store. So, I'm cool wit' it, we gotta put people in place that we trust so we can expand."

"My thoughts exactly. Hey, how about we finish this box up? Then head for some drinks. It's wind down time, and we both know sipping time comes after that."

"Whew, say that truth." Promise sighed and wiped at

her brow pretending she was sweating. "Because you are working me like a slave, I thought you might never suggest that."

"Girl, shut up." I playfully rolled my eyes and we both laughed. These were the times I missed, laughing and spending time with my sister. We were too much alike to be apart for too long. We fed off each other's energies. Money underestimated the love me and my sister had for each other. I always knew deep down she would sicken of him and when she did, she would call me. And she knew no matter what I would come. Running. As a bonus I brought Marlo with me, and he brought death in a chamber for Money.

Chapter 35

"Yeah, I need to get back with you on that. But go ahead and do some mixes and I'll drop by maybe tomorrow and we can do the testing." I told Sharita once again. She was mixing up some new drinks. She had just attended some new classes updating her mixology skills, anytime she wanted to take a class for that I paid for it. The girl was good and always looking to advance. It was just one more thing I liked about her ambition. If she stayed that way, I would make sure she succeeded by supporting her career.

I ended the call with her and continued to my destination. My plane had just delivered me back to LA from Miami, and already I had called Mob up and had him set up an urgent meeting with my main guys, Rob, Don P, and Case. The meeting I had with Marlo not even a full twenty hours ago had been major. We had a new job to do. In Georgia we had some territory that we had to go take care of ASAP. It was some major money to be made down south and we were just the crew to head it up, and make it happen.

I got straight to business as soon as I sat down, all the eyes on me in the room were inquiring, they knew I was about my business. Always. "So, it's time to pack some bags y'all, we are taking it all the way to the dirty south."

With their eyes never leaving mine they all smiled. I knew a few of them were hungry to see how the south was shaking when it came to the game. They were ready.

"Now, I can't send all you at once. As you know we still got shit here we got to keep on lock." They all nodded in agreement. "Don P, Mob, you two headed down to the A to jump shit off and shake it up. Phil is going to meet ya'll out there. Case and Rob you two gone be my main fronts here in LA. Everyone else will report to you all for reup."

"Aye we got you." Case spoke up.

"No doubt." All the other guys followed up.

"Gotta go out here and show these country niggas how to really get down. Nothin' but grind and muscle." Mob said then smiled.

"Nah, don't believe that Precious. That nigga tryin' to get to Magic City." Rob tossed in and we all laughed.

"Don't worry, when we get shit locked down, I'm going to shut that shit down just for y'all." They kept laughing. Every now in again we got to have a few laughs. I enjoyed it. "For now, though, let's rock. And as Mob said, the grind and the muscle. Oh, and also Marlo and I will be out there to handle the setup with distribution. I'll have dates for y'all soon when you are to leave and switch up positions." They all pretty much said cool. "Now I know y'all got business to handle, so back at it." I ended the meeting. We all scattered to move out.

"Aye, I need to speak to you alone." Case approached me before we exited the building.

"What's up?"

"I wanted to talk to you about Katrina."

My eyes took on a suspicious stare. I hadn't been expecting this. But I was worried something might be wrong with Katrina. "Okay."

"First, let me thank you for introducing us. We both appreciate the connection."

"Well, that really wasn't my intention." I smiled in spite of it.

Case's mouth widened into a grin. In the moment he looked school boyish, not the hustler that I knew. "Guess shit be crazy like that sometime. Or just fate." He shrugged. "Listen, I know Katrina is close to you."

To say she was close to me he was putting it mildly. I decided to be clear. "Katrina is my family, Case. Blood could not make her closer."

The look on his face turned serious again and I knew he understood where I was going. "She told me the same thing that is why I'm coming to you." He paused. "Listen . . . I know you know a nigga deep in these streets. But I ain't never had no choice in that. I never had no real family. My mother was a dope fiend, so the streets raised me. Until I met Katrina and Lalah, I didn't know I could love nobody. And I mean that." His eyes fell on mine, and I saw in them what I seen DaVon's. Case was in love with Katrina. "I guess what I'm trying to say is I want to marry Katrina." My mouth would have dropped wide open if I had not controlled it. I had guessed love and revealed marriage. He was not playing about her.

"Have you told her this or asked?" I managed to find the words while still being in shock.

"Not yet, I plan too though, soon. But with you two being so close and I know how much she respects your judgment. I mean she made sure that I knew that from day one. So, I figured I had to run it by you, first to get your blessing. And not just that. I know you know the real life I live. Katrina knows too but . . ."

"Hey, yes, I do know the life. I lived it with DaVon and had a front row seat to the game. If you worried this might affect her answer . . ." This time I shrugged my shoulders because that would be a decision Katrina would have to make. "I have to say I don't know what her answer will be. But I'ma tell you this, she been through enough shit. We both know this game can be tricky. Fast money, hoes, the grind, and loss of life. Her and Lalah can't be a casualty. Protect them at all costs . . . I can't accept nothing else past that. Anything else and all bets are off." And those words were my bond.

Case looked me in the eye like a proud man in love, and full of respect. "No doubt."

And with that the conversation ended. We both knew there was nothing else to be said on the matter. For me it was clear cut and to the chase. The rest would depend on Katrina's answer.

Chapter 36

Soon as the wheels on the plane touched down at Harts-field airport in Atlanta, Marlo and I geared up for the meeting. The hustle inside the airport was real but we were focused. We got our rental and wasted no time jumping into traffic. It was early but no sooner than we hit I-85 headed southbound than we got jammed into traffic. I figured then that we would be late. But through some force of nature traffic got moving at a good steady pace five minutes after we were at a standstill.

My cell phone rang just as we pulled into the spot. It was Mob making sure we were good, safe and in Georgia. Him, Don P, and Phil had arrived late in the night on a red eye. Marlo had stopped off in LA to meet up with me so we could discuss a few things before we boarded our plane.

Marlo parked the vehicle at the Holiday Inn & Suites where the meeting was being held in a room that Mob had reserved. Even though we were meeting Mike B who was the major contact in Georgia, we had made it clear that any business meeting would be set up on our terms. And since we didn't have spots set up around the city yet, I had instructed Mob on where to set up shop. None of us would of course be staying at the hotel, the meeting would just be held there.

"We thought y'all was lost out here for a minute?" Phil said as we made our way inside the room.

"Shit' nah, but I thought we was about to be held up in that weak ass traffic on the eight-five, but we navigated that shit."

"No doubt. Me and Don P was caught up in that shit three hours ago. Shit was crazy."

"Welp, I guess it's like that Miami traffic. All non-drivers, and crazy people," I teased.

"Ahhh, here we go." Marlo laughed. "LA people always hating on the three o five because they can't navigate rush hour. We can't help it we got our shit boiled down to ballin'."

"Yep, that's what they call it." We all chuckled, just as a knock came on the door. Mob, Phil, and Don P cocked their heat. Phill went to the door and looked through the peephole. He nodded. It was Mike B. Marlo gave the okay to open the door. The guys stayed in position because nothing was ever trusted.

This was my first-time coming face to face with Mike B. I had seen photos of him but in person he looked much thinner. He was brown-skinned, about six feet, and no more than two hundred twenty pounds. He had a low-cut fade and as I imagined his mouth was full of gold. His rite of passage for being in the south. Two guys that he had approved to bring with him stepped in behind him.

"What's up, fam?" is how he greeted us. His southern drawl was deep, but he owned it.

"What's good, Mike B.," Marlo said first. We all stayed quiet.

"Aye, this my peoples. Ed my right hand and Tyrel our tight end." He pointed at them both. They both nodded as they were introduced. "We welcome ya'll to the A."

"No doubt," Marlo spoke again. "So, the business at hand. As you know I already got territory that need to be moved around. And a spot here and there to open up, tighten up."

"And we got you," Mike B responded. "We will open any door that might think about being shut." Marlo nodded.

"Distribution will be coming through us from here, out for those territories." It was my turn to speak. Marlo watched me lay out the protocol. "When product drop it will have forty-eight hours run the chase then it needs to be gone. Collection will come the third day, no exceptions. As for the territories, there will be a cleaning of all that don't belong. Mike B, can you bring us up to speed on any urgent matters." I asked this because I could see it in his face, he had bad news to spread.

"These streets done fucked me bad. Supply down, as you already know. These niggas robbing blocks left and right. So, niggas been laying niggas down to make they point loud and clear." And we all knew what the killing meant. No money could be made. "I been beefing wit' this nigga Zeb, he out here sellin' bad product and stamping our name on it."

If I had horns, they would have raised up on my head. I had zero tolerance for that. Our product was our brand. Anybody fucked with that was a dead person walking. I gazed at Marlo because we had already heard about Zeb, who was once a big-time boss in the area and still was. But El Guapo had already given the word to shut Zeb down.

"Drop that location on Zeb to me before midnight tonight. Other than that work starts tomorrow. I already have a list of your guys who we will work with, and those who will walk. But no walkers shall breathe. They have cost us enough not to go on. I want them handled no later than tomorrow night. And you know who they are." He eyed Mike B and his guys with unforgiveable stares. "Phil, Mob, and Don P also have these walkers' names and faces, they will back you up. Product drops in two days and we will have a new city." Marlo ended the meeting.

Just as instructed, Mike B dropped Zeb's location around ten o'clock at night. And just like any arrogant skeezeball, he was out having drinks with no cares in the world. While we had waited to hear from Mike B. Marlo had shared with me more information about Zeb. He was familiar with him from the Miami area, had been out there for some time years ago trying to start a crew. Marlo said he was the same snake then as he was now. Never had loyalty and was always on some sneak shit.

He was sitting in the back of this rinky-dink bar that looked like it should have been shut down years ago. Mike told us in the parking lot that Zeb actually owned the bar, that he suckered the owner out of it. That the original owner had stepped out for a quick bathroom break which told us the spot was ours for business.

Zeb turned up a bottle of Hennessy to his lips and stared at us all as we approached. Two of his henchmen or at least so I assumed stood on either side of him. Clearly guarding him.

Marlo took stood in front to the table and looked Zeb square in the eyes.

"Well, well, if it ain't that nigga Marlo from the three o five up in this bitch." He laughed we all watched. Right away it was obvious he was a clown.

"Zeb, let me see." Marlo glanced at the time on his Rolex watch glistening on his wrist. "At 11:08 your business is in this city, or maybe I should say in your lifetime, is a wrap."

Zeb lip's parted to speak but a bullet raced out of Don

P's chamber and hit him right between the eyes before he could utter a sound. His head split open like a sliced tomato. His henchman appeared to be shocked but stood down and never made a move. And it was good they didn't because Phil and Mob had their eyes glued to them and was ready to match Don P's actions.

Marlo stepped around the table. Zeb's head or what was left of it lay back on the chair he had been sitting in. With one swoop Marlo snatched his diamond studded necklace from his stiff neck. Surprisingly, there was no blood on it.

"Which one of you is Calvin?" Marlo asked. Mike B had told him that one of the guys would be Calvin and he was Zeb's right hand.

"That's me." The medium-build, darker guy spoke up. His light voice didn't fit his muscular body tone.

"Set up a meeting with y'all crew. You will get instructions where to meet. As you can see, Zeb is done with business." He sat the diamond studded chain on the table. We exited.

Phil wasted no time. He got straight down to business setting up the meeting, we purchased a building in the middle of the night from a realtor Phil had got his people on. This would be only one of our spots in the city so far, but it was a start.

Twelve peons had been invited to attend the meeting. Mike B had identified all of them: Calvin, and Al, the guy who had been with Zeb the night before, were among them. According to Mike B, the rest of them had a loyal reputation beside the fact they worked for a snake who brought their name down, which had affected their business.

Marlo stood to address the peons and he cut straight to the chase. "For now, you have no leader, but supply in your territory is still in demand and we got it for you."

It was my turn to step in. "We will have the command over you. So that means your territory is being expanded into ours. And it's simple, whoever wants to work will. Whoever is against it dies." I hoped that part was clear because there was no debate. And it became clear right in the midst of the meeting who had problems with their new command. Calvin, Al, and a peon who went by plain E. All three were shot on sight. And I wasted no time addressing it.

"Anybody else have an issue can speak up now," I gave free opportunity. All three bodies laid out on display were the hard facts. Everyone gave me their undivided attention, so the meeting went on.

Two of the guys who Mike B had vouched for, Wacko and Trey, were given promotions and would work with Phil, Don P, and Mob to strengthen their territory which was now under Marlo's and my control.

Marlo and I stayed on for nearly two more weeks wrapping up odds up and ends. Marlo had three more guys come up from Miami to help lead, tighten, and open doors in the territories. Things were on a move, so he and I set out for home: him Miami and me LA. Not once did we get to enjoy even a minute of the city. It was strictly all work and no play. But I knew we would eventually have time to party in the city that was allegedly "too busy to hate." I was just glad I didn't get bit by some humongous southern bug.

Chapter 37

"Nope, if we start drinking that wine, we ain't gone never get out of here on time." I protested as Promise pulled out the bottle of champagne, ready to pop it open. We along with Katrina, Reese, Regina, Toya, Prel, and Lisa were getting dolled up. I was sitting in Reese's chair; it was my turn to get my makeup done. Promise had shut it down so everyone could get done at the same time. All the skilled people took turns doing each other and we were laughing, joking, and having way too much fun.

"Ahh, come on can we just all have one small sip?" Promise pouted. But I knew better, one sip would turn into three.

"Nah, I know I will want more than a sip. Put it away Promise, stop tempting me." Toya begged and told the truth at the same time.

"I swear y'all too light on your feet, but I guess I'll put it away since y'all can't hold your liquor." Promise put the bottle away and scurried back over to Regina who was in her chair, getting dolled up.

"Well ladies, I got some ice to show you." Katrina stood up and started bouncing around in circles showing all of us her ring. And the thing was beautiful, the diamond could only be described as sweet. "Yes, Case asked me to marry him, and I of course said yes." She was clearly happy, her eyes twinkled. He had done it.

"That is so sweet. That rock is to die for!" Reese grabbed hold of her hand and glared at it up close. "I hope my prince charming get me the exact same one." She smiled.

"Don't we all." Prel's eyes also gleamed at the sight of the ring. She was another single lady in the room. Her boyfriend was killed in Compton, shot right in front of her five years prior. Another guy had mistaken him for someone else and without so much as a second glance pulled the trigger, killing him dead on sight. Heartbroken and traumatized, she had not dated since. Said she was afraid of losing another man that she loved, they had been together since high school. But lately she had changed her mind. Said she was tired of being lonely and was considering taking a chance at dating.

"So have you set a wedding date?" Promise pried. But she knew it was the question we all had.

"No actually, that is something we need to discuss. But I'm sure we will get it to it soon. For right now we just been living on love bliss." She blushed. "I'm ENGAGED!" she chanted and showcased her ring again for all to admire.

"Well, now we have a reason to have a toast." Promise stood and retrieved that bottle of champagne again. "And this time I don't won't to hear no objections."

"Hmm, welp, I guess this is toast savoy." I teased as I reached for the one of the glasses she had filled. We all held our glasses in the air.

"Come on Precious, you say the words for the toast." Promise egged me on.

"No doubt, this I can handle." I smiled then gazed at

Katrina. "Katrina, I just want to say I am so happy for you. I have been knowing you since I was a teenager, and you were trying to drag me off to parties. Forcing me to have a social life." I chuckled and everyone laughed. I could remember it like it was yesterday. Katrina refusing to take no for an answer when I would come up with my many excuses not to hang out. "My dad put us together in that dry cleaner's, and we bonded like sisters. And today I want you to know are all here for you and to support you. To marriage." I raised my glass high in the air.

"To marriage," all the girls said, and we clicked our glasses together then sipped.

"And tonight, we going to party extra hard with this good news." Promise added.

"And I swear I can't wait." Reese polished off her drink. "Oh, Precious, what celebrity did Marlo pick for tonight? You never said."

"I can't help y'all wit that one. Marlo never told me. All he would share with me was to be ready to turn up." I said it just how he had put it to me. And to be honest I didn't think on it too long. I kept too busy to be wondering about a celebrity guest. El Guapo would be in the building so I just hoped he would enjoy it so once he turned up, he could get up outta LA.

"It had better not be nobody from the eighties. I ain't even playin','" Promise said, then added a fake frown.

"I know that's right." Toya threw in. "I love old school but I ain't tryin' to be dancing to Troop."

"Stop, y'all know better." I laughed. "While y'all worried about the entertainment you better be worried about being ready on time if you don't wish to miss anything. I have once again hired all you drunk heifers a car. Because I know having a celebrity in the midst give y'all extra excuses to get wasted." I teased them. But I really had ordered a car for them because I knew they would be DUI bound by the end of the night. I would be too for that matter.

"Hey' I'm going to be ready for sure because I love having a driver to pick me up, makes me feel special." Toya stirred in her seat.

"Me too." Prel threw in. Lisa then co-signed.

"Aww, Precious you can cancel mine. I'm riding wit' Case." Katrina jumped in. I wasn't surprised they were sticking to each other like glue with any free time they had.

"No problem I'll get that canceled." I assured her as my cell phone rang.

I answered. It was Mob on the other end ranting that we needed to meet up right away. I hung up the phone and sighed deep within'. I did not want the girls to see me in distress. Once again something was up. And to be honest I was not here for it. El Guapo was in the city and the last thing we needed was drama.

"Listen, I gotta run. You all finish up your hair and makeup then go get bossed up in your finery. And I will see you at the club later." Promise looked as if she wanted to ask questions, but she could see on my face that I didn't have time for twenty questions.

I didn't rush but I drove a good speed to reach the restaurant that Mob and I had agreed to meet up at. Mob was sitting at the table looking like he was ready to punch the first person that wronged him.

"Yo, shit done got stupid. Two of our blocks were shot up." The look on face said it was worse. "Only one our workers were shot in the leg. Flesh wound so he gone breathe."

"Who responsible?" Was my question.

"Right now, I don't know, but I got ears on the street working. They clearly forgot who they fuckin' wit' but they will be reminded real soon." And that was the exact reason why I wasn't worried. I eased back into my seat. Mob would get me information no matter what. Blocks being shot up was no small matter, it meant a breach in security. And that meant nobody was safe.

"Listen, you know we got that shit at the club tonight and you know who in attendance. Safety is key." I eyed him with significance. "So, I need you to get on a phone and beef up security even tighter." At this point we didn't know what was going on since we had no idea who was responsible for the shooting. So, we needed extra eyes, ears, heat, and of course our six senses. Mob knew the drill, so no more words were needed. Time was winding down, so I had to get home to get dressed.

I left the meeting and headed straight for my crib. I pulled in and parked beside Promise's Lexus convertible and made my way inside. Rose's car was not outside so I knew she had left for the day. I raced straight to my room. Promise texted my phone to see if I had made it in. I told her I was in my room. She tapped on my door not even three minutes later. I told her to come in.

"You good?" Promise stepped inside.

I really felt like saying yes. But my frustration came out before I could control it. "Girl . . . shit has been ridiculous. I can't for the life of me understand why some niggas just can't get money and leave that biggest nut shit at the crib. Niggas out here shooting up my blocks like we in Tombstone."

"Shit really? Anybody get hurt?" She sat down on my bed.

"Nah, unnecessary bullets flying and a leg wound. Nothin' serious, just damaging to the grind, which is a damn no-no." I rolled my eyes at the thought of the reck-lessness.

"I swear shit just been crazy everywhere."

"Tell me about it." I sighed. "Sometimes, I feel like I haven't known peace since DaVon." I couldn't believe those words had just escaped my lips, but they were so true. But

I knew in the back of my mind that maybe peace never had existed. DaVon just kept it at bay for me. And until now I didn't know how much I appreciated that.

"The way you say his name." Promise gave me a gentle smile. "Your love for him is still favored."

The words she had just spoken were so true. DaVon was my first real true love, my first everything. We had matched. A smiled creeped in on my face. "Always and forever. That will never change"

"Just the way you speak of him. Makes me wish all the more I could have met him."

"Me too. But . . ."

"Welp, I guess since I met Marlo he'd have to do" She cut me off and bounced up off of my bed with laughter.

"I swear if you don't stop with the taunting of my five good senses. Go and get dressed so I can do the same." I pointed towards my door for her to get out.

"I'm going, I'm going. So pushy." She left the room and shut the door behind her. I turned toward my mirror looked at myself and smiled.

Chapter 38

Shit may have been crazy, but I was feeling good as I stepped inside the VIP lounge in my all-white sleeveless jumpsuit by Tom Ford, with a pair of black three-inch Tom Ford high heels with gold metal heels, and gold chain ankle straps. Across the room Marlo was chopping it up with Phil, but his eyes lit up as they landed on me. Filing the bullshit that was going on in the streets behind me, I was ready to have a good time. But I would be watching because my guard was never down.

"First things, first, let's grab a drink." Promise leaned over my shoulder. She was rocking a pair of Versace fitted silk shorts, with a matching sleeveless Versace blouse, and of course Versace heels. And the rest was history.

Sharita had everything in our VIP area on point. The waitresses were inside serving up drinks and keeping everybody happy. I had yet to hire regular waitresses for the club, so we rented them out from a company around the way for Friday and Saturday nights or if we were having a party only, like tonight.

"Two shots of Apple Crown." I told the young waitress who stood in front of us, she went by Jade. Her and five other girls were always our regulars when we hired out. She strutted off to get our drinks.

I swallowed my drink quickly when Jade returned with it, and it hit my toes and rose through my soul. "That was good." I mouthed to Promise. She was still cradling her glass as her eyes darted across one side of VIP to the other side of the room. "Who are you checking for?" I asked.

"Girl nobody, just trying to see who up in here before I cut up. I don't want to behave too badly up in here tonight, in front of company." She laughed. "Bottoms up." She downed her drink. Her face twisted as if she had swallowed some sour lemon. "Yep, that was strong and good, and woke up all the right spots."

I grinned. "I told you." Marlo approached us. He looked so good I could eat him up. He was in Gucci from head to toe. And he smelled so good. I had to be calm.

"Hey ladies." His southern drawl fit him so well.

"What's up, Marlo." Promise smiled. Phil approached us.

"What's up, Ms. LA's," he teased us.

"Boy, I done told you I ain't from LA." Promise started in on him. They loved to play around and argue but they were cool. Never nothing else. Marlo eased over towards me a bit.

I looked in his eyes and wanted to just kiss him. He gazed at me, mesmerized as well. "Precious, you look so beautiful, everything about you." I wanted to laugh he was so sentimental. But his eyes told me he meant every word.

I smiled. "Thank you, but I know this already," I teased, then laughed.

"Aye, ain't nothin' wrong wit' dat." My smile faded though. I had to take a minute and clue him in on what was up so he could be aware. "Yo, I know security is supposed to be tight, but it looks like you got an army up in here tonight."

"That is what I was about to tell you. Two of my blocks were shot up earlier."

"Damn. You know who responsible?" Marlo jumped in before I could finish the story.

"Nah, not yet. But Mob on that asap. You heard any word from El Guapo?"

"I ain't heard from him personally but he touched down earlier so I know he is in the city. He'll be through this bitch probably any minute."

"What about yo' entertainment? You gone be able to deliver?" I joked with him; he had been keeping it under wraps. It was down almost to the moment, and yet he still had not shared who his entertainment would be.

He smiled as he knew my slick strategy was to get him to reveal. "That is covered," he assured me with a mischievous grin. "Yo and that DJ you got? He lit."

"As always. One of the best in the city. We do nothin' but the best up in here." I wanted to be clear.

"Aye, aye," I could hear Promise chanting all the way across the room and over the music, as "Up" by Cardi B blasted from the speakers. She dashed to my side. "Come on sissy, this is my jam." I laughed and started gyrating my hips to the beat. Marlo ate me up with his eyes and I knew he was watching so I entertained him on purpose.

"Do that shit Precious." Reese's voice chanted with excitement from behind me. Toya jumped beside me and started bouncing to the beat. And Promise followed.

Before long Regina too had arrived. We started taking shots and dancing nonstop. Marlo, Phil, and a few other guys with Marlo stood around enjoying the scene.

"Hey," Katrina popped up in the circle me and the girls had formed dancing. I noticed Case had strolled in with her, but he made his way over to Phil and Marlo.

"That's right, bitch. That is how you do it. Show up wit' yo' man on your arm. Let all these females know what it is," Promise teased. Katrina blushed. We continued to dance, and Katrina joined in.

I had just taken a break from dancing when I noticed security fall inside the VIP lounge, followed by El Guapo. At first, they had all been posted up outside the VIP entry door. I only had two guys positioned inside, standing in two different corners scoping everything. But now there three more who I was sure worked for El Guapo who had piled in.

Marlo and I both stood in the center part of the room. El Guapo parted between two of his guards and took steps toward us. "Precious . . ." His face spread into what I assume was a smile as he spoke my name. "Marlo," he followed up. His words were choppy with his accent but always clear enough to understand.

"El Guapo," Marlo and I both said his name at the same time. The music was loud, but we could all hear each other. I noticed one of El Guapo guard's eyes darted around the room catching sight of all the ladies. If you asked me, he wasn't focused on his job the way a guard should be. El Guapo was a target at all times in his position. I mean we all were but especially him. He had enemies we would never fathom. So, whoever was on duty for him should never be off their guard, unless they were off duty. I noted his security was weak and sloppy.

"Glad you could make it out tonight," Marlo said.

"LA always brings the festivity out in me." I wasn't sure if it was a joke or him really making conversation. I stood like a statue while he small talked, then spoke up.

"How about we have a seat?" I offered out of courtesy then turned and led the way to one of the plush couches we offered in VIP. Even if he didn't have a good time, which I doubted, he would be comfortable on the very expensive VIP furniture that I had flown in personally from Italy.

On cue as we sat down, and the waitress approached us with the bottle of champagne that had been ordered by us for El Guapo. The waitress just had to pay attention and know when to bring it over. And she had been on the money, her bag depended on it.

El Guapo sat up in his seat. He glanced at the bottle of forty-thousand-dollar champagne and grinned. The waitress picked it up off the ice and did her circular motion of advertising it then popped the bottle. Bubbly spilled over the top. Promise slid down next to me ready for her share of the champagne.

"The welcome is real." El Guapo accepted his glass of champagne the waitress handed to him. "Precious, your place is one of a kind," he complimented. He seemed comfortable and that was a good sign.

I could feel Promise's body's warmth as she leaned in closer to me then whispered. "He fine for a middle-aged man."

I nearly spit out the champagne I had just allowed to soak my mouth. But I caught myself. I turned to her slightly and smiled. "Don't you start," I said with a smile on my face, through clenched teeth.

I suddenly noticed Christopher as he headed in our direction. "Go get your company. Entertain him with your crazy self." I had to dig deep to keep from laughing.

Promise grabbed her glass, smiled, and stood up. She went off in Christopher's direction. I put my attention back to El Guapo and Marlo. Just as my eyes went to El Guapo I realized his were glued to the back of Promise. I hoped it was just a coincidence and not admiration. Marlo was talking but El Guapo was not listening to a word coming from his mouth.

I was surprised to see Christopher step around Promise and leaned down to speak. "Hi," he said in gentle tone. Security closed in on him before he could make another step. Christopher's eyes kind of bulged as he watched the men alongside him crowd his space. I told security he was good, so they could back off. The last thing I wanted them to do was scare the boy off. Christopher really was such a different kind of guy. He was a good one, respectable, and considerate. Marlo nodded a what's up. El Guapo of course said nothing.

"Hey, glad you came out tonight. Make sure you drink up and enjoy yourself." The poor guy had no idea the type of people he was faced with. If he knew he probably would have excused himself and never returned. El Guapo was like the murderer of the world. A dangerous guy to be seated with, no less known be in the game with. Christopher nodded and quickly stepped away. I was sure the vibe told him it was time. But he landed safe beside Promise who wasted no time handing him a glass of that expensive champagne.

Quavo stepped up. The bodyguards gave him the same body welcome Christopher had received that said back off. I waved him though also.

"Just wanted to say what's up?" He said to all of us. Then disappeared just as quickly as he had come over. I noticed Toya was his destination. She stood smiling and him co-signing whatever she was delivering to him.

El Guapo sat back and started enjoying the music and wasted no time starting his second glass of the good champagne. I walked back over to the bar in the VIP lounge to be sure everything was still on point, and we were stocked. I knew Sharita had made sure of that, but a host always checked themselves. It was only the professional thing to do. That and I wanted to sneak a moment of peace without El Guapo's presence in it. A quick glance around the room and I observed everyone was turnt up.

Marlo snuck up on me and stood beside me. He had still been sitting and entertaining El Guapo while I made my getaway. I could not fool him; I was sure he knew what I was up to. "I'm going to go down to the stage so I can introduce the entertainer," he announced.

I turned my face to him, only inches away and chuckled. "So, you gone keep me in the dark huh?" He had been determined not to tell me who was performing. He got a kick out of it.

Marlo grinned. "They say curiosity killed the cat."

"Whatever." I playfully pushed him.

He closed the gap between us. "Aye, and it's your turn to keep our guest company. Which means you will have to abandon this little bar island of safety, you tried to escape to." He teased.

"I guess since you got me stuck. Now go introduce your little secret entertainment." I teased back.

Marlo exited the room I made my way around to a few of the people who were standing in my way in the VIP lounge. El Guapo was sitting back watching everything. He really looked mellowed out. But I knew his brain was working overtime analyzing this and that.

It was turn to my put him at ease if that was possible. Ease didn't exist in my position so it would be crazy to think it could exist in his world. "You good?" I sat down close to him but not next to him.

"Of course. The one thing I can say . . . LA always treat me right." He smiled and I felt weird because of it. I sucked in my uneasiness and tried to be normal.

I was trying to think of what to say to him next because business was all I was ever prepared to discuss with him. But to my relief his lips moved first. "So, you never told me that you have a twin. Mirror image . . . Beautiful." This time I realized that he was speaking to me, but his attention is anywhere but there between us. My head followed his stare and found Promise connected to it.

Promise was across the room leaned into Christopher

with the biggest smile I had seen on her in a long while, she was really enjoying herself. I had to force my eyes back to El Guapo, but I spoke quickly. "Yes, I have a twin sister." I wanted to keep my answer at a minimum with the hopes we could move on from it.

"You never introduced her to me. I'd love to meet her." He fixed his eyes on me and I did not like it. It was clear to me and inside my head I screamed. "Oh nooo not this shit!"

I was too tongue tied to respond but was saved as Marlo's voice boomed out the microphone. "Aye, Aye," he said. "I want to thank y'all for coming out tonight to party with us. And from the looks of it everyone is having a good time. And that is not about to end now. We got some entertainment for y'all. So, get ready to turn up some mo'."

I paused for a minute as the beat started bopping, I looked over at Promise who was already twerking to "Bodak Yellow." A closer look at the stage and Cardi B came into view the crowd went crazy. I smiled so hard. Marlo and his petty games. The guy had a total crush on Cardi B. I gazed back over at Promise who was now grinding poor Christopher so hard I wondered if he could keep up. But the bliss on his face said he was enjoying every hump. I laughed.

El Guapo turned his attention to the stage as did everyone who wasn't dancing. Promise came out of nowhere and was dragging me off the couch. I could not lie that used to be my song when it was out. So, I was ready to turn up too.

"AYE, AYE!" Me and Promise started singing along. "I get the money and go this shit is hot like a stove," we chanted and twerked at the same time.

"This used to be MY SHIT!" Promise yelled over the music.

I felt Marlo all up on me. I knew it was him because nobody else would dare. I turned around. "You and your funky secret . . . maybe she will give you her number." I grinned.

"You think so? You think I'm handsome enough?" he teased. "You think a nigga really got a chance?" He chuckled.

"Shut up." I playfully pushed him out of my space.

He stepped back in my space, "Nah, I think yo' number good enough."

"Really, Ohhh . . . okay." I playfully rolled my eyes. We played around for a minute more than joined El Guapo again. He had stood up to watch the entertainment on stage. I was just thankful his eyes were no longer on Promise. Cardi B performed six songs and really showed out. Marlo had paid two hundred and fifty thousand dollars for those six songs. But everyone had enjoyed the performance. I had rejoined Promise, Toya, Reese, Regina, and Katrina by the third song, and we danced until we were out of breath. I was glad when it was over.

I sat down next to Marlo and mentally thanked the couch for existing. I could feel the throb roll out of the heels of my feet.

Marlo looked over at me and smiled, the exhaustion was clear. "You finally tired? I gotta say I think y'all like them songs a lil too much."

I could only laugh because maybe he was right. I eased back onto the couch; my mind shifted back to what I was sure I had seen while I was dancing. Black. It was a quick sighting because he had disappeared just as quickly as he had appeared. But I was more than certain it had been him. I would know that ugly ass face anywhere even in a deep crowd.

Duce, one of the guys that worked as my security, approached me. I stood up so I could be on his level and to hear him clearly.

"That nigga Black is trying to get up in here. Spittin' that he wants to speak with El Guapo. I escorted him away from this VIP area but he still in the club lurkin'." I could feel the blood rush to my face. I had to take a deep breath to keep my composure. If I wasn't sure of nothing else, I was sure Black had lost his damn mind. Duce stood back waiting on me to make my next move. I excused myself from Marlo and El Guapo. I didn't want to alarm them about my unwelcomed guest.

The club was packed but I spotted Black chilling close to the dance floor with his usual peons attached to his hip. The whole crew looked like dumb and dumber to me. I rolled my eyes as I approached them.

"What's good, Precious." He had his arms folded across his chest but released them in my presence. He knew that type of gesture was considered aggressive, and I was sure he didn't want that vibe around me. "I see you bringin' out celebrities and shit. Puttin' on for yo' city."

"You observant." My tone was ice. Because he was on some bullshit and we both knew it. I got straight to it. "Look, I hear you tryin' to get into my VIP spot to see El Guapo. But check this, he only here to relax and have a good time. No meetings tonight." I closed the gap between us, fighting back my aggravation, because I really wanted to slap the shit out of him.

He shook his head I could see the disappointment from the sag of his jawline. Blood was probably draining from his face, but he was too black for it to be seen. "Word . . ." He seemed to fidget. "You got that hot VIP."

This time I sucked my teeth and stared him down with the fuck you gaze. Because this fool was trying me, and he knew better. I had to keep my cool though. I was a business person, and my club was not the spot for drama. I searched for the calm in me. "Invites only allowed up."

He was so pissed I could see the anger that he was trying to hide, but it was in the twitch of his lips. "Look, ain't no disrespect intended a'ight. But I only wanted to speak to El." This time I saw something different in emotionless eyes. It was desperation. And that disgusted me. That was a sure sign of a weak ass nigga. And it was not a good look on no day.

I looked up as I felt Marlo over my shoulder. I figured he would probably follow me down because he knew when security approached something was up. I just didn't tell him because I didn't want to pull him away from El Guapo. Black and his bullshit presence was causing disruptions we did not need. I had to wrap this shit up so we could get back to the party and of course our guest.

I put my focus back on Black once again. "Look, you in the club . . . you are welcome to drink at the bar and vibe but that's it." I had to be clear. There would be no VIP or no El Guapo, at least not up in my establishment. Black's glare followed over my shoulder to Marlo just as Marlo stepped beside me.

A fake smile spread onto Black face. "My bad . . . it's cool. I'll fall back and have a drink or something." He signaled his crew and the walked away like they had been gut-punched.

"That punk ass nigga trouble." Marlo mouthed to me as we watched their backs bust up through the crowd.

"Watch him and his fuck boys until he leaves this property." I instructed Duce and another one of the security guys who had stepped out of VIP to guard me.

I was determined not to allow Black to ruin the good time we were having so I filed him away and we continued to party back in VIP. But it was getting late, and I could tell the crowd was dwindling down.

Promise had been off on the other side of the room doing her thing. I could see her steps were slow as she approached. It was clear she was tired, and those feet were hurting as were mine. "Hey, I'm out, I have enjoyed myself, hell maybe even too much." She smiled. "I'm going to ride with Christopher, he just went to get his car."

"Precious . . ." I looked over as my name jumped off El Guapo's tongue before I could respond to Promise. "I never met a more beautiful twin." He referred to Promise, again. One look at Promise and she had a smile spread across her face at his flattery.

"El Guapo, this is my sister, Promise." The words left my mouth reluctantly. El Guapo stood to his feet so fast one would have thought he jumped off a burning seat. Talk about thirsty.

"Your name is beautiful." The twinkle in his eye was too much for me. I wanted to snatch Promise by the hand and run. This monster could not be attracted to my sister, no fucking way.

"Thank you." Promise continued to smile as he reached to shake her hand. "El Guapo is not too bad." She joked then sighed. "Well, it was really nice to meet you." Her words became rushed, and her body language shifted, it was clear she was leaving.

"Wait . . . you leave now? You only just walked into my life. You can't leave so soon."

My heart must have stopped, suddenly I felt as if I could not suck air. If he didn't stop, I would scream or pass out.

Promise giggled. "Awe, that is so sweet of you but my boyfriend is outside waiting on me. I really must get going." I sighed when she called Christopher her boyfriend. Maybe El Guapo would back off. But I was also shocked that she had called Christopher her boyfriend.

"You break El Guapo heart." He raised his hands and

covered his black heart because there was no way that nothing red pumped in it.

Promise laughed again then smiled. "Goodnight." She backed up preparing to leave.

"Welp, I'll walk you out." I nearly jumped past them both. I grabbed her by the hand to get her away from him.

I signaled for four of the guards to walk down with us. We made it to the entrance and outside. The music was now in the rear view.

"Please go get outta here, that monster is hypnotized by you." I referred to El Guapo and his foolishness.

"Who me? Precious, that rich ass man got a thousand of me at his beck and call. He just used to getting what he want." She had a point. We looked at each other and laughed. "Relax, you have nothing to worry about. I'm good," she assured me.

Christopher pulled alongside of us. I hugged Promise and she climbed inside the car promising to call me in the morning.

Duce stepped up beside me. "Black left the building." I nodded, that was good news for me. As I turned to head back inside the club, I noticed Quavo and Toya. She was at his side, and they appeared to be leaving for the night.

I made it back inside. I was starting to feel really tired, I could imagine my bed and all the comforts it offered and me climbing in it. I made my way toward the bar to speak with Sharita for a minute. I was more than glad to catch a glimpse of El Guapo and his squad exiting the VIP lounge. Which meant they were on their way out of the door. Now that he was gone, I could wrap things up and do the same. But Black slid back into my mind for a moment. I couldn't help but wonder about his slick move. He had to know I wouldn't be cool wit' him poppin' in like that. Not to mention he had made himself a target. Not having a meeting with El Guapo and creeping in on his presence could cost you your life. His move had been risky. So why do it?

Marlo and I left the club together and my house was the destination. We had been all over one another in the back of the Maybach as the driver balled the down interstate. Inside the house he picked me up and carried me to my room where we all but ripped each other's clothes off. The craving we had for each other was immense. I'm not sure when but after rounds of riding each other we both must have passed out asleep.

When I awoke, I glanced up at the ceiling. It was daylight out and the sun was shining into my room as solid proof. Lying next to me still asleep, Marlo was resting well. I reached for my cell phone and couldn't believe I had forty-three missed calls. Promise's name was the first one I saw. I started to return the call. But I could hear from within my house Promise's voice loud and clear as she yelled my name.

I also noticed right away that the tone in her voice sounded urgent my heart raced as I jumped out of the bed. I nearly tripped over my own right leg and landed on my face I moved so fast, but I caught my balance. But steadying myself and not missing a beat, I rushed towards my bedroom door, at the same time I heard Marlo's movements as he bolted out of the bed.

I reached for the doorknob just as Promise burst through my door, without warning she threw her arms around my neck and hugged me tight.

"I thought something was wrong." The shaky tone in her voice said she had been crying. "Precious I was so worried. I've been calling you over and over like a thousand fucking times." She still held onto me for dear life.

I hugged her back even though she was hugging me so tight I could barely breathe. "I'm okay, see? I am so sorry, but I was knocked out from last night." I apologized and hoped to assure her at the same time. The last thing I wanted to do was worry her. I knew how that felt and that I didn't wish on anyone.

Promise slowly released her grip from around me, but I could feel her reluctance to let go, she sniffed back tears and stood back and looked me over. Her eyes were still red, and tears wet her cheeks. "I guess you haven't heard then?" She sniffed some more.

"What?" I asked my tone impatient.

"Quavo and Toya were in a shootout early this morning while having breakfast..." More tears flowed fast and freely down her cheeks. "Quavo is dead." I couldn't believe my ears. But I noticed she only said Quavo.

"And Toya?" I had to know but I stopped breathing as I waited for her reply.

Promise sniffed back more tears. "She is fine. Shook up a bit ... but fine." I glanced back at Marlo, he reached for his phone.

"Damn, I got like thirty missed calls." He mouthed and rubbed his head. Just as he said that his phone lit up with another call. "What's good?" He answered. "Yeah, she straight." He said then pushed the phone toward me. "It's Mob."

I reached for the phone. "Hello?" My mind was all over the place.

"Mane ... Precious, I been blowing you up, I'm almost outside yo' crib. I didn't know what the fuck was up, so I headed straight for you. Shit ignorant out here right now. Quavo was shot and killed this morning and your girl Toya, was wit' em." He was trying to fill me in.

"I already know Promise just got here ... she told me."

"Damn, this shit crazy. Shit outta line mothafucka."

I eyed Marlo; he knew I was tripping. "Listen, I'm good

out here at the house. But I want you to set up a meeting in an hour . . . you know who needs to be in attendance." With that I ended the call.

I watched Marlo as he laid back in the bed and stared at the ceiling. I turned back to Promise who pulled me into another hug. I hated having her shook up again with the bad news surrounding Toya. I knew that just triggered memories of her kidnapping. Which was not good with her battling the shock of the situation. But I also had to get control of this shit before bodies started poppin' up and interrupting business. I knew Quavo's crew would be out for blood and everyone in their path would be a casualty. And the last thing we needed was the whole city bucking. We could put down the problems in a quiet yet effective manner. Loss of life would be those responsible for taking Quavo's life and violating Toya feeling of safety and that would be the end of it.

Chapter 39

"That color is really pretty on you." Toya said as she sat down in her styling chair. Promise had just hooked me up with a twenty-four-inch ginger orange weave and I was loving it. I stood in the mirror in front of Promise station playing in it.

"Thank you. I'm really feeling it." I turned around and smiled at them. I then reached and picked up the glass of champagne I had been drinking.

Today was the first day in weeks since we all had been at the salon together. Toya had been out since the shooting, just getting her head together. And this was her first day back.

"So, Toya you good?" I finally asked.

"Yeah, I'm straight if that's what a person would be after a life altering ordeal such as this." She sighed and sipped her champagne. "But I ain't gone lie, that shit shook me up in ways I couldn't have imagined. I'm from the hood, lived in it all of my life, but that was the first time I ever been in the middle of gunfire. Bullets flying, things breaking, people scattering, and nowhere to run. At least that's how you feel in the midst of all the chaos."

"Trust me, I understand. And I think you should talk to someone to help you sort out your feelings about this shit. Describe to them how that shit made you feel like you just described it to us. I can hook you up with my therapist," Promise suggested.

"Nah, I don't think I need all that. I'm good."

"Listen, that's what I thought after the kidnapping. Thought it would just go away . . . disappear but it never did. It just became the bigger part of my life."

Promise was right, a therapist could help her navigate through her feelings. Trying to deal with her kidnapping on her own had almost ruined her. "Aye, I get it. I know you think you can handle this on your own. But Promise is right, sometimes we just need that listening ear and not just any ear. Someone who can help you learn how to process or sort out whatever you are experiencing. So, if you change your mind, I got you on the therapist. I'll handle all the expenses."

Tears formed in Toya eyes, but she sucked them back. She nodded, letting us know she had heard us. "Thank you all for being here for me. It really means a lot to me knowing you all support me."

"Absolutely, we always got you," Promise assured her, and we all chimed in, backing her up.

"Toya, your next client is here." Reese rounded the corner. She had been up front filling in for Prel who had left to handle some personal business.

"Okay." Toya sniffed back the choking up in her throat.

"What's going on in here? All the tears and such. What I miss?" Reese asked. "Soon as I leave the room y'all get all emotional." She fussed.

"Aww, you ain't missed nothing. We just talking about me seeing a therapist to get past this shooting and loss of Quavo."

Tears immediately formed in Reese's eyes. "Hey, I think that can be good. You should definitely do it. And you know we here for you." She walked over and hugged Toya. "Now stop all this crying and go get yo' nappy head client, with her bougie self." We all started laughing. We knew she was talking about Celeste. She was Toya's entitled client who was married to a doctor, and she was picky and always had issues with her so-called close friends allegedly hating on her. We all knew it was all her in her head. No one was really hating on her, she desired to be hated on. We just ignored her and smiled.

"A'ight. Welp that is my cue to leave. I will leave you all to deal with her. I'm out." I stood up and gave myself one last glance in the mirror.

"Wait, I thought you were hanging out for a late lunch?" Promise asked. It was like three o'clock, we had been drinking champagne, talking, and skipped all over lunch.

"I would but it's late now and I gotta get home to pay Rosa, she is going out of town."

"Oh, okay I guess you can go then. And tell Rosa to enjoy her getaway, if anyone deserves a vacation it's her."

"No doubt." I headed out.

Rosa was packing up and waiting on me when I arrived home. I hadn't expected her to, but she had thrown me some Buffalo dip, tuna fish, and pasta salad together, and packed it up in Tupperware so I could put it in the refrigerator. She said she wanted me to have some quick snacks I could grab for the next couple of days. I paid her her regular pay then gave her a couple extra stacks, hugged her, and told her to enjoy her trip.

Hungry, I went to the kitchen and put some of that Buffalo dip which was still hot onto a plate and smashed it. Just as I reached into the refrigerator to grab me a bottle of cold water the doorbell rang.

I sat my bottle of water on the counter and headed for

the front door, I opened the door to find Katrina standing before me.

"What's up K?" I said, I surprised to see her. For one she had just shown up without calling or texting me. I noticed right away she seemed all out of sorts. I could tell she had something on her mind.

"I gotta talk to you." She stepped inside and walked past me and headed for the den. I followed behind her.

"Can I get you a drink?" I asked. This was serious. She sat on the couch but stood back up.

"Yes. I'll take a shot of Apple Crown Royal if you had that."

"I got you." I walked over to the bar. "So, what's up? What's bothering you?"

Katrina fidgeted with her hands. She paced, I reached for the Apple Crown Royal and started feeling the glass. "I don't know if I can marry Case." She released, then looked at me and paused. "I'm not even sure about being in a relationship with him after what happened to Quavo." And that was her dilemma. Truth be told I had thought about Katrina when the incident had happened, but she and I had never discussed it or asked me any questions about it when I saw her at the dry cleaners. "Toya could have been killed. I can't go through that. I can't live my life like that . . . BEING SCARED ALL THE TIME!" She raised her voice but tried to calm down. "Feeling like a target is on my back . . . on the back of the ones I love." The fear she was speaking of was in her eyes.

I approached her and handed her the drink. She held the shot glass tight. I had given her a glass instead of a shot. I figured she might need more.

I stood before her. This would be the hard reality that she would have to face. "Like I told you before, there are no guarantees. This is the game . . . it loves no one, it is not safe for no one. There are no exceptions." I know I was being blunt but there was no way around it. "That reality is Case's lifestyle. You date him, you marry him, you inherit it. Your family inherits it." Katrina's eyes followed my every move. "So, in making the tough decision of what to do. You will have to follow your heart. Your basic instinct." The reality of the game was a heartbreaker. There was no peace, no solace. And neither could be afforded.

Tears swelled up in Katrina's eyes. Her hands were shaking as she lifted the glass to her mouth and swallowed it all drop by drop. Her hand slowly lowered with the glass in it. She cried out. "I swear, I don't know what to do."

"But you will. Only you can know," I said as calm as I could.

"And Toya?" She asked. "How is she today?"

"She is fine. Under the circumstances."

"That's good." Katrina nodded.

"Would you like another drink?"

Katrina sniffed back her tears. She looked down at the glass in her hand then back at me. "Yeah, I would. But make it water this time."

"Sure. Let's go into the kitchen."

Chapter 40

It had been two days since Katrina had stopped by with her concerns about whether to marry Case. It still bothered me that I had not been able to set her mind at ease or give her the assurance that she was seeking. But telling her anything different than what I had said would have been a fantasy or a complete lie. The best thing I could do for her out of friendship and love was to tell her the hurtful truth. Her heart and basic instinct.

But even though it bothered me I wasn't worried. The one thing I knew for certain was that Katrina loved Lalah and she would do what was best for her. After sitting down in the kitchen, she drank the water that she had wanted, and she calmed down. We both were hungry, so we ate some of Rosa's food that she had prepared for me and continued to talk. She felt better when she left my house and thanked me for always being honest with her and not sugar coating what had to be said. That didn't bring me much comfort, but it was what it was.

Today I was taking some time to chill and hang out with Promise even though she had no idea. I had checked with Toya, and she had confirmed that she had no appointments today and wouldn't be coming in until late afternoon. I knew to catch her I had to be quick and early.

I showered, dressed, jumped in the Ferrari, and sped off towards her house. Traffic was thick but the Ferrari made sure to get her respect as I balled down the interstate. I arrived at Promise's condo in no time. I adjusted my Tom Ford sunglasses and strutted up to the doorbell and pushed it twice. Promise would curse me out for sure when she finally opened the door. With no answer after the first two rings, I hit two more times.

A smirk spread across my face as I heard the deadbolts being unlocked. Promise's eyes blinked and squinted up at the site of the light as it slapped her dead in the face. Her hair was disheveled, her robe pulled extra tight, it was clear she had still been in bed.

Leaning her body up against the door entrance, she rubbed her right hand through her hair and tightened her eyes. "Really, Precious?" She sighed. "Is it even noon yet? I mean really there are other ways to torture me than to snatch me awake with this devilish doorbell? I thought that bell was ringing in my head," she whined.

I just glared at my sister. Even though her hair was wild, and she looked like she had been asleep for three days, she was still beautiful. I enjoyed hearing her whine, just having her at home and safe was all I could ask for. I shook my head at her, pretending to be disappointed.

"I swear you a such a big baby. It is time for you to get out of that bed so suck it up and get movin'." I stepped inside and maneuvered right past her as I usually did. "I don't smell any coffee up in here."

"Really, you don't say. Maybe it's because I'm asleep as some people do at this hour. By the way exactly what time is it?" She asked on my trail.

"Eleven o'clock. And since you don't have any clients and nothing pressing at the salon to do, I'm taking you out. Now." I turned to her and smiled. "Go shower, brush your teeth, wash the sleep from your eyes, and get dressed."

"Why, where are we going?" She stood back on her legs and pulled her robe tighter around her.

"Out. Now get dressed. In the meantime, I will make myself a quick cup of coffee." I turned towards the kitchen.

"Pffft. So, bossy." I heard her grit her teeth from behind me. I smirked at her complaint and continued towards my coffee.

"I'm so glad you brought my baby out today. As usual she smooth as butter. Go on faster." She urged me on as we balled down the interstate to our destination.

"Promise, I'm already going ninety-five. Would a hundred be better?" I played at being sarcastic.

Her eyes gleamed. "Hell yes. Do it, Precious." She begged and braced herself I checked traffic around me and put the pedal further to the medal. The Ferrari seemed to breathe in deep and silently exhaled. The ride was just smooth, and it felt like we were floating past the other cars.

"That's what I'm talking about that FAST AND FURIOUS SHIT, I LOVE IT!" Promise's smile stretched from ear to ear. I laughed.

"Yeah, keep that same energy when the whole LAPD behind me," I joked.

"Hey, I'll shoot, and you drive, no worries," she joked as well. I started to break down the speed as my exit was fast approaching. I gazed in my rear view mirror several times and my side mirrors. For one I wanted to check to be sure no cops were behind me for real. And two I wanted to be sure no other cars were to close by me. Because my speed was so fast that everything I drove past was a blur in hindsight.

"You are so crazy." In truth I was enjoying the speed just as much as she was, and she knew it.

I veered onto my exit and continued to our destination. The Ferrari sang as I broke it down to a complete stop as we pulled into the customized car lot called Exquisite Ferrari.

"Oh shit, what we doing here? You about to cop you another one of these hot ass rides?" Her eyes dotted across the lot as with excitement as I pulled into a free parking space. I shut off the engine and jumped out. Promise followed.

"Precious." The owner Josh Soprano was coming out of the building as we exited the car. DaVon knew him personally and we had attended some of the same social gatherings when he was alive.

"Hey Josh." I spoke, as he stopped in front of us and smiled so hard at Promise I knew it was a cue to introduce them. "This is my sister Promise. Promise, this is Josh Soprano he is the owner of this fine establishment."

"Hi." Promise extended her hand. The girl was man crazy. And Josh was easy on the eyes. Italian, he was every bit of six feet, four inches tall, bronze skin, slim, and just plain handsome. Not to mention he was rich. But he was also every bit of a ladies' man, and I would shoot his pinky toe off if tried anything with my sister.

Josh reached for her hand and held on. "Precious never told me she had a twin." He smiled like a school picture.

"Well, she does." Promise was too giddy. I had to break this up and Zach saved us.

"Precious, how are you?" He approached us just in time. Zach was Josh's top salesman and cousin.

"Hey Zach, you ready for us?" I hoped Josh got the

picture. He continued to smile at Promise, and she engaged him innocently.

"Yes, let's look around."

"Well Josh, we have to get going. But it was good seeing you."

"Oh yeah, it was good seeing you too, and nice meeting you, Promise." Another miracle happened when his cell phone rang.

Josh looked over at Zach. "I have a meeting. I'll be back later." Zach bid him bye.

"So, Promise, I hear you've come out today to drive off with great speed?" He joked about the speed but was serious about her driving off. This was my surprise for her today. I was going to let her pick a Ferrari of her choice. I had promised her one and today was the day.

Promise turned to me. "Precious, you didn't?" She beamed and held her chest.

"You're right I didn't. Because I decided to let you pick, I figured it was best."

"Aw, you are too good to me. Shit which one would I pick." She turned around and gazed over the lot.

"How about we start with the show room floor." Zach suggests with a grin.

"Please do I just hope my legs hold me up for the excitement." Promise said.

"I'll catch you if you fall." I giggled. We both followed Zach inside.

"Ohh, I promise I can smell the Ferrari in here." Promise was impressed for sure. But it was beautiful inside. Talk about plush. The floors were real marble, just beautiful. The cars on them were the icing on the cake. I had felt the same way the first time I was inside. Zach showed us around, it didn't take long. Right in the center of the showroom floor was a 2021 Chrome Ferrari

Portofino M with red interior, 620v to die for, and Promise did just that. "It's this one Precious, this one, this one." She had to bite her lip to keep from jumping up and down. "I absolutely fucking love it." She beamed.

"The key is on the seat. Enjoy it." Zach smiled and gazed at me. I winked at him.

"Zach will you have them open this place up so my sister won't tear this new whip through the window?" I teased.

"Because I will." She opened the door and hopped inside.

"Yeah, we better handle that. We need these windows to look out of." He laughed.

While Promise oooh'd and aaah'd over her car, Zach told his team to ready the doors so Promise could drive off the showroom floor. Meanwhile I went to my car and retrieved my checkbook and filled out a check. I then handed it off to Zach who had finance type up the papers to show that the car was paid in full.

Finally, the paperwork was handled, and we stood outside and prepared to leave. "Thank you so much, sissy. Now can we put this thing on the interstate so I can see what it can really do."

"Sure, tell you what. Why don't you follow me I got something I would like to show you."

"Hey, I'll go wherever you go." She smiled.

"Let's do it then." I turned and headed for my car.

"Oh, by the way," she said to get my attention. I turned around. "That Josh didn't have a chance. He fine as hell, I can't lie. But I see LA's biggest whore written all over him." She chuckled, turned, and jumped in her car. I laughed so hard as I strolled off to my car. That girl was something else.

I was no competition for Promise on the interstate. She

matched my speed and kept up with me every step of the way. Finally, we were back in the Bel Air area, so we topped our speed to regular. As we drove through the prestigious neighborhood, I pulled into a huge driveway of a beautiful home with a visible *sold* sign out front. I stopped my car. Promise pulled up beside me, and we both turned off our ignitions. I climbed out first then she followed.

"Who do you know that lives here?" She asked.

"The new owner is you," I spilled.

Promise's eyes shot back towards the mini mansion, her mouth was wide open. Slowly she twisted her head back in my direction. Tears flooded her face. She took both hands and covered placed them over her eyes and sobbed into them.

"Wait, why you crying?" I rushed off towards her. "Hey, hey, I didn't mean to make you cry." I reached for her and as she continued to cry, her head fell to my shoulder. I hugged her tight. "Come on, now. Stop that crying." I rubbed her back and tried to soothe her. I had expected her to be happy, but hadn't planned on all this emotion. Tears formed in my eyes I tried to blink them back, but they still came down. "Come now," I crowed again.

She sniffed. "I'm sorry. I didn't mean to do all that." She slowly lifted her head and stepped back. "Precious, you are just too good to me. I mean how? I mean when?" Her questions were indecisive.

"I found the time whenever I found the time. Look, I wanted to do this for you. I wanted you close."

Again, she covered her face and cried into her hands.

"Come now. No more tears," I said.

"You know when Momma died I was miserable and alone for so long. I would lay awake at night when I was in a different foster home and think no one would ever love me. No one would ever be there. I would always be alone. There were times I wished I would just get hit by a car and it would be all over. Then nobody would have to be bothered with me." The tears once again flooded my face. I could barely breathe thinking about how my sister had suffered. Just thinking about her not being on this earth was enough to end me.

"I'm so sorry that you ever had to feel this way," I managed through choked up tears.

She sniffed back her tears then sighed. "It's okay because you're what I come to. I find you, my sister, who has done nothing but showed me and given me her bare heart. And I give you mine. Thank you so much for caring for me and taking care of me. I love you, Precious." She reached out and hugged me tight.

"I love you too. Now, let's stop all this and go see this house."

"Ohh yessss," she sang and strutted up the driveway. Inside she fell in love with the beauty of the house.

The house was a four-bedroom, four-and-a-half-bathroom, three thousand-two-hundred-and-seventy-one-square-foot piece of heaven with French doors throughout, a full gourmet kitchen, and more.

"Precious, this place is huge. How am I going to sleep here all alone?" She said as she stepped outside into the backyard and discovered the pool. "The water in this pool is so blue, OWWW!" She suddenly shouted. "A cabana built in my backyard. I take that back. I know how I'm going to live here alone. Please don't worry about me I'll be just fine." She giggled. I laughed at her dramatics.

"I'm sure you will. Besides I'm only five minutes away now." I was happy about that as well.

"Right. Welp, guess I'll be bugging you more now."

"I guess." I smiled. "Now we got to find you a good housekeeper. I already talked to Rosa, and she knows a few people you just need to choose."

"Dang sister, you be on it."

"No doubt. I got you boo." We hugged again. "Now how about we have some snacks and a drink? Rosa hooked us up." I pointed towards the other side of the pool, and you could see the set up.

"Rosa be on top of it. Well let's pop this bottle." Promise picked up the bottle of champagne.

Chapter 41

Fully clothed in a wifebeater and some boy shorts, I sat on the toilet and read the stick over and over again, the same thing I had done for the past three days, and for the past eleven sticks. It was positive and it was not going to change. How it happened was more the mystery to me seeing as though precaution was taken every time to avoid this outcome. But I could not deny it. I was pregnant.

The feeling I had all over me as I accepted the facts was instant and forever unchangeable. I was in absolute love with this love inside of me, now a part of me. Tears stung my eyes as I thought of and pictured the look that would have been on my father's face from the news. No matter what the situation, he would have loved a grandchild.

Then the one thought that had not crossed my mind. *Marlo.* The father. My doorbell rang.

"Marlo." Slid out of my mouth. It was him who was ringing my doorbell, I was sure of it. He was in town to check on things but only for a day. Slowly I stood up, sat the stick on top of the box it had come out of, and washed my hands.

Ding dong, my doorbell chimed once more. Then it hit me. Rosa was not here. I would have to get it. I raced out the bathroom and to my front door. I pulled it open just as Marlo's finger was fixed to press the bell again.

He gazed at me. "I considered kicking this door in but figured I would only break my foot so I thought I might try the bell again first before I injured myself."

I smiled. "My bad. And yes, your foot would have been injured. To be specific it would be broke in several places." I laughed. "Come on in. I was all the way in my room, and I forgot that Rosa was not here.

"Girl, you had a nigga worried out here."

"Why worry?" I asked. "Trust, I have a military up in here to handle most situations. You know I dead them on sight." I chuckled. "There is no need to worry." I smiled again but he knew I was serious. I turned from the door and headed for the kitchen. I was thirsty for some Tropicana orange juice. Marlo was on my trail in no time and wrapped his arms around me from the back.

"Aww, I missed you. It's been one month too long." He kissed my neck.

"Stop being so sentimental." I teased him. I turned around kissed him on the lips and broke away from his embrace and ran into the kitchen. He tried to catch me and tickle me. "Stop it." I cried out laughing.

"I don't smell pancakes up in here." He stopped tugging at me and stood by the stove. I opened the refrigerator.

"Welp, you didn't bring any so that would be the outcome." I grinned. I opened the cabinet and fished out two glasses. "Can I offer you some very cold and sweet Tropicana?"

"Sure, I'll take what I can get it." He smiled as I poured. I passed him a glass then picked up mine. I emptied the glass quickly I was so thirsty. "Ummm, that was so good.

I was so thirsty. Felt like I haven't drank anything in a week."

"Yeah, if that is the case maybe you should have another glass." He teased. I playfully pushed his shoulder. He was now standing next to me.

"But perhaps you are right." I filled my glass again. The smile on my face suddenly faded. I had to tell him my news. And I honestly did not know how he would feel about it. "Come on let's go into the den so we can talk"

"Oh shit, who been shot or stabbed." He chuckled.

"Boy, shut up and get in the den." I led the way, my glass full of orange juice and the bottle of Tropicana in the other hand. In the den I sat down and ushered him to sit across from me. This time he looked me in the eyes.

"Why so serious? What's wrong?" He asked.

I didn't know how to tell him, so I said it straight out.

"I'm pregnant."

Marlo looked at me and blinked his eyes. I stood up and walked over towards the bar. I needed a second away from his stare. The shock on his face was clear. But I had to face him, so I turned back to him.

"With a baby?" Finally creeped from his lips.

"What else would I be pregnant with?"

This time he raised out of his seat and slid over to me and hugged me so tight I couldn't breathe.

"Marlo, I need air." I said in a wheezing manner.

"Oh, oh, I'm sorry." He stepped back and I was surprised to see his face was now wet with tears. "Are you okay? How do you feel?" He reached for my flat stomach, but I stepped back.

"I feel fine. I am fine." I wanted to be clear. "Just pregnant."

Without warning he pulled me back to him and kissed me deep. "Thank you so much," he spoke.

"Why are you thanking me?" I asked.

"For giving me the one gift, I never knew I would have. To be a father."

"So, you are okay with this?"

"Of course . . . the one thing I have always wanted to be was a dad."

"Aren't you concerned how this happened when we always used protection?"

He laughed. "Well, I guess we both know that condoms are not one-hundred-percent guaranteed. No birth control is. Can I . . . can I touch?" Again, he reached for my six-pack stomach this time. I stood still and allowed him to touch where our baby was growing. More tears flooded his eyes, and my heart skipped a beat. It felt good to see him so genuinely happy. But suddenly I was also sad. Our lifestyle did not fit a baby.

"Now I see why Katrina was so conflicted about being with Case. I mean I understood all along but not in the same way as I understand it in this moment."

"What do you mean?" Marlo asked, his hands still on my stomach, his eyes on mine.

"Lalah. She was worried about Lalah, the one person she lives for. Did you know she broke things off with Case? The incident with Quavo being killed and Toya in the middle of the gunfire freaked her out. She just couldn't handle it."

Marlo pulled my face up to meet his. "You do what's best to protect the ones you love."

"Right . . . so what about us? Our lifestyle."

Marlo gazed into my eyes he looked down at my stomach. "We might have to get out of the game." We both knew what that meant or could mean. In most cases there was no getting out.

"That can't be done." I said it out loud, what I knew he had to be thinking.

"Yeah, stepping down can be complicated, consequences . . . just things."

"So how?" I looked to him, but I knew he had no answers nor did I.

"I can't answer that for sure right now. But what I do know is you and this baby come first from this day forward." He smiled and I would have, but for some reason I could not find the energy. Instead, I looked down at this hand that was still on my stomach. My heart was kind of troubled by his suggestion. "Listen, I have to go to Peru to meet up with El Guapo, but I will be back in the states in a few days. I will come straight to LA. We will talk and plan out our next move at that time."

Chapter 42

"So, finally you meet with me."

I sat down at the table and still wondered why I had agreed to the meeting. It was one I had avoided and was still unsure of but still I was here.

"I've been busy, but I made the time," I responded. I was meeting with one of the most notorious drug women in Spain and probably the world. Es Talita Gotti. Penelope used to share stories with me of her long ago when I first stepped in the game. She had killed top drug lords in the past with her bare hands. There was no question that she was feared. But her word was bond and she lived by the sword. And that the moment she was in LA to see me and me only. Which meant I was important. But I did not want to be having her attention. It was nothing I would ever have wished for. Her presence to most people was scary.

"I know I have a reputation that travels mouth to mouth as people try to know Es Talita. But I'm sure Penelope made sure you knew who I was from her account and what that meant." Her eyes seemed pleasant, but there was something dark behind them. I wasn't sure if it was personal pain or her killer instinct, but whatever it was, it was embedded deep and would never be touched.

I nodded my head to answer her question while trying to break away from my thoughts. "I think anyone who is in the game and wishes not to cross you knows who you are." I smiled but was unsure if I should.

She shook her head and returned the smile as she adjusted in her seat. "Hmmm . . . you're probably right." She agreed. We were at one of my warehouses for the meeting. I had ok'd for Mob to set it up. The agreement was it would only be us inside, no henchman from either side. "I come a long way to see you. And I get to the point. I want to know when you are going to take your own destiny?" She said the words simply, but they seemed to explode in my head. Had she really traveled a million miles to ask me that?

And to be honest, I was clueless to her straight-out question. Not that I expected her to beat around the bush to whatever her goal was.

"What do you mean? I run three cities as I'm sure you are aware?" Even she couldn't say that was a small thing.

She looked off then back at me. "With your boyfriend?" That statement pushed me back in my seat. I wasn't sure if I should be offended or pissed. The words had come out of her mouth like stone. Harder rocks couldn't bruise me worse.

"Even though that could be considered a bit personal and offensive. He is not my boyfriend." I hoped I was clear. I still claimed that even though no one else besides Promise would dare say that to me. And now of course Es Talita Gotti. And now that I was pregnant by Marlo, what would I say?

"That does not matter much . . ." Her Spanish accent was choppy but super dope and even though she was offending me I loved her voice. "I will tell you like I tried with Penelope, a woman must rule her own kingdom or spend her time running a man's kingdom her way but with limited benefit. While he is the King Kong of the operation with a fist to his chest."

Ouch. Her words had all the truth in it. But really what was the alternative? When DaVon was alive I never even considered the game for myself. And probably never would have. I never wanted a part of the game. Why would I?

"El Guapo is king, you know that."

"A man is always king, at least that's the way he is programmed. But lucky for you, or any boss queen, you have me. And I know you have the power to rule the world, DaVon groomed you, and Penelope made you."

My eyes went to hers and locked. Never had I thought of that. But her words held more truth than would have ever cared to imagine. DaVon and Penelope had been the root of me. "I...I..." I stuttered, unable to get my words together. She saw the wheels spinning in my brain.

"Precious, a woman must pick up her throne and hold it with both hands and nothing should be in the rearview mirror." That statement rattled me. Opened my mind yet challenged me. Or at least I was sure that is what had happened.

The meeting ended as swiftly as it had started, and me as clueless as I had come in. I knew Es Talita was handing me my destiny as she saw it. I knew her presence meant something big. But Marlo and I, we were opening new territories growing and becoming more powerful in our domains. And contrary to how she saw my role, I did not work for Marlo: we worked together. El Guapo was our supplier. Business was tight and going where we took it. Solid was a good way to describe our success.

Chapter 43

I was excited although weary in some ways, but I had to stay on top of business. No matter what, the grind never rested. Today was delivery day at the club so I headed over as I always did to help Sharita out because it was also a night the club but would be open for happy hour. Which meant Sharita would be extra busy and could use the help to get the order verified and put away. I really had to hire another set of hands to help out but just hadn't had the time to do it.

"Precious, do you want a drink?" Sharita looked over at me. "You look a bit tired; a good strong drink would give you a boost."

"Nah, I'm good, I just woke up early this morning. Had to get an early start, just so much to do, and the day don't seem long enough."

"Trust, I understand." She smiled. "That's why I had me two shots at noon." She chuckled. I noticed she had been doing that a lot lately. She was always in a good mood, but she just seemed different.

"So, what's up wit' you? You have been in a sunshine

mood all week. Singing, hell damn near dancing around here." I teased. "Gone spit it out who is he?" I knew that had to be cause, a man.

"Who . . . me. Pffft." She sucked her teeth. "I'm always in good spirits. I don't need no man for that." She laughed. "But girl, I ain't gone lie, he is fine."

"Humph . . . I knew it. Spill and don't leave out no details."

"Precious, his name is Justine. I met him at the gym like six months ago. We kinda been working out together, you know getting fit and having good company. Well, he finally asked me out. And yes, I went . . ." There was twinkle in her eye it was clear she had fallen hard. "I tell you he is special, and a good guy."

"Okay, okay, I need more details before I decide that. Now . . . what does he do?"

"I knew you would ask that. He is a fire fighter. A captain I might add."

"Really, a captain huh? I never met a real fireman in real life." I chuckled. "That's what's up."

"Precious, I think I really like him. He's different from all the other thugs who are always trying to push up on me." I was about to respond when the door opened. I was surprised, no one ever came by this time of day. We normally kept the door locked but I had forgot to lock it when I came in. It was dark in that area with the lights off so we couldn't see until they stepped into the light. We still had some of the overhead lights off but enough to see once they were in the clearing. Finally, Shasha's face appeared out of the dark.

"Oh, what's up Shasha." I spoke first.

Sharita grunted and said, "Girl, why you didn't announce yo' self-standing in the dark like that? Poppin' up all random."

"Why you scared or somethin'?" Shasha gawked at Sharita. But the look she gave her was not a friendly one. I thought it was odd, but quickly dismissed it. I knew they were not the best of acquaintances so a little stank attitudes towards each other was probably normal.

"You come in early to help out?" I snatched the conversation away from both of them.

Shasha's eyes were still on Sharita. She pulled them away from her to me. "Something like that," she said, then pulled a nine-millimeter out of thin air and pointed at us. At first, I almost laughed. Were we really staring down the barrel of a gun with the club promoter Shasha standing behind it?

"What the fuck is that? A toy gun?" Sharita said, her voice trembling.

"Oh, I guess you are scared." Shasha smiled. "Bitch do I look like I carry toy guns?" Her tone said she was offended.

"Yo, Shasha wha's going on?" I asked.

"Precious, just shut the FUCK UP!" This time she yelled and thrust the gun towards us with force.

"Aggh." Sharita screamed out and her body sunk. "Please don't point that thing at us. It might go off."

"Sharita, please just shut up you don't run shit today, okay. You can't control this . . . and as for you, boss bitch." Shasha put her eyes on me. "This empire of yours is about to go down." Stunned, I watched as a guy appeared from behind the darkness with a gun also pointed at us.

"What the fuck," I mouthed. What the was going on?

"You a bomb bitch, Shasha," Sharita yelled. "Precious, I always knew this grimy bitch was shady. I knew it," Sharita accused through clinched teeth.

Shasha just stared at Sharita but said nothing.

"Aye, who the fuck are you?" I looked past Shasha at

the guy who was now standing just beyond her off to the side.

Shasha arm twitched as she looked from him then back at me. "Never mind who he is . . . just know he here to end you. Is that enough information?"

Boom. The loud banging like the doors were coming down startled all of us but Shasha never took her aim off Sharita and me. A second of silence and then a gun shot, and Mob stepped into the light.

"AGGHH, AGGHH!" The guy with Shasha fell to his knees blood was gushing out the back of his leg where Mob's bullet landed like a water fountain. The pain that I was certain was intense caused him to squeeze his trigger, a bullet released from the chamber and flew past me. I watched in slow motion as that same bullet hit Sharita between the eyes. Somehow my body moved, and I grabbed her before her body dropped.

My heart skipped a beat as I watched the promise of life and love ripped from Sharita's innocent body. I looked towards Mob as he stood over the unknown guy with two guns in his hands, one pointed at the guy the other at Shasha, he ordered her to drop her gun.

"MANE WHO THE FUCK ARE YOU? WHO IS HE?" he demanded from the guy and Shasha at the same time. They were both quiet as the guy sat on the floor losing tons of blood and the color draining from his skin.

"I said who is he?" Mob's gun's aim moved from Shasha's chest area to her face, at the same time I heard it as he allowed a bullet to slide into the chamber. This was her last chance to speak.

"He's my boyfriend," she finally admitted in a hurried tone. "Who the fuck sent you?" His gaze fell again from Shasha to her boyfriend back to Shasha. Once again remained quiet.

"Fuck this shit mane, I ain't dying for nobody . . . tell

em' Shasha, go ahead, spill that shit." He begged her his entire body shook as the loss of blood was taking its effect.

"Nigga fuck this bitch . . . you tell me?" Mob demanded.

"Mane, I promise I would, but I can't." He cried like a bitch. "I ain't neva knew who this was for, she never told me. I'm just helping her. I was just supposed to come through help her tie up the bodies and once she shoots them, I was to set the bodies on fire . . . and then set the building on fire." He added as if he almost forgot that bit of information.

The plan he shared shocked me. Who the fuck was Shasha . . . why the fuck was the bitch here to burn me? Who was my enemy? It couldn't have been her because I didn't know her from Adam at least I didn't think I did.

Mob looked at Shasha I continued to hold on to Sharita's lifeless body. "Bitch, you need to spill it before you lose a kneecap and an eyeball. Because this weak ass nigga you fuckin' ain't got no grime or grit."

Shasha had snot and tears all over her face. And something told me that whoever she was holding out for was dear to her. She was ready to die to keep them safe. So, I decided to make it easy for her.

"Mob I'm not in the mood to deal with this shit, today. It's light out for the both of them." I gave my order. And at the exact same time both of Mob's gun released a bullet from the chamber. The boyfriend's bullet landed in the top of his head. And Shasha's complementary bullet landed between her eyes. All for one.

Chapter 44

My body felt as light as feather as I entered my house. Thankfully Mob had shown up when he did. In the midst of talking to Sharita about her new love I had forgotten all about Mob, who was supposed to stop by the club to discuss collection because I had a few changes I needed to make for our upcoming pickup. It just so happened, he had showed up in the middle of Shasha's plan and interrupted it. Mob said he knew something was up when he saw the unknown boyfriend entering with a visible in his hand. From that he locked loaded and got ready to intervene. And thankfully he had. But I still could not believe that Sharita had been killed. And I felt horrible about it. She was so young and had so much promise with her future ahead of her. And a piece of shit who never should have had a gun in his hand had shot her. And because of the situation in which she was killed we couldn't return her to her family. The situation was unfortunate but far from finished because people like us didn't deal with the law, we handled our own revenge. And cleaned up our own mess.

*   *   *

I made sure my house was on lockdown, and even secured my security gate which would let me know if somebody so much as stood outside it for more than a few seconds. Someone was out for my life, and they had sent the weakest link to get me. The joke was on them and so would blood be. I went to my room, sat on the bed, strolled through my contact history until I found Marlo's name and touched it. His phone rang and went to voicemail. I threw the phone on my bed next to me.

Exhausted, I jumped in the shower so I could wash off the bullshit of the day and fell into bed. I was asleep in no time and the dreams started. Suddenly I bolted straight up in bed. I looked at the big screen tv on my wall which was on the tv guide channel, I saw the time: 2:14 AM displayed in the corner.

My thoughts quickly reverted to my dream, and I remembered it just as if it were yesterday where I had seen Shasha before. All that time she had been working for me at the club I had not once remembered her, never had she looked familiar to me. But suddenly I knew. It seemed like a lifetime ago but back when I worked at my dad's dry cleaners after graduation. One day I was at work and Black who used to frequent the dry cleaners strolled in casually, with an arm full of clothes to drop off. While in the store he received a call from someone. I was off preparing his ticket, but I couldn't help but overhear his conversation. He answered the phone and said, "I'm comin' girl. Calm yo' ass down." I assumed it was one of his girlfriends rushing him, but after he ended the call, he called out to me because my back was turned to him. "Aye, just hold on to the ticket, I got my sister in the car, and she is a rush and shit."

I turned to him and to say, "Okay." But he was halfway

out the front door before I could. I did notice sitting in his car, which was parked right in front of the dry cleaners by the door, a girl sat in the front seat of his SUV. That girl as I now recall was Shasha. A younger version but it was definitely her. How had I forgotten her face? How had I not remembered her when I next laid eyes on her in my club?

I reached to my right side and grabbed my cell phone. Again, I dialed Marlo's number but once again I got no answer. Nor had he called me back from the last call I had put into him. He should have been back in the states but maybe something had come up in Peru that kept him longer. Things were known to go down like that and if that were the case, I also knew the connection in Peru could be not worth shit compared to the states. So, instead of dwelling on it I dialed Mob.

"I figured it out." I told Mob he answered the phone on the first ring. I told him who Shasha was and how I knew.

"No fucking way." Was Mob reply. "I know a lot of motherfuckers in LA, but I never knew that ugly ass nigga had a sister."

"Well, he does, so check this out we got to handle this shit tonight. Now, Black has a beach house that he stays in at night with only two guards posted, one outside, and one on the inside. I will shoot you the address. I need you to come alone and meet me there in an hour. On the dot." I instructed. I had made it my business a long time ago to know where Black slept because never had I trusted him. I was glad I did.

I jumped outta bed and dressed in record time, raced out to my car garage, pulled out the Range Rover, and balled to my destination. Mob and I arrived on schedule just as I had hoped. We both were booted up with guns complete with silencers. We scoped the scene and Black's so-called security, which was weak and as I had expected from a bitch ass nigga.

Right outside there was a guard securing the garage. Mob quickly and quietly pumped him with two bullets putting him down for life. We then made our way through the opened garage door and just like that we were inside in his beach house. Easy as pie. I peeked around a corner that was off a small hallway from where we entered and there was the kitchen. And to my surprise Black was standing at the stove stirring something in a pot. I should have known his fat ass could cook.

I turned and winked at Mob and gestured for him to go find the other guard who should have been somewhere close by. There were two ways to enter the kitchen. Another wall separated the other side. I decided to go in from the other side which would give me a better drop on Black. I rounded the corner and could see like a living room type area. Black's girlfriend popped up from nowhere. She froze in her tracks as she caught sight of me, and I saw the fear edged in her eyes as she recognized me.

Her lips attempted to move but I released two hot bullets from my chamber that opened her chest. The thud of her body meeting the floor caught Black's attention. He turned around swiftly in the direction of the sound, to find me sitting at his island with a gun pointed at him.

A hot skillet in his now unsteady hand nearly hit the ground but he gripped it in time. The shock etched on face looked as though he had seen a ghost. Truth be told he had.

He looked so pitiful, in any other situation I would have laughed. Instead, I sucked my teeth and said, "anybody ever told you, that you are ugly as fuck when you shocked?" He looked as if he wanted to answer my question. I laughed. "Sit down right there." I motioned with a nod of my head, to reference the other end of the island where I sat. He followed my directions, never taking his eyes from the gun, but he also never sat down.

"I thought you were dead," he finally mouthed. "Where is Shasha?" He then asked.

"You tell me?" I followed up. "You a slick nigga you know that? I remembered who that bitch was. I just hate it took me so long and a dead employee. No, friend. But damn if I didn't figure it out."

"Where is Shasha?" He stared at me and asked the same question again.

"Nigga didn't I tell you to sit yo' ass down? Make this the last time I say it." I waved the gun at him, and he sat. "Now tell me why?" I said.

He looked me square in the face. "Why you think? Because you were in my way, still is. Like a fucking cold I can't shake." He was blunt and I was glad for it. Nothing ever pleased me more than the real. "LA one of the most lucrative drug games in the US. It shouldn't be run by no BITCH! Clearly, yo' nigga El Guapo weak and can't see that . . . but one nigga don't stop no show." He sucked his teeth. I waited. "See, I got his connection down in Spain, but they won't want to fuck wit' me because of you. And you run around LA like a queen on sitting on your FUCKIN' THRONE!" He barked. "Nah, you in my way. And you got to go. Ain't no other way." He gritted his teeth at me.

"So, that's yo' conviction?" I was still calm.

"Damn right. See I tried to get yo' attention the nice way. I shot up yo' blocks . . . and killed that nigga Quavo. But still you ain't distracted." Now it all made sense the crazy shit that was going on.

"Nah, that shit you did is on some other shit that don't include me. See you . . . you a greedy motherfucker." I gave him facts.

He grinned at me and looked like the devil. "Yeah, that sissy dressing ass nigga said the same thing right before he was knocked into a nap."

Marlo popped in my head. My heart skipped a beat. Before I can respond Black charged for a gun off the counter by the stove. As his hand touched it, I landed a bullet in the back of his shoulder blade.

"AGGHH!" He screamed and buckled to his knees, unable to grab the gun because of the pain.

Mob rounded the corner with the guard marching in front of him and Mob's gun at the back of his head. The guard attempted to speak but Mob pulled the trigger, and a bullet opened the back of his head. We all watched as his body fell forward unto the floor.

"Where is Marlo?" I barked at Black. He was trying to hold his shoulder blade tight, blood was starting to smear his hand.

He smirked, "Close by." He toyed with me.

I stood up and pointed my gun directly at his forehead. "The bullet that leaves this chamber will land directly between your eyes. Then your brains on this cheap ass flooring."

"Where is Shasha?" He asked again. As if it were a bargain.

"You will get that little bitch when I get Marlo." I hoped I was clear.

"A'ight I'll take you to him." I could see the desperation on his face. He loved his sister, but I wasn't surprised because every monster had a soft spot.

"Don't make me shoot you nigga by doing something

stupid." I warned him with my gun at his spine as we followed him into what looked like the basement.

My stomach contents nearly spilled out of my mouth as I noticed Marlo's beaten and battered body tied up in a corner. I rushed to him. I was unsure if he was dead or alive. But as my hands touched his cold body, I knew. He was gone. The room spun, I stopped breathing. I had to close my eyes to gather my bearings. To reopen the passageways to my lungs. I breathed again but it was shallow.

"WHERE THE FUCK IS MY SISTER!" Black's voice boomed across the room.

I gazed up as Mob's gun cracked him across the back of his head. "You better take some of that base out yo' bitch ass voice." I heard him lift the safety off his gun.

The hate I felt for Black was at an all-time high. My blood rushed to my brain. "You want that bitch . . . well you might have to dry her out first. I got that hoe soaking on chemicals to keep the ROT OF HER BODY DOWN!" I hoped my words tormented him.

"AGGGH!" He cried out like a wounded brute. "You killed my baby sister, my mother's child, and she will never forgive me. You evil bitch." The fight was knocked out his tone. He continued to sob. "I've been wanting to kill you . . . I shoulda killed you a long time ago . . . but it ain't too late. I'm still gone body yo' half-white ass. Or whatever the fuck you is," he threatened.

"Precious, please let me pump this snake ass nigga full of lead?" Mob begged.

I didn't answer Mob. Instead, I stood up and walked over to Black. "Nigga you still don't get it. Death on your doorstep in the form of a BITCH!" I spat the words at him with so much venom my entire body shook. "And there ain't shit you can do about it."

Black opened his mouth and a screeching laugh erupted

as tears stained his face. I leaned into Mob and whispered to him. Mob marched off on my mission.

Without saying a word, I slowly placed the tip of my gun in between Black's eyes. He ranted on about Shasha, all the while crying. Mob returned and stood next to me with the can of gasoline and matches I had requested. He sat the gasoline down and passed the matches to me, then pointed his gun at Black head. Black stopped rambling and his eyes bulged, then darted back and forth between the gasoline and the matches. To my surprise he seemed to soften. "See Precious, it's not like that. Listen, we can talk about this. Even the business about my sister." At that I could have laughed.

"Stop crying like a pussy. Having balls are the basics in the game, you damn fool," I snarled at him. This time I reached down, picked up the gas can and started to douse him with it until he was soaked.

I continued to douse him until the can was empty. "I think it's important to mention that you murdered my child's father."

His face twisted with confusion. "What?" he asked.

I turned my attention to Mob. "See Mob, this dumb weak ass punk wants to be a kingpin but can't even put two and two together. But I have an idea, let's give him another chance." I picked up the matches and pulled two out of the box, scratched them until they lit up with fire. I watched the fire blaze off the matches.

I took one of the lit matches and threw it on him. He screamed a piercing sound that burned my ears as he attempted to beg. I watched as the flame grew.

"One," I mouthed then threw the other on him, it flamed, "two." I mouth again.

The fire was so swift and thick I could feel the heat from it. Black fell to the floor, fighting, and kicking from the hot flames. I watched him.

"You can't count very well but you can scream." I taunted him. "Now let's see if your brain can scatter." I took steps to get closer to him but careful not to get too close to the fire. As one could, I pumped two bullets into his forehead. His head was so full of blood and guts, they could be heard as they spilled onto the floor. The fire was growing bigger. Mob and I carefully grabbed Marlo's lifeless body and pulled him from the burning house just as it started to spread.

Chapter 45

"I swear this view is so beautiful I could look at it all day. It's just calming." Promise's eyes darted around the scenery. We scanned the perfectly sitting sand that stretched out from all sides and led into the blue water that shined so bright and looked clean enough to bathe in. Just looking at the water cooled me all over even though the humidity was quite warm. The calmness of it all soothed me in ways I could not explain.

"It is." I agreed in a soft tone standing right next to her, one of my long box braids trying to dip over my shoulder. I pushed it back from my face. We stood outside on the deck of the beachfront house I had purchased in Hawaii. It had been two months since Marlo was murdered and five weeks since I had miscarried our baby. I had told Promise the very next day after Marlo's untimely death about the baby. And she had pleaded with me to rest in hopes the baby would be fine. But the pain of losing Marlo just proved to be a bit much for me. For days afterward I tried to remain as calm as possible all the while handling business. I had to make a quick trip out to Miami to handle some things. Then jumped on a plane to Georgia to do the same. But on the inside, I was a complete and utter wreck.

Still, I carried on as normal as possible. I couldn't allow things to fall apart and with the assistance of Mob and the rest of the guys I did my thing. But still my body knew the truth. I was torn apart and in the end my body had let me down. Fresh off a plane from Georgia I went home to shower and catch some sleep before I headed off to a meeting with the crew. But in the midst of my sleep, I had woken up in so much pain I couldn't move. I called Promise over since she was now living in her new house a few minutes away. By the time she got there I was still in pain, but I told her I felt like I had to use the bathroom. But as I tried to stand the pain only got worse, so she insisted she take me to the emergency room. By the time we arrived, and I was placed on the gurney, I started to bleed. Before the doctor could see me, I miscarried. I was distraught. Not only had I lost Marlo. Now our baby was not meant to be.

After being released from the hospital I had to get away from LA, so I hopped on a private jet with nothing but myself and my sister and fled. I could no longer breathe in LA; I needed a break. I now understood whole heartedly when Promise had told me she had to be in Miami for a while. I just couldn't swallow the air in LA for now. I had to have a break.

Mob was holding down business in LA. Phil was holding down Miami and together he and Mob were holding down Georgia. So that was that. I left the club in the hands of Katrina. She knew how to order stock and I had put her in charge of hiring two bartenders which was now handled. I trusted her and knew she could handle it and the dry cleaners. I had promoted Regina to Manager at the hair store, which she proudly accepted, and she was thriving. Promise had of course made Toya manager at the salon, and she was holding that down.

I had business in Hawaii, and I wanted to tend to it while clearing my head. And the calmness of the beach, the cleanliness of the air, and the beauty of the scenery, were proving I had made the right decision every day. Hawaii had rejuvenated me and given me back my sense of reason.

"Maybe we can go for a run on the beach today?" Promise smiled.

"Why not." I looked at her and nodded in agreement. These days it was her most times who suggested we worked out. Talk about a change in attitude, she was showcasing it. Another positive about Hawaii: it had given my sister a new outlook on health. And I was glad to have her by my side. Both of us had been through so much, but there were still reasons to smile, laugh and giggle like schoolgirls. "I still can't believe you and Christopher eloped on me." I had been more than surprised when she had flown back to LA three short weeks ago for two days and come back hitched. Not once had she even given me a hint that she was considering becoming a wife. But I was so happy for her. According to her I would have insisted on a wedding, with all the trimmings. And to be honest she was correct. I would have loved to see my sister walk down the aisle with me as her maid of honor. But I respected her wishes as long as she was truly happy. It appeared she was.

"I know. I know. I can't believe I'm an old married woman either." She gazed her ring and smiled. "He'll make me the happiest of women." She was giddy.

"Hey, you two." Christopher stepped out onto the deck with us. He had joined us a week after they were wed. He was getting his real estate company up and going in Hawaii and I already had dibs on some properties for some new business ventures we had in store in the area.

Christopher's expertise in real estate and connects in the business were already paying off and opening up doors.

"Morning babe," Promise turned to him just as my cell phone rang.

I had stepped away from LA, but I could never fully step away from the game because I was the leader. And now with Marlo being gone I lead alone. So, I was now El Guapo's one and only contact and his standards of course were the same.

"Hello," I answered his call and stepped back inside the penthouse and headed for my room to distance myself. I had contacted him and made him aware when Marlo was murdered. Then went on with my scheduled collection right after and made sure he was paid and on time. But since that meeting I had not spoken to him. It had been complete silence, but I knew it was him giving me time to grieve without actually saying it. He also knew he had nothing to worry about when it came to business, and that I would make sure everything else was handled.

"Precious . . . it's been a while."

"Well, time does fly." I kept it short. I preferred when he got straight to his point. Small talk of any kind was a waste of both our times. And I would not pretend to be interested, Marlo still occupied a great portion of my mind.

"I know you got away take some time . . . but you know your reign is even greater now. Now you have the power and respect. You Precious Cummings are the most notorious and connected women on the West Coast and as well as the South . . ." He paused then ended the call.

I turned to look at myself in the mirror that was attached to the wall in my room. I saw myself at first as my daddy's little girl. Innocent and curious. I saw myself running the register at the dry cleaners while Dad greeted and talked with his long-time customers. Then I saw me now. Me the person El Guapo had just described. His so-called validation of me, or which at least he thought and assumed I should be proud of. But I was not impressed. So instead, I put one foot in front of the other went back out onto the deck where Promise and Christopher no longer occupied the space and stepped onto the beach. I walked out onto the part of the beach of which I now owned, occupied with birds, seagulls, sand, and blue water.

My mind bounced from DeVon and then to Marlo. I could hear both of their voices in my head. I learned the most from DeVon when it came to the game, he had made me into the hustler queen I was. It was him I had started this journey for, it was him I still did it for. It was his legacy I could not walk away from until it was fulfilled. And that had not been done yet.

Marlo had also taught me some things as we ruled together. But if I had learned anything from the both of them it was that being on the top meant being ON TOP! Trust and partnership were a minus.

Yeah, I was a hustler and Queen of the South and West Coast, but I had lost too much to stay in that lane. I had much to still gain. Now international was on my list and the rules would be my own. Es Talita was right about one thing. There comes a time when "a woman must pick up her throne and hold it with both hands and nothing should be in the rearview mirror."

And to that my solution would be this. El Guapo would be no longer in charge when I was done. Yes, I would reign over my own kingdom and my new title will be The QueenPin King.